"My code name is Coyote,"

the man had said.

"Why am I not surprised?" Beatrice had murmured in response. "A lone wolf, cut off from the pack, stalking his prey with slyness and agility."

He'd cocked an eyebrow.

And Beatrice had felt a flush building. She'd meant for the description to have a sting. Instead, it had turned complimentary...and much too dramatic.

But then, the man she had married had always had that effect on her. He'd awakened her imagination...and her desires...in ways no male had awakened them before.

Abruptly Beatrice's mind returned to the present. And her jaw firmed with resolve.

Now that she knew the truth, she'd find the man...and set herself free.

Once and for all.

Dear Reader,

Fall is in full swing and so is Special Edition, with a very special lineup!

We begin this month with our THAT'S MY BABY! title for October. It's a lesson in instant motherhood for our heroine in *Mom for Hire*, the latest story from the popular Victoria Pade.

Three veteran authors will charm you with their miniseries this month. CUPID'S LITTLE HELPERS is the new series from Tracy Sinclair—don't miss book one, *Thank Heaven for Little Girls*. For fans of Elizabeth August, October is an extraspecial month— *The Husband* is the latest emotional and compelling title in her popular SMYTHESHIRE, MASSACHUSETTS series. This series began in Silhouette Romance and now it is coming to Special Edition for the very first time! And Pat Warren's REUNION series continues this month with *Keeping Kate*.

Helping to round out the month is *Not Before Marriage!* by Sandra Steffen—a compelling novel about waiting for Mr. Right. Finally, October is premiere month, where Special Edition brings you a new author. Debut author Julia Mozingo is one of our Women To Watch, and her title is *In a Family Way*.

I hope you enjoy this book, and all of the stories to come!

Sincerely,

Tara Gavin,
Senior Editor

Please address questions and book requests to:
Silhouette Reader Service
U.S.: 3010 Walden Ave., P.O. Box 1325, Buffalo, NY 14269
Canadian: P.O. Box 609, Fort Erie, Ont. L2A 5X3

ELIZABETH AUGUST
THE HUSBAND

SPECIAL EDITION®

Published by Silhouette Books
America's Publisher of Contemporary Romance

To Lily Lee...a woman of spirit and perseverance

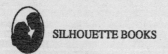

SILHOUETTE BOOKS

ISBN 0-373-24059-7

THE HUSBAND

ELIZABETH AUGUST

lives in western North Carolina, with her husband, Doug, and her three boys, Douglas, Benjamin and Matthew. She began writing romances soon after Matthew was born. She's always wanted to write.

Elizabeth does counted cross-stitching to keep from eating at night. It doesn't always work. "I love to bowl, but I'm not very good. I keep my team's handicap high. I like hiking in the Shenandoahs, as long as we start up the mountain so the return trip is down rather than vice versa." She loves to go to Cape Hatteras to watch the sun rise over the ocean.

Elizabeth August has also published books under the pseudonym Betsy Page.

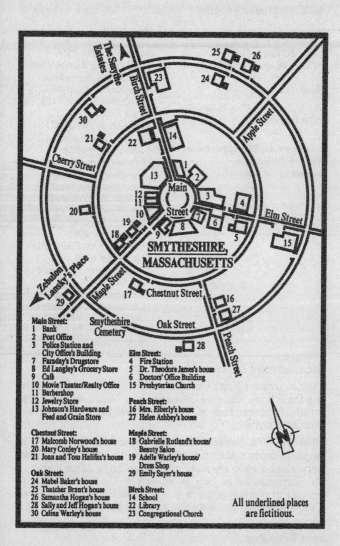

SMYTHESHIRE, MASSACHUSETTS

Main Street:
1 Bank
2 Post Office
3 Police Station and City Office's Building
7 Faraday's Drugstore
8 Ed Langley's Grocery Store
9 Café
10 Movie Theater/Realty Office
11 Barbershop
12 Jewelry Store
13 Johnson's Hardware and Feed and Grain Store

Chestnut Street:
17 Malcomb Norwood's house
20 Mary Conley's house
21 Joan and Tom Halifax's house

Oak Street:
24 Mabel Baker's house
25 Thatcher Brant's house
26 Samantha Hogan's house
28 Sally and Jeff Hogan's house
30 Celina Warley's house

Elm Street:
4 Fire Station
5 Dr. Theodore James's house
6 Doctors' Office Building
15 Presbyterian Church

Peach Street:
16 Mrs. Elberly's house
27 Helen Ashbey's house

Maple Street:
18 Gabrielle Rutland's house/ Beauty Salon
19 Adelle Warley's house/ Dress Shop
29 Emily Sayer's house

Birch Street:
14 School
22 Library
23 Congregational Church

All underlined places are fictitious.

Chapter One

"I hope you don't mind my stopping by unannounced."

Beatrice Gerard smiled at the thirty-one-year-old black-haired, gray-eyed woman on her doorstep. "No, of course not. Please, come in."

The smile had been automatic. In this rural community nestled in the mountainous region of northwestern Massachusetts, it was natural to put on a friendly face. But Samantha Brant's visit was a surprise. The Gerard land was several miles outside of Smytheshire, the town that formed the heart of their small sphere of civilization. People did not normally simply drop by. And although she and Samantha were the same age and both had been born and raised here, they'd never had more than a passing acquaintance. There was no dislike or animosity between them. They had simply been too occupied with their own families and circle of friends to have had any time to get to know each other.

Accepting the invitation, Samantha glanced around as she stepped over the threshold. "I was wondering if I could have a word alone with you."

Beatrice realized Samantha had been looking for Justin Gerard. "My grandfather is over at my brother's place playing with his newest great-grandchild."

Samantha relaxed noticeably for a moment, then tensed once again. Stopping in the hall rather than proceeding into the living room, she turned to face Beatrice. "I'm really not certain how to say what I've come to say."

An uneasiness spread through Beatrice. Samantha was married to the chief of police. Had there been an accident? Had Thatcher Brant sent his wife to inform Beatrice because the news was so bad it needed a woman's touch? "I prefer straightforward honesty."

For a moment longer Samantha hesitated, then said, "I know you and your family have spent three generations denying the accusations against your great-grandfather."

Beatrice's gaze turned cold. "You came here to discuss my great-grandfather?"

"No, not really," Samantha replied hurriedly. "I just mentioned him to let you know that I understand how you feel. People look at you strangely if they think you might have some sort of ability they don't understand. And, I'd rather people didn't look at me that way."

Beatrice's expression became shuttered. "Are you confessing to having such an ability?"

Samantha's nervousness visibly increased. "I'm not certain I should have come. It's just that I can't get rid of the image."

The strain the other woman was under was obvious, and Beatrice felt guilty for appearing so cold. It had been a protective, knee-jerk reaction. "Whatever you tell me won't go any further," she promised in milder tones.

Samantha sighed. "You'll probably think I'm as crazy as a lot of people thought my grandmother was, playing around with her Ouija board all the time."

"Your grandmother was correct a great deal of the time," Beatrice reminded her.

"Most people only remember the mistakes."

Mentally Beatrice kicked herself. It was safer not to appear to believe so readily in things that went beyond the ordinary. She gave a nonchalant shrug. "I prefer to look at people in a positive light. Now, please tell me about this image that's been bothering you. I know you must feel it's important or you would never have come here."

"It's a man. He looks near death ... or, at least, in great pain. His face is swollen on one side and the eye is black. He's in an enclosed area, a small, narrow windowless room. It's not a hospital room. I have the impression it's some sort of cell ... that he's a prisoner. His hair is either very dark brown or black and the color of his eyes is so dark they look ebony. He has high cheekbones and a strong jaw. His clothing is that of a Mexican peasant—loose-fitting pants and a tunic top. They're dirty now, but my impression is that they were once white."

Beatrice fought back a wave of nausea. "How did this image come to you?"

Samantha's shoulders straightened defiantly as if she expected ridicule. "My grandmother had a crystal ball that had been passed down through her family for generations. To her and others, it was simply a pretty ornament. But ever since I was a young child, I've seen images in it." A plea entered her voice. "My grandmother was the only one of my family to know about this. I don't want the others to find out. They already think my grandmother had too much influence over me, and they worry about me becoming like her. They were all certain she was missing the top rung on her ladder."

Beatrice knew Samantha's family had been embarrassed by the old woman's behavior, and she couldn't help wondering how Thatcher Brant would feel if he knew about his wife's "talent." She could easily visualize a skeptical glitter in his eyes. Samantha was right to keep this knowledge to herself. "I gave you my word I wouldn't tell." Fighting to maintain a level tone, she asked, "How did you know of my connection to this man?"

"You were there, a sort of misty image in the background. I got the impression he was thinking of you."

Beatrice told herself that Samantha's crystal had to be wrong. Even if the man was still alive, which he wasn't, she was the last person he would have been thinking about. "The man you described is dead." She'd had years to get used to this knowledge and yet the words had threatened to stick in her throat.

Samantha was silent for a moment, then she shook her head. "Are you sure?"

"I saw him die." But even as she spoke, Beatrice was beginning to have doubts. Her expression hardened. "Please, don't mention this to anyone."

"You have my word on that," Samantha assured her.

"Our secret." Beatrice held out her hand.

Accepting the handshake, Samantha smiled. "I suddenly feel very relieved. I need to be getting back to town."

Watching her depart, Beatrice felt anything but relieved. Samantha had described Joseph Whitedeer to a tee. On his father's side he was Crow. His mother had been of English and Spanish ancestry. Her genes had softened his features just enough so that he could pass for several different nationalities, including Arabian and Mexican. That had been a help in the work they had done. Could he really still be alive? If so, he was clearly in trouble. But then he'd always had a way of finding trouble.

Continuing to stand on the porch of the old farmhouse, she frowned with indecision. For nearly five years, she'd been certain Joe was dead. Most people would have discounted the story Samantha had told and called the woman mildly mad. But Beatrice knew her to be a rational person. Even more, she was well aware that those powers people labeled "extrasensory," could and did exist.

Going inside, she dialed a number she had not used in four years. Abruptly she hung up before the first ring. Calling could be dangerous to maintaining her anonymity. Numbers today were quickly and easily traced. Mentally she smiled at herself. Old habits died hard, but then it was those habits that had kept her alive.

Again picking up the phone, she punched in her brother's number. When her sister-in-law, Emily, answered, she said simply that she had to leave town for a couple of days and asked Emily to keep an eye on Justin. Then she hung up and went to her room to pack.

Emily Gerard stared at the receiver that had gone dead so abruptly. Her sister-in-law was not a woman prone to spontaneous acts. Even more puzzling was the fact that Beatrice had overlooked saying where she was going and hadn't given Emily a chance to ask.

"You look worried," the tall, muscular, dark-haired man watching from the doorway said. He'd just come in from the fields. Taking off his Stetson, he wiped the sweat from his brow with the sleeve of his shirt.

The sight of him brought a warm smile to Emily's face. Before Ryder had forced himself into her life, she'd begun to think that she would never find this kind of love and happiness. Then her smile turned into a thoughtful frown. "That was Beatrice. She's leaving town for a couple of days and wants us to keep an eye on Justin."

Ryder Gerard raised an eyebrow in surprise. "Where's she off to so suddenly?"

The frown on Emily's face deepened. "She didn't say."

"What's this about Beatrice getting a sudden notion to travel?" Justin Gerard joined his grandson in the doorway. White-haired, his eighty years of hard work under the sun evident on his face, he still stood straight and tall, exuding the air of authority common to the Gerard men.

"All I know is that she called and said she had to leave town for a couple of days." Emily smiled warmly. "You're welcome to stay here until she returns."

"I appreciate the offer, but I can take care of myself just fine," the old man replied, then added quickly, "I'm not saying I haven't appreciated having Beatrice looking after me these past few years since she got her divorce and left the military, but I don't need a nursemaid." He turned to Ryder. "I think we should head over to my place and find out what this is all about."

Ryder nodded.

As she watched from the porch while they drove away, Emily's frown returned. Beatrice had a mind of her own, and Emily had the distinct impression that her sister-in-law had no intention of telling anyone where she was going.

Beatrice had finished throwing a few things in a suitcase and was carrying it downstairs when her grandfather and Ryder pulled up.

"You look like a woman with a purpose," Ryder remarked as she stepped out onto the porch.

"Don't ask me any questions and I won't tell you any lies," she said stiffly.

"I want to know what this is all about," Justin demanded.

Beatrice met his gaze. "This is a private matter I have to handle on my own. I love you both and respect you. I'm asking that you do the same for me."

Ryder grinned. "Guess we'd better," he advised his grandfather. "My sister can be more stubborn than any mule ever born."

"Takes after her mother's side of the family in that respect," Justin muttered.

"I'm a lot more Gerard than Mallery," Beatrice returned, continuing to her car and tossing her luggage inside. Starting to climb in, she caught sight of her jeans-clad leg and booted foot. An impatient frown knitted her brow. She couldn't go like this. Joe Whitedeer had always had a way of sending her off half-cocked. "I've got to change and then get going," she said over her shoulder, heading back to the house.

"Beatrice." Ryder spoke her name sharply.

Prepared to fight any further inquiry into her activities, she turned to face him.

"If you should need me, just call," he said.

"Thanks," she returned with a sigh of relief, then hurried inside to change.

As Samantha Brant mounted the steps of her front porch, Thatcher came out to greet her. Concern was etched deeply into the ruggedly handsome features of his face. "Did you speak to Beatrice?" he asked.

"Yes, I felt I had to."

The lines of concern on his face deepened. "How did she react?"

"She didn't treat me as if I was crazy. In fact, she was very kind and I got the feeling she believed me. We both agreed to keep my visit a secret." She smiled. "Of course, telling you doesn't count. You already knew. But I didn't tell her you knew about the crystal. She thinks I'm keeping that a secret from everyone, including you."

He visibly relaxed. "That's probably for the best." His expression became thoughtful. "Her reaction suggests that there is more truth to that story about her great-grandfather than the Gerards would have us believe."

"Perhaps," Samantha agreed.

"But that's their business and none of ours," he added.

A knowing look passed between husband and wife. Then, wrapping his arm around her waist, he guided her inside. "The children are with your parents, and I've arranged to take an extra-long lunch hour," he said huskily as they crossed the threshold.

She grinned up at him. "How lovely."

It was midnight when Beatrice's plane landed in Washington, D.C. Her hair covered with a scarf and oversize sunglasses hiding the majority of her face, she disembarked with a decided limp. These were small tricks she'd learned to hide her identity from any surveillance cameras recording the arrival of passengers.

From the airport, she took a taxi to a hotel in Georgetown, registered as Sarah Jules and paid cash for the room. Once in her room, she placed a call to the number she'd dialed from her grandfather's farm.

"Versatile Pest Control. How may I help you?" a familiar female voice asked in friendly chipper tones as if it was the middle of the day instead of the middle of the night.

So Susan still worked the 11:00 p.m. to 3:00 a.m. shift at The Unit, Beatrice noted. But then the pretty, thirty-something blonde had always claimed that night was her favorite time of day. Beatrice had wondered if the woman was an insomniac, but wondering was as far as it had gone. No one pried into anyone else's business. Everyone was on a first-name basis, not because they were all friends but because that, too, provided a certain privacy. Secrecy, even in personal matters, was the watchword. Of course, if the office staff wanted to fraternize, they were allowed. It was only the agents who were encouraged to remain totally insular. Even their given names were not used. They were known only by their code names.

"Is The Manager in?" Tobias, the head of this small elite operation, worked long hours, sometimes sleeping in his office, and Beatrice hoped this would be one of those nights.

The voice on the other end of the line became cool and crisp. "No. May I take a message?"

"This is Thistle." Beatrice identified herself.

The voice on the other end of the line became even crisper. "It's been a long time. What is your message?"

Good old Susan. Always down to business, Beatrice mused. She remembered the first time she'd met her. Susan liked to wear massive amounts of makeup and tight, sexy clothes that showed off her curvaceous figure. At first sight, she gave the impression of being airheaded and available. Both qualities, Beatrice had learned, were as far from the truth as possible. Tobias had a knack for surrounding himself with people who weren't what they seemed.

"All of us have some part of ourselves we keep hidden," he'd told her once. "That's what makes people so interesting."

Using the code Joe had taught her, Beatrice delivered her message in precise tones. Only she, Joe and Tobias knew this cipher. It had been derived from a mixture of Crow and English. "Would you see that The Manager gets this message as quickly as possible?" she requested. Without waiting for a response, she hung up. Worried that she'd been on the line too long, she grabbed her bag and left the hotel.

As she took a taxi across town to Arlington, memories assailed her. It had been Joe who had chosen her code name. He'd said she was like a thistle—pretty to look at but dangerous if one got too close. She wished he'd heeded his own advice and kept his distance.

The taxi pulled up in front of the motel she'd requested. Jerking her mind back to the present, she paid the fare, went inside, registered as Mary Clemens and went to her room to try to get a couple of hours' rest. Working with Joe, she'd learned to sleep whenever possible and had caught an hour here and there during her flights. But her body ached to stretch out in a prone position for a short while.

Joe Whitedeer fought to keep his mind clear. It wasn't easy. The drug they were using to try to break him down was powerful. A woman's face filled his mind. It was pretty; not beautiful, but pretty. Long, thick, brunette hair caught in a gentle breeze blew lazily around the face. Her lips—full and sensuous—were a soft shade of pink. She'd hated bright red lipstick, he recalled, and had only worn it when it was necessary for a disguise. Then there were her eyes. At times they reminded him of the sky on a warm summer day. At others, he could almost see the storm clouds brewing in their darkening blue depths. He focused his mind on the face... Thistle's face. During the past few years, he'd conditioned himself not to think of her. But right now he needed the memory. It kept him alive and sane.

Beyond the door of his narrow cell he heard the guards laughing and joking. Housed in his windowless prison, unable to tell day from night, he'd lost track of time. One thing he did know for sure, he had to escape soon. He was weakening, and the mountainous terrain between him and civilization was thickly forested and would be hard going. He ordered his body into a sitting position. Dizziness assailed him. He tried to rise but was forced to sink back onto the narrow cot. He would rest awhile, then try again, he decided.

* * *

Dressed like a tourist, a camera slung around her neck, a wide-brimmed straw hat shading her face and the sunglasses again covering a major portion of it, Beatrice entered the Capitol building. Weaving through the tour groups already filling the passageways, she made her way to the basement.

"I was told I could get to my senator's office from here." She addressed the guard seated at the desk. Her voice had a Southern drawl and gushed with enthusiasm.

The man smiled patronizingly. "Who is your senator?"

She named one from one of the Southern states.

He gave her the senator's office number, told her which building she would find him in, then nodded toward a small, elegant, open tramlike railway vehicle. "You can take that train over there."

"You're ever so kind," she cooed over her shoulder, hurrying to climb aboard.

Smiling brightly at the female operator, she told her where she wanted to go.

Barely more than a couple of minutes later the woman brought the railway vehicle to a halt at the underground entrance of the requested location. "Have a good day," she said as Beatrice disembarked.

"I hope to," Beatrice replied, but doubted that would be the case.

Once inside the building she made her way to the top floor. There she walked quickly down the hall, rounded a corner, noted that there was no one to see her and slipped into a door marked Private.

"Right on time, as usual," a male voice greeted her.

She frowned. The face was familiar, but it wasn't the one she'd expected. "Where is Tobias?"

"Not even a 'Harold, how nice to see you'?" the man asked. "Coyote was right, you do deserve your code name."

Coyote was Joe's code name. Beatrice found herself wondering if even Harold had been kept from seeing their real names. When Tobias wanted to be secretive he was very good at it. Of course, even if Harold did know, he would never use them in public. He'd been taught by Tobias and was a professional in every sense of the word. And he was right. She had been impolite. "It is nice to see you again," she said in milder tones.

From behind her sunglasses, her gaze raked over the man who was second in command and Tobias's faithful right hand. He was in his early fifties, dressed in a nice-looking suit—nothing fancy or so expensive it would garner a second look, but well-cut. His once-blond hair, now nearly pure white, was cut in a conservative style. He'd kept in shape, but she'd expected that. His face was pleasant but nondescript. He had the ability to hide his air of authority and blend into any group, becoming one of the unnoticed. Tobias had valued him for that. Concern entered her voice, "Has something happened to Tobias?"

"He retired a couple of years ago. Coyote's death hit him pretty hard."

Beatrice recalled how withdrawn Tobias had been when she'd returned alone from that last fatal assignment. The car bomb had left little to be recovered of Joe's body. Tobias had been the only one in The Unit to know of her and Joe's marriage. After the small private funeral service held at Arlington, he'd suggested that she tell her family that she'd gotten a divorce. As a widow, she would be expected to talk about her husband. People would ask questions and she would be forced to lie, make up stories. That was always dangerous. A divorce, he'd pointed out, if she let people think it was an unpleasant one, would eliminate a great many problems. If asked about her husband, she could simply say she didn't want to talk about him. He'd also suggested she take back her maiden name. That would be evidence to the nosy that she wanted to put the marriage behind her. It would also eliminate any connection between her and Joe, should his identity ever be discovered by those they'd sought to stop.

She'd never doubted that Tobias's concern for her safety and the safety of her family was real. And considering the strain that had existed between her and Joe at the end, she guessed Joe would have preferred to have been disassociated from her, as well. So she'd agreed to all that Tobias had suggested. He'd had divorce papers drawn up, along with a court order allowing her to reclaim her maiden name. Thus, officially, Joseph Whitedeer had been erased from her life for all time.

And until yesterday, she had almost managed to put him out of her mind. Only at very weak moments had he crept back into her thoughts. Now she couldn't push him out. She needed some assurance that it was him in that grave in Arlington.

"I contacted Tobias when your message was delivered to me," Harold continued. "I realized it was meant for him. I recognized the code as being the one Coyote used when he sent something for Tobias's eyes only. Even I was never given the cipher for that one."

She caught the faint hint of anger in his voice and realized he'd felt slighted by this omission. She, herself, was a little surprised. Tobias had his reasons for everything, though. Besides, with Joe dead and her out of The Unit, there would be no one left to use it.

"Tobias prefers to remain retired. He asked me to meet with you. How can I be of assistance?" Harold finished.

The hint of anger was gone. In its place was a friendly, even fatherly smile of encouragement, and the words to ask him about Joe formed on Beatrice's tongue. But before they could be issued, she swallowed them back. If Joe wasn't dead and Harold knew, he wouldn't tell her, and she didn't know him well enough to detect if he was lying. "It's a personal matter. Some unfinished business between myself and Tobias. I was pretty broken up by J—" She bit back the name. Quickly substituting the designation she knew Harold would expect her to use, she continued, "Coyote's death. I owe Tobias a thank-you I never gave him. Since I was in town, I thought I'd tell him."

"We were all pretty shaken by your partner's death, but Coyote knew the chance he was taking. When any of us went into the field, we knew we might be coming back in a body bag."

His voice, Beatrice noted, held just the right touch of sympathy but she wasn't buying it. She knew he'd never liked Joe. He'd thought Joe was a loose cannon, undisciplined, a risk taker. And he was right. But Joe had always gotten the job done. "Would you mind getting another message to Tobias for me? I'd really like to see him."

Harold's fatherly smile returned. "Yes, of course. Where can I reach you?"

Giving him a specific location where she could be reached went against her training. She told herself she was being overly cautious. After all, he was The Manager now. Still, she heard herself saying, "I've already checked out of my hotel. How about if I give your office a call in a couple of hours?"

"Fine." He extended his hand. "You're looking fit. I'm glad."

"Thanks." She accepted the handshake. "You look very well yourself."

He nodded, then left.

She waited a full five minutes before opening the door a crack and looking out into the hall. It was empty. Making her way back to the train, she returned to the Capitol building and left it in the midst of a tour group.

Mentally she mocked herself for continuing to hide behind the sunglasses. She could have walked barefaced down any street in Washington and never been recognized. Her military record read that she'd spent the last years of her service in a rather dull, uneventful assignment at the Swiss embassy. There were no more than a handful of people who even knew she'd been with The Unit: Tobias; Harold; Grace, Tobias's secretary; Susan; Julia, the 7:00 a.m. to 3:00 p.m. receptionist; Lucinda, the 3:00 p.m. to 11:00 p.m. receptionist, and three of the other operatives besides Joe.

The images of the three receptionists played through Beatrice's mind. They knew everyone who worked for Tobias by sight. They had to. They were the first line of defense, should an unauthorized person try to trespass uninvited into his inner sanctum. They simply didn't look like a first line of defense.

Lucinda, in her late twenties, slender to the point of looking like a twig, with eyes too big for her face, always seemed mildly harried as if constantly trying to catch up with herself. And there was Susan, with her bright open smile giving the impression she was ready to be picked up by any good-looking man who entered. Then there was Julia. In her mid-fifties, on the slightly plump side with white hair and a bright smile, she was the epitome of the storybook grandmother.

But near at hand, in a holster on the underside of their desk, was an Uzi, loaded and ready at all times. And no one doubted that any of the three would use it. All had been personally recruited by Tobias from the various branches of the service and all were crack shots.

Returning to her hotel, Beatrice checked out. Precisely two hours from the time she'd parted from Harold, she placed a call to his office. Julia answered. The message she relayed was in the same code Beatrice had used on first contact. Tobias would see her.

Chapter Two

When Beatrice stepped off the small commuter plane at a private airstrip near Craftsbury Common, Vermont, a car was waiting for her. She recognized the driver as Raven. That wasn't his real name, just his code. She'd never known his real name. Tobias preferred for his operatives to remain anonymous even among themselves.

Raven was, to her knowledge, considered by Tobias to be one of the very best. She judged him to be about four years younger than Joe, in his early to mid thirties. Like Joe, he had black hair and brown eyes. From his carriage she could tell his tall athletic frame was still in top form. Today he had on his comfortable face, the one that didn't intimidate. When he wanted, with just a look she'd seen him cause strong men to quake. This ability to appear mild-mannered or dangerously homicidal depending on the situation was, according to Tobias, one of Raven's most useful qualities.

"Thought I'd take on a safe, dull assignment for a while," he said in answer to the question on her face.

"I never thought you'd leave the field," she admitted honestly, as they drove away from the airport.

"The Old Man needed a bodyguard, someone he felt comfortable with. I volunteered. I owe him my life several times over."

"We all do." It was sad, Beatrice thought, that the team of operatives Tobias had built and who had come to rely on one another so completely could not even visit like old friends. Even to see Tobias, who had been as close as a father, she'd had to go through covert channels. Joe had been right about one thing: as long as they'd stayed with the agency, they could never have had a family or even a semblance of a normal life.

"Tobias is in his greenhouse. It's around to the left. I'll put your suitcase in your room," Raven said, parking in front of the manor house of Tobias's county estate.

Beatrice thanked him, then followed the brick path in the direction he'd indicated. She was barely halfway to the greenhouse, when Tobias came out. He'd aged. The last time she'd seen him, he'd looked a good ten years younger than his mid-sixty years. Now he looked his age and more. His brisk gait had slowed and he required a cane to walk.

"You're looking as lovely as ever," he said, smiling fondly upon her. "To what do I owe the pleasure of this visit?"

They'd never beaten around the bush with each other. "I want to know if Joe is alive."

His gaze narrowed on her. "That's a peculiar question to ask after all this time."

He was hedging, feeling her out. She had her answer. "He is, isn't he?" she demanded.

For a moment Tobias hesitated, then said, "He was until five days ago. My guess is that he isn't any longer."

A surge of pain shook her. She'd thought she'd finished with her grief. Now it felt as fresh as ever. "Why fake his death?"

Tobias's manner became fatherly. "He and I thought it was for the best. He'd realized that your marriage was a mistake for both of you. I wanted an experienced operative to go deep and for that I needed someone no one would be looking for. It was his contact who was killed in the explosion. Joe was injured but managed to find a safe hole to hide in. He was afraid you'd get tagged if he contacted you, so he contacted me. When we realized we could make it look as if he was the one who had died, we followed that route."

Beatrice fought back the hot tears at the back of her eyes. She wouldn't cry over a man who'd wanted so badly to be free of her, he'd been willing to fake his own death. She suddenly remembered an elderly Indian on a lonely hilltop in Wyoming. "How could he do that to his grandfather? Frank Whitedeer had no one else."

A glimmer of guilt showed in Tobias's eyes.

The truth dawned on Beatrice. "His grandfather knew he was alive."

"As you said, Joe was his only family," Tobias said, apologetically.

A new thought caused her gaze to narrow in anger. "Joe's bank and savings accounts. You gave all that to me. And there was that ten thousand you said was from an insurance policy." She'd tried to give the money to Frank Whitedeer but he'd been insistent that she kept it. Now she understood why. She'd been the pawn in their game. And she didn't like it.

"The insurance money came from cashing in some bonds he'd had. As for his accounts, he wanted you to have them."

Her mouth tasted bitter. Joe had settled his conscience by thinking he could buy her off. Silently she cursed herself for ever having cared for the man. Next, she congratulated herself for having put the money away in a rainy-day fund. It was still intact. When she found him, she would return all of it, plus the interest. She wanted nothing from him. A sudden realization hit her. "So you haven't retired."

"Officially, yes. Unofficially, I'm handling one final assignment. Joe was my only operative."

"You mean he went out without a backup?"

Tobias frowned at her naiveté. "He's been operating on his own ever since you and he parted company. I couldn't send backup with a dead man, and being dead was Joe's major trump card. And it worked well."

Beatrice's jaw hardened with purpose. "I have to find him. I have reason to believe he's still alive. And if I'm right, he needs my help."

"You're out of the business now."

"I may be out of the business, but I'm going after Joe."

"You have no idea what you're up against."

"Then tell me."

"That's classified information. Besides, as I've told you, I doubt he's still alive. The people he was dealing with do not play games."

Beatrice's stomach knotted tighter. "He's not an easy man to kill. If he's alive, I'll find him. If he's dead, I want to see the body. I have to know for sure."

For a long moment, Tobias studied her, then said, "I had him associating with mercenaries, trying to get a line on problems before they developed. A little less than three years ago, he managed to hook up with a couple of men who were contacted to participate in the robbery of one of our arsenals out west. It was after that incident that he and I began to suspect that the robberies, while they were being carried out by different groups of thieves, were being orchestrated by a single person. But what really had us rattled was that our people were being more and more effectively eluded. Joe became convinced there was a mole in The Unit who was fingering our agents.

"I retired to take myself actively out of the loop and the mole's attention off me and my activities. This also allowed me to take an outsider's view of our little community. But our mole is clever. Perhaps, even more so than I even suspected. I thought we were merely dealing with an informant. However, during the past few months, Joe concluded that this elusive mole we are seeking is also the one masterminding the thefts. The last time I heard from him, he was sure he was on the right track to discovering the traitor's identity. Then he vanished."

"Where was he when he vanished?"

"San Diego, waiting to catch a plane for Mexico City."

Not much of a lead, Beatrice thought. "I'd like a bag. With or without it, I'm going to find him."

Tobias's gaze narrowed on her. "Why did you come here asking about Joe after all these years?"

For a moment she considered making up a story, then decided that the truth would do. He would never believe it. He would think she was evading his question with a jest. Still, she couldn't take any chances. "I have your word that what I tell you will go no further?"

"You have my word," he replied.

"A seer with a crystal ball described him to me. She said she was sure he was alive."

For a moment interest sparked in his eyes, then abruptly he laughed. "You always did have a knack for the dramatic. However, I know you well enough to know that you're not going to tell me anything you don't want to. So,

I'll just hope your source is right. I'd go after him myself if I could. Maybe you showing up here is prophetic."

Or maybe just her bad luck, Beatrice thought two hours later as Raven drove her back to the airport. This need to find a man who would prefer never to see her again was nuts. Even more, she was again armed with the tools of a trade she'd taken great precautions to put behind her. In addition to her luggage was a black leather knapsack with a high-tech radio transmitter, a .32 automatic with extra clips and three packets of IDs hidden in a secret side panel. In her wallet was a bank card for an account she could access for funds. For now, she'd chosen the Treasury agent persona. She was Claire Homes, Special Investigator. The badge gave her the authority she needed to carry a weapon onto a plane.

Tobias had been very little help in discovering Joe's whereabouts. Although Joe had said he was headed to Mexico City, he could have been taken prisoner in San Diego. Or maybe Mexico City had merely been his jumping-off spot to somewhere else.

Joe Whitedeer stared at the tray of food in front of him. Time was a difficult thing to judge in this black hole of a cell. For hours—perhaps even a full day—he'd been lying in the dark. His captors had stopped their questioning. They had, in fact, seemed to have lost interest in him altogether and were simply allowing him to slowly die. Now, suddenly, his guards had brought him a lamp and a meal of lamb stew, fruit, coffee and a large jug of water.

His last meal? he wondered.

"Eat," one guard ordered.

Joe suspected it was drugged. Still, the people who held him had less palatable ways of getting drugs into him if they were determined to do so. They already had. He scooped up a bite of the stew. Either he was in for a quick trip to la-la land or his captors had decided they needed him in a healthier state. Mentally he tossed a coin. He didn't wait for it to drop. Without food and water, he would die soon anyway. He shoved the bite into his mouth and chewed. It tasted good and he took another....

When Raven dropped her off at the airport, Beatrice did not catch a flight for the coast. Instead, she bought a ticket for Boston. There she switched IDs and rented a car, paying with cash.

But as she slid into the driver's seat, that there had been no bug detector in the black bag nagged at her. It was standard equipment. She told herself that Tobias had not had time to organize her travel kit as efficiently as in the past. Not including the bug detector could have been a mere oversight. But the memory of Joe reciting his rules for survival continued to play through her mind. Rule number one was, "Never fully trust anyone but yourself." Of course, she had trusted him and Tobias completely. And in spite of the game they'd played, where her safety was concerned, she still did. However, she didn't know all of Tobias's household staff. For all practical purposes, even Raven was a stranger to her. She knew Tobias trusted all of them, but anyone could be fooled.

"Better safe than sorry," she murmured. After a quick check of her clothing, she opened the trunk and examined her carry-on and its contents. Next came her purse. Nothing. Her attention turned to the black bag.

Sitting in the back seat of the car, she began a thorough search. Inside the tiny portable radio transmitter, she found what she was looking for—a high-tech bug. Fear for Tobias swept through her. He had a traitor under his roof.

Going back inside the airport, she found a pay phone and dialed his number. When he came on the line she said, "I'd suggest you get an exterminator. You have a bug problem."

From the other end came a chuckle. "I forgot you were trained by the best. Don't worry. It was a friendly insect."

She glared at the array of shiny metallic buttons in front of her. "You?"

"I didn't like the idea of you going off alone. I wanted to be sure there was an angel on your shoulder."

Beatrice knew he was only being protective, but she planned to seek out people and go places that even he didn't need to know about. "I'll be fine on my own," she assured him and hung up.

Back at the car, she made a second thorough search to be certain she hadn't missed anything, then drove to Greenfield. She'd taken several side roads on her across-state trek and kept an eye on the traffic behind her. She was convinced she hadn't been tagged. Still, she didn't want to lead anyone to her doorstep. In Greenfield, she parked the rented car in the airport parking lot and switched to her own car. Tomorrow she would return and use the rental car to drive back to Boston.

Her instincts had brought her back to Smytheshire. They told her that if she was going to find Joe alive, she'd better find him soon. For that she needed help. It was in the early hours of the morning when she drove up to her grandfather's farmhouse.

Hoping not to wake him, she entered and made her way to her room.

"You ready to tell me what this is all about?" Justin asked, coming out of his room as she reached the door of hers.

"There is someone I need to find," she replied simply.

"This someone have a name?"

"It's my ex-husband. I thought he was dead. But maybe he isn't. I need to find out."

Justin frowned. "When you never brought him home to meet us, divorced him after barely a year of marriage, took back your maiden name and never spoke of him, I figured he must have mistreated you badly—so badly you were too embarrassed and humiliated to tell any of us about it. So I'm finding it a little hard to understand why it's so important for you to find out if he's dead or alive. Are you afraid he might come looking for you?"

"I've never worried about that," she replied dryly. "And he didn't mistreat me. He just simply didn't want to be married to me. But that doesn't change the fact that I owe him. If he's alive, he could be in trouble." Her shoulders straightened with purpose. "I'm going to ask Zebulon for help."

"If you're going to Zebulon, then finding your former husband must be mightily important. And I hope you do find him. I'd like to ask him what kind of fool would give you up."

"We gave up on each other." Although she'd managed to sleep on the planes, exhaustion threatened to overwhelm Beatrice. "I'm too tired to talk anymore."

Justin nodded. "Get some sleep. We'll finish this conversation in the morning."

Going into her room, Beatrice stripped and crawled into bed. There was no conversation left to finish. She'd said all she could or would. A shiver of fear for Joe traveled through her. The desire to go to Zebulon's place right away was strong, but he would be asleep, and waking him at this hour of the night might anger the old man and cause him to refuse to help her. Besides, she admitted, she was too tired to move. Her eyes closed and in the next instant she was asleep.

* * *

The sun was fully over the horizon when she rose. Impatient with herself for having slept so late, she was strongly tempted to dress and leave without eating. But her stomach growled, reminding her she had eaten very little the day before. Suddenly Joe's scowling countenance filled her mind. "Never pass up food when it's easily available," she could hear him cautioning. "Once you're in the middle of an operation, you can't always count on having time to eat or even being able to find food."

Justin Gerard was in the kitchen when his granddaughter entered. After a monosyllabic greeting of, "Morning," he waited until she'd sat down to eat, then, seating himself across from her, said, "You've never volunteered any information about your marriage and I've respected your privacy. But now I'm asking. Before you take off again, I want to know a little about where you might be going."

Beatrice looked up from the plate of scrambled eggs to meet her grandfather's gaze. Although Tobias had zealously guarded the identities of his agents as a safeguard for their families as well as themselves, she did not want to take any chances. If there was a mole in The Unit, there was always the possibility that even Tobias's carefully devised security had been breached. "There are things you should know," she said. "I have not been completely honest with you and the rest of the family about my tenure in the military. I was in the military police but, during my last years of service, I was not stationed at the embassy in Switzerland. I was part of a small group of specially trained operatives who investigated the stealing of arms and munitions from military bases, drug operations on our bases, anything that required undercover methods to solve. We worked within all the branches of the military, wherever the problem was. It was a covert operation. My real identity was hidden at all times so that when I left The Unit, I could resume a normal life and neither myself nor any of you would be threatened by retaliation. Joe was my ranking officer. We worked as a team. We didn't get along too well at first. He could be real stubborn.''

Justin grinned. ''It's my guess he met his match on that point in you.''

''That's what he claimed.'' A sharp image filled Beatrice's mind. It was of Joe. They'd been arguing, then the mood between them had changed. A moment later, he was kissing her. That was their first kiss. If they'd been smart, it would have been their last.

''You said last night that you'd thought he was dead.'' Justin coaxed her mind back to the present.

Beatrice stared down into her coffee cup. ''On our last mission together, the people we were after rigged his car to explode. As it turns out, it was his contact who was blown up. Joe managed to escape. He and the man we both worked for decided to let everyone believe Joe was dead. It allowed them to make him into an invisible man.''

Justin scowled. ''And he never even let you know the truth?''

''By then we'd realized that our marriage was a mistake. I guess he figured faking his death was an easy way out. At the time, our boss told me he'd worked up the divorce scenario because it would be easier to avoid questions when I returned home. His logic seemed reasonable to me.''

Justin nodded. ''It worked with me and the rest of your family. We figured the experience had been too painful to talk about so we never asked any questions.'' He studied her. ''I know you said you were only going looking for him because you think you owe him. But you don't look like a woman going after a man you dislike.''

"I never said I disliked him. I just said our marriage was a mistake." Falling silent, she finished her breakfast quickly, then rose. "I've got to go see Zebulon. I took precautions. I doubt anyone will find their way here, but just in case, keep an eye out for strangers and warn Ryder and the others. If anyone asks about where I am, just say I'm on vacation, traveling around, you're not sure where. The last part will be the truth. If anyone asks about Joe Whitedeer, just tell them you've never heard of him. Our marriage was a better-kept secret than the location of King Solomon's mines. Whoever does the asking will assume we were never more than partners and that I followed procedure and never spoke of him to you."

"We can take care of ourselves," Justin assured her. "But I don't like you going off alone."

"I have to do this by myself," she insisted.

As she drove to Zebulon's place, her mind again went back to that first kiss. It had been a shock to both her and Joe. They'd jerked apart like a couple of embarrassed teenagers.

"It's not safe for me to be thinking about you as a woman. It diverts my concentration from more important things like keeping us both alive," he'd said. Then he'd added that he planned to forget the kiss had ever happened and ordered her to do the same.

"Consider it forgotten," she'd replied. Now she wished she'd been more successful at obeying that order.

In hindsight, she was certain Joe had never allowed himself ever to be truly emotionally involved with her. And what she'd felt for him was nothing more than animal passion, she assured herself. But it had been incredibly strong.

She brought her mind fully back to the present. Ahead of her was the gate that led to Zebulon's land. Coming here would be the first time in several generations that anyone in her family had openly acknowledged their heritage. But Zebulon and his kin before him knew the truth. It had simply been a silent understanding that it would not be spoken aloud.

Beyond the gate, the gravel road wove through thick woods until it ended in a large clearing. Within the clearing was a sprawling structure. The original portion had been a one-room log cabin, but through the years it had been added to as whim or need dictated. Sitting in a rocking chair on the railed, roofed front porch was a man with a head of white hair that hung well below his shoulders. His face was obscured by a thick mustache and a beard as long as his hair. Only the Lansky blue eyes were clearly distinct. He wore jeans, a red-and-black plaid cotton shirt and hunting boots that laced to his knees. Beside his chair was a long-haired dog, medium in size, brown and black in color.

The dog rose. His ears back and his teeth bared, he took a protective stance at the top of the short flight of stairs leading up to the porch.

"Sit down and relax, you fool dog," Zebulon said as Beatrice climbed out of her car. "We've got a female caller. Mind your manners."

The dog immediately became indifferent and returned to his position beside the rocker.

Rising stiffly, Zebulon eyed his visitor with interest. "Morning, Beatrice," he said.

"Morning," she replied. At the foot of the steps she paused, waiting for an invitation to proceed. She knew Zebulon was not as crotchety as he acted, but she also knew it was best not to cross him if you wanted a favor—and she wanted a favor.

"Come on up and sit awhile." He waved toward a second rocker beside the one he'd occupied. "Would you like some coffee?"

"No, but thank you." Continuing to the level of the porch, she seated herself as he eased himself back into his chair.

"You've come here with a purpose, girl. I can see that." He shifted his chair so that he had an easy view of her face.

Normally Beatrice was a very straightforward person. But she was uneasy about breaking the code of silence that had existed for generations among the residents of Smytheshire who knew of their heritage. She felt fairly confident in believing that most of the populace whose families had been linked to hers in centuries past, were oblivious to the truth about their ancestry and about the purpose behind the founding of the town. Certainly Samantha's behavior was proof that neither she nor her family was aware that having a talent was a very natural part of their nature.

On the other side of the coin, Beatrice was equally certain that Zebulon knew that and much more. She was aware of his family's ancestral duty and did not doubt that he was carrying out his appointed task. Still, it wouldn't hurt to proceed slowly with her request. "My family has always believed that Angus Smythe chose this place to set up his own little town because it was secluded and because you and your kin were already established here?" She spoke in a tone that made this a question.

"My family and the Smythes go back a long way," Zebulon replied, a gleam appearing in his eyes as if he guessed where this was going and was excited by the prospect.

"Centuries, perhaps?"

"Centuries," he confirmed.

"Back to pre-Christian days? Perhaps as far back as when the Druids thrived?"

"So I've been told."

"The history books have very little in them about the Druids. They say that the people of the time believed them to have strong paranormal powers. However, those powers have never been officially verified."

The gleam in Zebulon's eyes grew. "Centuries ago, people were less skeptical of things they did not understand. Today, everything has to be proved scientifically before people will allow themselves to believe."

Beatrice was well aware that some people in town thought Zebulon was a brick short of a full load. But they were wrong. He was wily and clever. And he was toying with her, making her do the revealing. "The history books also claim that all the Druids were killed, slaughtered by conquerors who feared their powers."

Zebulon's mouth formed a thoughtful pout. "So I've heard."

"But I have also heard tales that claim that is not entirely true. They tell of some of the Druids escaping and assimilating into other cultures, denying their heritage and hiding their talents until those talents became weak, then lay dormant within them."

"I've heard that, as well."

"According to these tales there was one family who ignored the agreement that their people would disperse and forget the names of the others. This family kept track of as many of their brethren as possible. Twice in past centuries, they tried to gather the descendants of those ancient Druids together and twice the colonies failed. The first time was because outsiders discovered the truth of their heritage and out of fear, wanted to kill them."

"There are always those who perceive what they cannot understand to be a threat. They are unwilling to accept the great versatility of the human mind," Zebulon noted.

Beatrice waited a moment for him to take the lead. When he didn't, she continued. "The second failure was due to internal strife. Most were strong Christians by then and understood that the powers they possessed were inherited talents that could not be made stronger nor conceived by any pagan ritual. But one who had been born without any special abilities, grew resentful and wanted to reinstate the old pagan ways with hope of achieving the powers. It was his actions that sent them apart yet again."

Zebulon smiled. "Interesting tales. Are there more?"

"The saga ends here in Smytheshire. It was the Smythes who kept track of their brethren after each dispersion. Toward the end of the 1800s, Angus Smythe decided to again attempt to bring the Druid descendants together. Only this time, there would be a code of silence. No mention would be made of their heritage. His hope was that once they were all gathered together, their powers would again come to life. He sought out those he wanted to settle here. Without making any reference to their ancestry, he encouraged them to move here. To people who were in business, he said he needed their talents for his town to survive and flourish and offered to help them set up shop. With others, like my family, he claimed a long-lost relative had left us a great deal of land—enough to make it profitable for my great-great-grandfather to pull up stakes and relocate here. Of course, my family had other reasons for coming, as well."

Zebulon grinned. "I heard my daddy and Angus talking about your great-great-granddad. Seems he'd remembered the Smythe name and guessed Angus's intent. Seems he also didn't trust Angus. He made Angus give his word that this would be a God-fearing community and their heritage would remain a secret kept by those who knew and never revealed to those who didn't. And, of course, there'd be those who lived here who didn't have any Druid ancestry.

Angus needed people with all kinds of business and care-giving skills to make his town work. He couldn't fill all the positions with his own ilk. And he couldn't throw out those families already living in and around our valley.''

Beatrice breathed a mental sigh of relief. Zebulon had stopped playing his cat-and-mouse game.

"You said your family had other reasons for coming here.'' The old man's gaze bore into her. "Can I assume the claim made by Thaddeus Sayer about your great-grandfather Zachariah Gerard was true?''

"Let's just say that the talents of some families didn't ever become dormant.''

Zebulon smiled broadly. "A belief I've held for a long time.'' His expression became serious. "But you would not have come here and admitted to something your family has kept private all these generations without good cause. Why have you come?''

"Most people here in Smytheshire think of you as a hermit who pays little attention to anyone. But we Gerards have always believed you and your kin to be the Observers.''

Zebulon shrugged. "I do like to pride myself on being more observant than most people think.''

"You have the ability to detect those with talent?''

"My family has always been able to sense certain auras. We cannot tell how strong the talent is, though. For that, I can only listen and watch.''

Time to get to the point of her visit, Beatrice decided. "I need a Finder.''

"That's a very vague and iffy talent,'' Zebulon cautioned. "There are a couple with a mild ability here in Smytheshire. Are you seeking animal, vegetable or mineral?''

"A man.''

"I believe there is one who might be able to help but she doesn't live here."

"I don't mind traveling."

"She's a MacGreggor. Her married name is Stone... Amanda Stone. She lives on a ranch in South Dakota somewhere near the small town of Redig. You can contact her cousin, Madaline Darnell, if you want more explicit directions. But I would not reveal my reasons to Madaline for seeking her. Madaline, as well as her husband, are of the lineage. But they are not yet ready to accept the full truth. From what I've heard, however, Amanda recognizes her ability and is not as secretive about it as some. She does not flaunt it, but if asked outright, she will admit to it."

"I'll find her on my own."

"I would advise you to take something that belongs to the person you're seeking. Something that holds a strong, special meaning to that person would be best."

Beatrice thanked him for his help. As she started to leave, she turned back. "I'd appreciate it if you'd consider this conversation confidential."

"I consider all my conversations confidential," he replied.

She nodded her gratitude and continued to her car.

Chapter Three

Back at her grandfather's farm, Beatrice stood in her room in front of her bureau and opened her jewelry box. From inside, she extracted a necklace. It was old—a single strand of beads on a leather thong with a tiny wooden replica of a coyote at the center front. Her hand closed tightly around it as memories flashed through her mind.

Soon after they were married, Joe had taken her to his grandfather's ranch. "If you ever need a safe haven, come here," he'd instructed her. "My grandfather claims the spirits of my Crow ancestors guard this place. I don't know about that, but I do know it's isolated and anyone approaching is easily spotted."

She'd heard the indulgence in his voice and knew he didn't share his grandfather's belief in the spirits. If he had, she might have confided in him.

Her mind traveled further back and she recalled the first time she'd meet Joe Whitedeer. She'd been lying in a hospital bed recovering from a concussion caused by a bullet grazing her head. He'd been dressed in the uniform of a major. The lack of battle-obtained metals suggested he'd spent his career doing tasks that held no risk. But that and the uniform, she would eventually learn, were merely a sham. He was a ranking officer but not in the army. He'd been a navy Seal when he'd been recruited by Tobias. He'd earned his rank in battle and had a chest full of metals for bravery. But that was the real Joe Whitedeer, and it took her time to make those discoveries. At that first meeting he'd stood over her bed, those cold, dark brown eyes of his boring into her, and introduced himself as Major Jones.

"I've been sent from Washington to investigate this robbery. The top brass is very concerned about thefts of this sort. I need to know exactly what happened," he'd said. "I want every detail you can recall about the men you caught stealing from the armory."

"She's just regained consciousness. Give her some time to recover," the doctor insisted. He was standing on the other side of the bed, scowling at Joe, clearly displeased with the major for making demands so soon on his patient. "That bullet grazed her head pretty deep. She's lucky to be alive. She might not even remember the incident for a while, if ever."

"You're wrong, Doctor," she said. "I do remember." In spite of the dull throbbing in her head, the image of her partner, Sergeant Bruce Wood, was sharp in her mind. His body was doubling over and there was blood. Her gaze narrowed on the man in white. "How is Sergeant Wood?"

The sympathy on the doctor's face gave her the answer before he spoke. "He didn't make it."

She thought of Bruce's wife and kids. Tears flooded her eyes. "We walked right into it."

Joe took out a notebook and pen. "Describe what happened."

"She needs time to recover," the doctor insisted. "She's still weak."

Joe's cold gaze turned on him. "We've lost several hours as it is. If we're going to catch these men, I need information now."

"I want to help," Beatrice said, interrupting the dispute. A tear trickled down her cheek. "I have to help."

The doctor frowned, but made no more protests.

For a long moment she was silent, trying to think past the building headache, then said, "We recognized Private Harrison sneaking in the back door of the armory and figured he was meeting some buddies for a poker game. He has a gambling problem. Whenever we heard of an illegal game on the base, we'd just follow him for a few days. Eventually he'd lead us to it. But neither of us ever saw him as a threat. We both agreed that if he ever went into battle, he'd get killed because he'd never be able to harm anyone, even in self-defense. We were wrong on all counts."

"Never underestimate anyone." It was Joe who spoke. This was another of the rules he taught and possibly, she thought, the most important she'd ever learned from him.

"I won't ever again," she assured him.

The hint of a smile tilted one corner of his mouth, then it was gone. "You saw Private Harrison sneaking into the armory. What then?"

"Even though we didn't expect any real trouble, we followed procedure and called for backup. The other units had been called to stop a break-in in the officers' quarters. We chose not to wait for them to finish there. It was near the end of our shift and Bruce—Sergeant Wood—wanted to get the bust over with so we could get the paperwork done and go home."

"The break-in at the officers' quarters was a diversion. It was meant to keep all the MPs occupied," he informed her.

She frowned at her own and Bruce's naiveté. "A thoroughly planned job."

"You were dealing with professionals. Did you recognize anyone other than Harrison when you went inside?"

"There wasn't any time. They were waiting for us." The truth dawned on her. "It was our call for backup that nailed us, wasn't it? They were scanning our patrol band."

"You catch on quick."

She thought of Bruce and another tear escaped. "Not quick enough."

Joe turned to the doctor. "You may have your patient back."

As he started to leave, she forced herself into a sitting position. "I want to help catch the men who did this."

He turned back. "Good, because you're going to. You're my bait."

Her anger flared. "You mean you were going to use me and not even tell me?"

He shrugged. "You're a soldier. You've promised to lay your life on the line for your country. But I would have warned you." He turned to the doctor. "I'm leaving a couple of MPs on her door. Until I get back, no one, not even a nurse, gets inside unless you know them personally."

"I have other patients. I can't stand guard here," the doctor protested.

Joe's jaw twitched, letting the doctor know he was not pleased. "Then you march whatever nurse might be needing to come into this room down here and introduce her to the MPs."

"That I can do," the doctor agreed.

An hour later, Beatrice had been lying with her eyes closed, concentrating on remembering the events of the night before, when she heard someone entering the room. She opened one eye just a sliver to see Major Jones returning. Closing the eye again, she continued to concentrate on a face that would not come totally clear.

"Nice dead possum," he said, approaching the bed. "Anyone less observant than me would think you were asleep."

She opened her eyes. "I wasn't trying to fool you. I was trying to think. It isn't easy with what sounds and feels like a drum corps marching through my skull."

The hint of the smile returned. "Lucky for you, you have a thick one."

"My family has always accused me of being hard-headed."

The smile lingered just long enough for her to note that he actually looked handsome in a rugged sort of way. Then it was gone.

"I've changed my mind about using you as bait," he said. "You're in no condition to defend yourself if the bad guys should get past my lines of defense. I told the base commander that you didn't see anyone other than Harrison and I've taken the MPs off your door as proof I don't think you know anything important."

"What about Harrison? Do you have him in custody? Did he tell you anything?"

"He was found dead a little ways outside the post gates. I'm fairly certain this is the same group that robbed an armory in Texas. They don't leave any witnesses. Harrison was as good as dead when they recruited him."

"I suppose he did it for the money. He was a gambler and always in debt."

"Just the kind of weakness they'd look for."

Her gaze narrowed on him. "I'm sure the others were in uniform."

"And I'm sure you're right, but anyone can purchase a uniform. They were civilians using phony IDs to move around the base. If we check the personnel, we'll find all of them accounted for and the men we want won't be among them."

"They're not going to get away with killing my partner. I want to be used—" Her demand was cut short by the sound of the door opening and something being dropped.

"Damn! Fire in the hole!" Joe yelled.

Beatrice barely got a glimpse of the grenade before he lifted her out of the bed on the side opposite the door, dropped to the floor and fell on top of her, covering her with his body.

Seconds later came the explosion. The windows rattled, then shattered. Silence followed.

Joe lifted his head and looked around in confusion. "What the devil?" he muttered. The room, except for the broken windowpanes, was in the same condition it had been in before the grenade exploded.

"He must have tossed it too hard," Beatrice said. "And it went out the open window."

"That was one hell of a toss," Joe observed.

The two MPs he'd just dismissed came bursting through the door. "What happened?" the first demanded.

"Someone tossed a grenade in here from the hall," Joe said, getting to his feet. "He put too much energy into it, sent it out the window."

The other man gave a low whistle. "Talk about luck. You two could have been killed if it'd exploded in here."

"Did either of you see anyone in the hall?" Joe asked curtly.

"An orderly passed us when we were leaving." The first MP had approached the window and was looking out.

"Looks as if it exploded in midair. There's no sign of damage on the ground."

"Was anybody hurt?" Beatrice demanded, trying to make certain the hospital gown wasn't exposing too much as she eased herself into a sitting position.

"Not on the outside," he replied.

In the next instant, Joe was scooping her up. The back of the gown opened and she was aware of her nakedness against his arms. But her embarrassment was overshadowed by a rush of heated excitement. The reaction startled her. He was a fine specimen of manhood, she admitted, but she wasn't the swooning type. As he laid her on the bed, then released her, she experienced a sense of desertion. Then thoughts of him were forgotten as her concern for others took precedence. "What about inside? Was anyone injured inside the building?"

The MPs shrugged in unison. "We came directly in here," the second one responded.

"Looks like there were a few more windows broken," the first offered.

The doctor entered at that moment. "How's my patient?" he asked, hurrying to her bed.

"Her IV's been ripped out," Joe said. He frowned down at her. "How does your head feel? I tried not to let it hit the floor."

"It doesn't feel any worse than it did before," she replied, amazed by the honest concern in those eyes that had seemed so cold only moments before. It took effort to pull her gaze away. But she had to know if any other occupants of the building had been injured. She turned to the doctor. "Was anyone else hurt?"

"I haven't had time to check. But I'm sure everyone is fine," he soothed.

"I need to know," she insisted. "This attempt was meant for me."

Picking up the phone, he called the main desk. A moment later, he hung up. "No one was injured."

Beatrice breathed a sigh of relief.

"Are you sure nothing got broken or sprained?" Joe demanded.

She turned to him to find his gaze raking over her. Never had an inspection felt so personal . . . so intimate. It was almost like a physical touch. She was just shocky, she told herself. "Nothing's broken."

"Step aside and let me have a look at my patient," the doctor ordered, shining a light into her eyes.

Joe turned to the MPs. "Put in a call for backup units. It's probably too late, but I want a search made for that orderly. I'll guard Corporal Gerard. You two get going."

"Yes, sir," they responded in unison.

As the MPs hurried from the room, Joe took a position by the door on the inside of the room.

The doctor frowned at the IV. "I'll get a nurse in here," he said, starting to press the button.

"Unless she really needs that, leave it out," Joe ordered. "I may need to transport her quickly and I can do that easier without tubes attached."

The doctor took her pulse and blood pressure. "Her vital signs are stable. She'll be all right without it."

"Go check on your other patients." Politely but firmly, Joe was telling the doctor to get out.

The medical man frowned down at Beatrice. "I'll be close by. If you begin to feel queasy or dizzy, you ring for me."

"I will," she promised.

Alone once again with only Joe, Beatrice gently rubbed her temples, being careful on the left side where the bullet had grazed her just beyond the hairline.

"That was one damn lucky bounce." Joe broke the silence between them. "I saw that grenade hit the floor. Whoever tossed it must have really spiked it for it to have hit something and gone out the window like that." He frowned at the metal underworkings on the bed. "He must have wanted it to go under you and forgot about the metal railing and the mechanics of a hospital bed that could stop it."

"I guess my guardian angel was looking out for me," Beatrice replied.

"Luck's a peculiar thing," he muttered, frowning at the window.

"It would seem I get to play the bait after all."

His gaze returned to her. "More than likely they just hadn't gotten the word that you don't know anything. Once they do, you should be safe."

She noticed that the cold indifference had returned to his eyes. A few minutes ago, he'd placed himself in the line of fire, been willing to exchange his life for hers. Now he was behaving as if she was totally unimportant. "But I do know something."

Striding to the phone, he punched in a series of numbers. "This is Major Jones. I want a helicopter on the pad outside the hospital in ten minutes or less," he said without any preamble. Hanging up without waiting for a response, he turned back to her. "What do you know?"

"There were two men who approached after Bruce and I were shot. I was barely conscious and I'd lost my gun when I fell. All I could do was lie there and wait to see what happened. One leaned down to check Bruce. 'No sense in wasting another bullet on this one,' he said. When he spoke, he turned in my direction. That's when I saw his face."

"Why didn't you tell me this before?" Joe growled.

She scowled back. "Because I didn't remember before. Like the doctor said, I'd been through a lot. It took my brain a little time to start remembering the details I'd rather forget.''

"You said there was a second man. Did you see him, as well?''

"No. He was the one who came to check me. I was too groggy to turn my head upward so I didn't see his face, but I did see a part of a tattoo on his forearm. A snake. No, that's not quite right." She paused and concentrated harder. "I remember thinking it had sort of a mythical quality. Maybe a dragon's tail.''

"He must have realized you were still alive. Why didn't he finish you off?''

"His gun jammed. Then they heard sirens and took off. That's when I lost consciousness.''

"Apparently you lead a charmed life, Corporal Gerard.''

"Not charmed enough to have saved Sergeant Wood,'' she replied.

A silence fell between them and he glanced at his watch.

From outside she heard the sound of a chopper approaching. Apparently, when Major Jones called for action, he got it. Without preamble, he bundled her in a blanket and lifted her from the bed, cradling her in his arms. "Hold on,'' he ordered. She wrapped her arms around his neck and he strode from the room.

"What's going on?'' the duty nurse demanded as Joe started down the hall.

"I'm transferring Corporal Gerard to another facility,'' he barked back.

Beatrice was certain she saw relief on the woman's face. She couldn't fault her. She was feeling relieved herself to be taken someplace where, hopefully, she would not be putting other patients at risk.

Bypassing the elevator, he carried her down the stairs and out to the helicopter pad. There he handed her to one of the soldiers inside. She had not been thinking about his arms until they were no longer holding her. Suddenly she was feeling abandoned and scared. Then he climbed into the helicopter with her and the fear subsided.

"Get us airborne, now!" he yelled at the pilot.

Immediately they began their ascent.

The soldier strapped her into a seat, while Joe put on a set of headphones that allowed him to talk to the pilot. Only then did she notice that the men were wearing Special Forces insignias on their uniforms. Apparently Major Jones had been given carte blanche to protect her.

Sitting beside him, she watched him out of the corner of her eye. That his presence made her feel so safe stunned her. The only other time she'd ever felt this way was when she was in Smytheshire, in the midst of her family.

The noise from the engine was making her head throb worse and she was feeling dizzy.

The soldier who had helped her to her seat, carefully placed a pair of ear protectors over her head. "This will help keep the noise level down," he shouted above the roar.

She gave him a grateful smile, then, leaning back, closed her eyes and tried to think of something pleasant. Being carried out of the hospital in Joe's arms was the thought that filled her mind. She opened one eye a crack to study him once again. He was concentrating on talking into the head-set, making arrangements. She had the feeling he barely realized she was there.

I'm simply having extreme reactions to him because I got shot in the head and my brain is still jostled a little, she told herself. Closing her eyes once again, she pictured her favorite spot on the ridge overlooking her father's house.

A little less than half an hour after takeoff, the helicopter landed in an open field. There an ambulance was waiting for them. Two marines with weapons at the ready stood guard. She wanted to climb out of the chopper and make it to the vehicle on her own, but when she started to rise, the dizziness became worse. She teetered forward. Joe caught her. "Sit," he ordered.

She obeyed.

He jumped down, then motioned for one of the soldiers to hand her to him.

"I'm really not the fainting type," she said, as he carried her to the ambulance.

"I never thought you were. Most women would have been hysterical after that grenade incident. You took it like a man. In fact, you took it better than most men I know."

"In spite of your chauvinism, I'll accept that as a compliment," she returned. She'd expected a small smile, at least. Instead, his expression remained grim.

Laying her on the waiting stretcher, he motioned for the marines to lift her inside the ambulance. As soon as she was secured, he closed the doors, leaving her alone with the medic and her bodyguard. In spite of the presence of the three men, again she felt deserted. Then she heard the passenger door in front open and close. She could not see him, but she knew he was there. And once again she felt safe. *That bullet really did throw my brain out of whack*, she thought wryly.

"How do you feel?" the medic asked.

"Like I've been in a war zone." Her gaze traveled to the two marines, their guns still at the ready. "Like I'm still in one," she corrected.

The medic smiled encouragingly. "Don't worry. You're safe. Now, I need to know if you're dizzy or nauseous."

"A little dizzy," she admitted. "But then I've never liked flying and I have a pounding headache."

"I'm going to give you something for the pain." Continuing to smile, he gave her an injection. In moments the world went blank.

She awoke in a queen-size, four-poster, cherry-wood bed. A white cotton canopy arched overhead, while matching curtains hung at the windows. The bedspread was a handmade quilt. The rest of the furnishings in the room matched the wood of which the bed was made. She knew good furniture when she saw it and she was surrounded by that of the highest quality. *Elegant* was the word that came to mind as her gaze traveled over her surroundings. Not at all what she'd expected. She'd expected to wake up in something that at least resembled a hospital room.

Her mouth was dry. Seeing a pitcher of water and a glass on the table, she shifted into a sitting position and poured herself a drink. Her hospital gown, she noticed as her mind cleared further, had been exchanged for a soft, white cotton nightgown.

Maybe this was one of those very realistic dreams, she thought, returning the glass to the tray. Then the door opened and Major Jones entered. He had discarded his coat and hat. But even in shirtsleeves, he didn't look any more casual than when he'd been in full uniform. His broad shoulders were stiff and his back straight as he approached. She found herself wondering if he ever relaxed.

"How are you feeling?" he asked, his manner coolly unemotional.

"Confused. I'm wondering if I'm in a dream."

"It's not a dream. You're in a safe house. There's a nurse here and a doctor on call twenty-four hours a day, should you require him."

"I don't think I will. I'm feeling much stronger." She looked out the window. The sun was shining. It had been the beginning of evening when she'd been lifted out of the helicopter. "How long have I been asleep?"

"Nearly twenty-four hours. The doctor insisted you needed the rest."

She caught the impatience in his voice. "You didn't think so."

"I wanted to get a drawing of the man and the tattoo you saw on the second man as quickly as possible. But a day won't make any difference. They'll need some time to set up a new operation at a different base." He approached the bed and reached for the phone. "I'll have food sent up. Once you've eaten, I'll call in an artist to work with you."

She started to say she would work with the artist immediately, but her stomach growled loudly, stopping her.

"We are on a need-to-know basis here," he continued in the same grim tones. "The staff knows you as Mrs. Jones. They have been told that you are my wife and were injured in an attempt on my life. Your base commander thinks you've been transported to a military hospital, the identity of which is being kept secret to protect you."

"In other words, for the moment, I've vanished."

"It's safest that way."

This was almost like being in a James Bond novel, she thought. "I suppose the next thing you're going to tell me is that your name really isn't Jones."

"You will keep thoughts like that to yourself, Corporal," he ordered.

She'd been teasing. The realization that she'd stumbled onto an unexpected truth, shook her. However, if the military was willing to hide Major Jones's real identity, it wasn't up to her to expose him. She covered her surprise by adopting a stiff military bearing. "Yes, sir," she returned crisply.

Stifling her curiosity, she added matter-of-factly, "If I'm to play your wife, sir, then I need a first name to call you by. Unless you prefer I refer to you as Major or sir, sir."

"You can call me Joe. I'll call you Tess."

Her paternal great-grandmother had been the only one she'd ever allowed to call her that. But coming from his mouth, the nickname sounded natural. It didn't grate on her nerves. *Because my nerves are beyond being grated,* she reasoned. She'd been shot, had a grenade tossed at her and was still suffering from a dull headache. He could have called her whatever he wanted and she wouldn't have minded.

The food arrived on two trays. As the maid and one of the security people carried them in, she caught the aroma of steak and potatoes. Her mouth began to water. "That smells delicious."

The maid's expression became apologetic. "Sorry," she said, setting Beatrice's tray in front of her. "The doctor says you can't have solid food until tomorrow."

Beatrice looked down at the bowl of broth and crystal goblet filled with Jell-O, then looked to the small round table by the window where Joe's tray was being placed. There was a huge piece of sirloin steak, a baked potato, salad and a wedge of what looked like homemade apple pie.

As the door closed, leaving them alone, he frowned at the accusatory pout on her face. "I would have eaten elsewhere but people expect us to eat together," he said, taking a seat at the table.

"After all we've been through, you could give me just a couple of bites," she coaxed.

He frowned impatiently. "Eat."

"Do you always follow all the rules?" she asked, grudgingly taking a sip of the clear soup.

"When it's the right thing to do," he replied, then turned his full attention to his own meal.

As they ate in silence, she felt tension building in the room. Again, she studied him covertly. The hard set of his jaw told her he didn't like being idle and he didn't like baby-sitting her. Pride caused her shoulders to straighten. "I'm sure I'll be fine here on my own. No one is going to expect you to remain by my side when you have a duty to per-form."

"I can't do anything until I've got the drawing of the face you saw and a sketch of the portion of tattoo."

"Then call in the artist," she ordered, shoving the last bite of Jell-O into her mouth.

Immediately, he reached for the phone.

For the next two hours she and the artist, a Lieutenant Loydd, worked to get the face and the tattoo as close as possible to what she saw. For the first half-hour, Joe hov-ered behind them until her nerves couldn't take it any longer. She'd cast him a "get lost" glance. He'd grimaced sheep-ishly as if realizing he was being a nuisance, and left.

He'd returned momentarily with a book, seated himself in a wing chair in the corner and read. After a while, he dozed.

She lowered her voice so as not to disturb him and Lieu-tenant Loydd did, as well. Finally, she decided the sketches were as good as they were ever going to be. As the lieuten-ant bade her a whispered goodbye and rose, Joe was sud-denly on his feet, striding toward them.

"Let's see what you've got," he said.

Beatrice jumped slightly and saw her own startled ex-pression mirrored on Lieutenant Loydd's face.

"Yes, sir." The man snapped to attention, extending the drawing pad in Joe's direction.

"At ease," Joe ordered, taking the pad and studying the face portrayed there.

Beatrice noticed that the lieutenant relaxed only partially. She guessed no one ever felt completely at ease in Major *Jones's* presence. She didn't. But she wasn't going to let him know that. The males in her family could be just as intimidating and, from experience, she was certain the major would bully her if he thought he could get away with it.

"I want these circulated among the MPs on all our military bases in all the services, not just the army. Tell them they will be looking for civilians, either newly hired or new friends of one of the soldiers. The soldier will, most likely, be one who has either a drug, gambling or drinking problem. I don't want the men responsible for my wife's injury to know we have any clues to their identities. Any reports of anyone answering this description or anyone having a tattoo that might match the one Mrs. Jones described is to be kept confidential and brought immediately to me."

The lieutenant snapped back to attention as the pad was returned to him. "Yes, sir." He gave a brisk salute and left at close to a jog.

Working on the face had brought the memory of Sergeant Wood back full force. As soon as the door closed, leaving them alone once again, Beatrice's gaze leveled on Joe. "I want to stay on this case until the men are caught and brought to justice."

"You've done all you can. I'm going to get some sleep. I used your head wound as an excuse for requiring separate quarters." He started toward a door to her left. "My room is adjacent. I'll leave the door open. Yell, if you need anything."

She scowled at his departing back. He wasn't going to dismiss her so easily. "You still need me."

He turned around, his expression the cold impatient look she was growing used to seeing. "Have you remembered something else?"

"No. But that drawing could be of a hundred different men. It's simply a sketch. You need me to actually finger the real culprit."

"And what makes you so certain you could pick the right one out of a bunch of look-alikes?" he challenged.

"Because I saw his eyes. They were icy, even colder than yours. Well, maybe not colder. Just different. More cruel. You're simply arrogant." She ignored his raised eyebrow. She'd meant to let him know that he couldn't make her cower, that she'd sized him up and wasn't afraid to admit it. "Anyway, I'd recognize that look anywhere. And I heard his voice."

For a moment he regarded her in silence, then said, "You've got a point. I'll consider it."

"Only a stubborn blockhead would refuse my help," she called as he turned to leave again.

He paused in the doorway. "I'm sure I've been labeled that at one time or another," he returned coolly, before completing his exit.

With or without his permission, she was going to help catch Bruce's murderer, she vowed silently to the empty space Joe had recently occupied. Nature called and she rose slowly.

"Where do you think you're going?"

She looked to the door through which Joe had departed and saw him striding toward her. The man had ears like a radio antenna, she thought. "I need to use the bathroom."

"You were told not to get out of bed without assistance," he growled, taking hold of her arm to steady her.

The momentary dizziness she'd experienced upon first standing was gone. "I can make it on my own."

His hold tightened. "I'll walk you there."

She expected his touch to be irritating. *He* certainly was. Instead, his hand felt warm and sent a soothing heat along her arm. "If you insist," she muttered, not having the energy to argue with him.

"I do."

"Bet you'll never say that at the end of a church aisle." She couldn't believe those words had come out of her mouth. Why she'd even thought of him and a church aisle bewildered her. She felt a flush coloring her cheeks. "Sorry," she apologized. "I don't know what caused that thought to even pop into my mind. It must be the drugs."

He remained silent, clearly feeling the remark merited no response. Alone in the bathroom, she fumed at herself. She wanted him to let her help. Alienating him wasn't going to win him over. "Look, I really didn't mean anything by that earlier crack," she said, as he helped her back to her bed. "It only popped out because you're being so insistent about being a loner."

"No offense taken," he replied.

His voice was an indifferent monotone, giving her no clue to his real feelings. *Maybe he doesn't have any,* she mused dryly as she slipped back into her bed and he went into his room. Her fair side reminded her of the concern she'd seen in his eyes right after the grenade explosion. He probably considered that a momentary lapse and cursed himself for it afterward, the side that was feeling frustrated by his attitude rebutted.

Her head began to throb. The nurse had come in while Lieutenant Loydd was there and left some pills to be taken when needed for pain. She swallowed a couple, then snuggled into the bed. Her trip back from the bathroom had been steadier and without any dizziness. After another night's rest, she was determined that she would be getting around just fine, certainly well enough to accompany Major Jones wherever he might go.

From his room, she heard his shower running. As she closed her eyes, a nude male image filled her mind—Major Jones's image. She couldn't know if it was correct, but using what she did know—the broadness of his shoulders, the strength of his arms, and so on—a fairly explicit form had taken shape. It wasn't like her to have such intensely sensual flights of fancy. And about Major Jones to boot! "These drugs must be really powerful," she grumbled, forcing her mind to the calm, soothing vision of the view from the ridge on her father's property. But the tranquil scene she'd used to lull herself to sleep at other times, only irritated her tonight. Major Jones again came into her mind. This time, at least, she envisioned a towel wrapped around him at the waist. Frowning at herself, she fell asleep.

The next day, he entered her room, stood looking down at her and said, "If you're determined to come with me, you'll need a haircut."

She considered asking why but didn't. She would show him that she could follow orders and would be a help, not a hindrance. "Yes, sir."

Within the hour, a hairdresser had appeared. Minutes later, her long brunette tresses were lying on the floor. When the hairdresser left, she looked in the mirror to discover she had a soft bob with a long bang combed to one side to cover the area that had been shaved to allow the doctor to care for her wound. *At least it will be easy to manage,* she reasoned.

Two days later, Joe announced that he had five sightings of possible suspects. "The doctor says you're strong enough to travel. I'm taking you along to spot the man for me. After that, you're on your way back to your current post. I've made it clear to everyone there that you know nothing, that you were merely put in protective custody as a precaution.''

She responded with a demure smile, letting him take that as acceptance of his plan. Inwardly, she promised herself she would not be going back to the status quo until the men were apprehended.

"The nurse will bring you some civilian clothes," he said. "I took a guess as to the sizes."

For someone who'd seemed to pay as little attention to her as possible, he'd guessed pretty darn accurately, she thought a little later as she fastened the bra he'd chosen. He'd also stayed true to form. The underwear he'd selected was simple and plain, nothing that could even remotely be considered sexy. She had just finished dressing in the slacks, light summer sweater and sneakers, when he knocked, then entered.

He, too, was wearing civilian clothing. But even in the slacks, loafers and button-down shirt, he had an air of command that caused others to snap to attention in his presence.

An hour later a helicopter landed them at a nearby airport where a military transport awaited them. The copilot greeted them as they boarded. "Your luggage is on board, sir," he said, indicating with a wave of his hand two trunks strapped to the wall in the starkly equipped belly of the plane. Joe nodded his approval of the arrangements and within moments, they were taxiing down the runway.

Once they were airborne and could move around safely, he walked over and opened the nearest trunk. "This one is yours," he said. "Our first stop is at a naval base, so dress appropriately. There, I will be Commander Jones. You'll be Ensign Barnes, my secretary, driver and all-around girl Friday."

Excitement bubbled within her. She was actually going to be a part of a covert operation! Approaching the trunk, she looked inside. There were three wigs lying on top of the neatly organized array of uniforms from the various services. One was short, curly, and chestnut in color. Another was long, wavy and auburn, with an emphasis on the reddish highlights. The third, a brownish blond, was long and straight.

Joe nodded toward the wigs. "I want you in disguise. We'll lose our advantage if our man recognizes you. There are glasses in there, too, regular and tinted. You'll wear them at all times."

Now she understood the reason for the haircut and was glad she hadn't challenged him on that point.

"Get changed," he ordered, opening the other trunk.

She looked around for a place of privacy. The toilet was out; it was barely big enough to turn around in.

"Consider yourself under battlefield conditions."

She looked to see Joe regarding her with his usual cold impatience.

"Don't worry. I don't have time to leer," he assured her. "I'll respect your privacy. You respect mine and we'll get along fine."

That he could so easily be oblivious to her as a woman, carried the sting of insult. "I think I can keep myself from peeking," she returned, determined to let him know that he held no interest for her, either.

He made no response other than to again direct his full attention to the contents of his trunk and she had the feeling that for the moment she was totally forgotten. *I should feel relieved, not insulted,* she admonished herself, then began to change quickly.

She'd ordered herself to ignore her stoic companion but the licentious image that had taunted her a couple of nights earlier came back to taunt her again. He probably has scrawny legs, she told herself. Unable to stop herself, she peeked. *Definitely not scrawny,* she admitted, catching a glimpse of muscular thighs and calves as he stepped into his pants. In fact, she didn't think she'd ever seen any man in better physical condition. A heat began to travel through her. Quickly she returned her attention to her own undressing and dressing.

Still, she could not entirely forget that he was there. She wasn't used to taking her clothes off in the presence of a man she barely knew—or in the presence of any man, for that matter. As she was slipping out of her slacks, she again glanced toward him, this time to see if he was respecting her privacy. He had his back to her, displaying no interest in her. She'd never thought of herself as a raving beauty, but she knew she wasn't difficult to look at. Abruptly, she frowned at herself. He probably had a girlfriend or even a wife. Her feminine pride healed, she finished changing and then, seating herself in front of the mirror provided, began to adjust the blond wig. "I always wondered what I'd look like as a blonde," she said, finishing and standing for inspection.

His gaze leveled on her. "That won't do. You look too hot. You need to blend into the background. It's safer that way."

The masculine glint she saw in his eyes before they again became shuttered, brought a flush of feminine satisfaction. So he thought she was hot as a blonde, she mused.

"Try the curly wig," he ordered.

Obeying, she grimaced at her new image in the mirror. "I look like an overage Shirley Temple."

He nodded with satisfaction. "That's better." From an overhead rack, he lifted down an attaché case. "This is yours. Get acquainted with the contents. A good attaché knows where her notepad, pens and pencils are. The papers are irrelevant.''

"Aren't there any secret compartments housing small quantities of explosive or springs that can shoot poison darts in case of emergencies?'' she asked, examining the exterior with interest.

"It's just an attaché case.''

She looked up at him.

"This isn't a game,'' he finished curtly.

Her eyes narrowed in anger. He was treating her as if she were an unruly child he'd gotten stuck baby-sitting. "Don't you ever joke around?''

"I don't like working with novices,'' he growled. "They can do stupid things and get themselves and others hurt.''

"You were a novice once.''

"I had training before I went out into the field.''

"Well, I've had training. I am an MP,'' she returned. He didn't look impressed and her ire rose. "I suppose you were a navy Seal or a Green Beret or in some other elite unit.'' She wasn't certain exactly what it was—the slight flicker of his eye, perhaps—but in that instant she knew she'd hit on at least one truth about Colonel Jones or Commander Jones or whoever he really was.

"In the future you will keep your speculations to yourself,'' he said. "There is no need for you to know anything about me. When this assignment is over, you will forget everything about it, including me and anyone else you have met or will meet. Do you understand?''

"Yes, sir.'' She saluted him in her sharpest military manner as a sign that he could count on her for that.

He saluted back, then seated himself and closed his eyes.

Three bases and two disguises later, she'd identified the man they were seeking at an installation in Texas. Joe tried to send her packing then and there, but she dug her heels in and refused. In the end, he gave in, either because he'd grown tired of fighting with her or because somewhere deep inside he respected her need to avenge a fallen comrade. She wasn't certain which. Probably a little of both, she decided.

"You'll need a code name in case anything happens to me and you have to contact my superior," he said. "He and I are the only ones who need to know your true identity. It's his policy for his field agents to work in anonymity. It's safer for our families this way. For the duration of this operation, you are to consider yourself one of us. Thistle seems appropriate as a code name for you—pretty to look at but, definitely, a flower one should never touch."

"I'm not that difficult," she retorted.

"Maybe Burr would be better. Once you get attached, you're impossible to shake off, even if it means being carried along into harm's way."

She frowned at his continued anger over her insistence on staying. "I know you're being boorish because you're worried about my safety. But, I assure you, I can be an asset." Sergeant Wood came into her mind. "I'm not perfect." She forced that image out and recalled the grenade. "But as you pointed out in the hospital room, I have luck with me at times."

"Skill is a great deal more reliable than luck."

Regret caused hot tears to burn at the back of her eyes. "I am skilled. And, if I'd had a second or two of warning, I could have saved Sergeant Wood."

He frowned at this declaration. "You can't know that for certain. And you can't blame yourself for what happened. He was your superior. It was his decision to go in. He chose his own destiny."

Her jaw firmed. "And I'm choosing mine."

He issued a resigned snort. "Then choose your name. Thistle or Burr."

"Thistle. The big purple kind has always been one of my favorite flowers."

"Why am I not surprised?" he muttered. His voice again took on command. "Memorize this phone number." He recited the sequence and had her recite it back. "The person answering will say you have reached Versatile Pest Control. You will say you are dissatisfied with their service and wish to speak to The Manager. They will ask your name. You will say Thistle, nothing more. They will direct you from there. If you need to mention me, my code name is Coyote."

"Why am I not surprised?" she said sarcastically. "A lone wolf, cut off from the pack, stalking his prey with slyness and agility."

He cocked an eyebrow and she felt a flush building. She'd meant for the description to have a sting. Instead, it had turned complimentary and much too dramatic. But then he had that effect on her. He awakened her imagination in ways no man had awakened it before.

Signaling the end of this conversation, he returned his attention to the plan he was devising to capture their thieves. She tried to focus on the work at hand, but his mention of "families" taunted her. For all she knew, he could be married. He wasn't wearing a ring, but then she wouldn't have expected him to. He was very insistent about keeping his private life private. He could even have children. His personal life didn't matter, she told herself sternly. Still, her curiosity grew. "I suppose the kind of work you do makes marriage or even long-term relationships difficult to manage." She'd openly pried! Keeping her head down, she feigned intense interest in the blueprint in front of her as if his answer were inconsequential.

"That's why I'm not married and do not participate in long-term relationships."

She heard the finality in his voice and knew he was letting her know that if she was thinking of their having any romantic involvement, to forget it. "I doubt anyone could put up with you on a long-term basis, anyway," she returned dryly. Promising herself she would do no further prying into the man's life, she added that once the bad guys were caught, she and Major Jones would part company, never to see each other again, and that suited her just fine....

But that wasn't the way things had happened. Tobias had liked the way she handled herself. He'd also liked the way she and Joe operated as a team. He'd offered her a position in The Unit as Joe's partner and she'd taken it. Joe had been there and hadn't looked pleased.

"I should have named you Burr," he'd said when they were alone. "You're proving impossible to shake loose, even if it is for your own good."

"And I would have been smart to have let him shake me loose," she murmured, her mind returning to the present and the necklace she was holding, coming back into clear focus. But she hadn't, and now he was again in her life. Her jaw tensed with resolve. She would find him and set herself free, once and for all.

Chapter Four

"I realize you've got your mind set on this trek, but I still don't feel easy about it," Justin said as Beatrice stepped out onto the front porch, suitcase and black leather bag in hand.

She read the worry on his face and guilt assailed her. He was an old man. She did not want to cause him undue stress. There was a time when secrets needed to be shared and this was one of those times. "Would it ease your mind to know that Ryder and I have a great deal more in common than the rest of the family realizes?"

Relief spread over the old man's face. "Yes, it would." His gaze narrowed on her. "I suspected that at one time. But you never said anything or showed any signs."

"I felt that some things were better kept private. I still do. I would like this to be our secret."

He nodded knowingly, then gave her a hug. "You take care."

"I will," she promised.

* * *

Flying west, she gained three hours. Even so, night had fallen when, according to the directions she'd gotten from the gas-station attendant in Redig, she turned her rented car onto the hard dirt road leading to Hawk Stone's ranch. Rounding a curve at the base of a hill, she saw the lights of a house ahead of her. Drawing nearer, she could see it was a large, frame, two-story affair with a long, wide-roofed porch. There were corrals and several outbuildings beyond. Stables, a barn and a bunkhouse, she surmised.

A tall, strongly built man came out the front door as she parked. In the glow from the porch light, she could see he was of Native American descent. As he continued toward her, she looked beyond him to see that a pretty, burgundy-haired pregnant woman had followed him out of the house. Unlike the man, the woman stopped at the top step of the porch.

"Looks like you're lost," the man said, coming to a halt beside the car.

Meeting his cool gaze, Beatrice felt a strong wave of déjà vu. His eyes reminded her of Joe. His manner did, as well. He was polite but there was also a strong "Go away, you don't belong here" message in his tone. "Maybe," she replied. "I'm looking for Amanda Stone."

"I'm Amanda."

Beatrice saw that the woman had approached and realized the man had held her attention so strongly, she'd missed the movement. Joe had had a way of holding her attention like that. On missions, she'd had to fight doubly hard not to concentrate on him. She smiled hopefully at the woman. "I've come all the way from Smytheshire, Massachusetts, to see you." Wanting the man to know that he could not intimidate her into leaving before she'd stated her business, she opened her door, forcing him to step back a little, and climbed out.

Amanda frowned in confusion. "Why would you come all that way to see me?"

"I didn't catch your name." It was the man who spoke.

For a moment Beatrice hesitated, then decided that an alias would not do. Amanda might take it into her head to check. "I'm Beatrice Gerard." She extended her hand to the man. "And you?"

"Hawk Stone," he replied, accepting the handshake but continuing to remain guarded.

Like a sentry protecting his queen, she thought, and felt a twinge of envy for Amanda. Returning her attention to the woman, she said, "I believe we met a number of years ago at a church social when you were visiting your cousin, Madaline Darnell. Of course she was still a MacGreggor then."

"That was a long time ago. At least fifteen years." Amanda's manner remained as guarded as her husband's. "I'm surprised you remember me."

Beatrice had spent a lot of time learning to read people. With these two, she knew that only the truth would get her what she wanted. "I don't really remember you," she admitted. "But I am aware that you have a talent for finding things and people, and there is someone I need to locate. I think he may be in trouble."

Amanda's expression immediately softened. "I can't promise you that I can be of any assistance, but I will try. Please, come inside."

Beatrice immediately accepted the woman's invitation, accompanying her to the house. Out of the corner of her eye, she watched the husband. His expression had become shuttered and she could see that he continued to be on his guard.

The interior of the house had a warm cozy air.

"We were eating dinner," Amanda said. "Won't you join us?"

"I really didn't mean to impose," Beatrice replied, coming to a halt just inside the door.

"Really, you won't be imposing," Amanda assured her, casting Hawk a "Be nice" glance.

"Yes, of course, you must join us," he said, echoing his wife's invitation.

In spite of the politeness of his tone, Beatrice sensed restraint. There was a protectiveness toward the burgundy-haired woman in his eyes that reminded her of the way Joe had looked at her. Only in Hawk's case, she did not doubt his concern was born out of love. In Joe's case, at one time, she'd convinced herself he'd felt that way about her. But, in the end, she'd been forced to realize that he'd seen her as a nuisance he had to protect. He'd felt responsible for getting her into The Unit, and he'd felt responsible for keeping her alive while she was there.

Beatrice focused her full attention on Amanda. "I know my coming here is an inconvenience and I would never have imposed if I wasn't seriously worried about the man I seek. If you could give me some clue as to where to start my search, I'd be grateful and on my way."

"It's obvious this means a lot to you." Amanda's expression became apologetic. "But I'm really not certain I can help. The truth is, I've rarely been able to use my ability on command."

"If you could just try," Beatrice pleaded. Taking the necklace from her pocket, she extended it toward the woman.

"That's Crow." It was Hawk who spoke, studying the necklace with interest.

"The man I seek is half Crow. This necklace was made by his great-grandfather and given to his great-grandmother. It holds a great deal of significance for him."

Hawk nodded. "The coyote is a strong totem."

Accepting the necklace, Amanda motioned toward a nearby upholstered chair. "Please, sit down," she coaxed.

As Beatrice accepted the invitation, Amanda seated herself in the rocker in front of the fireplace. Hawk took a position a little to her right, continuing to remind Beatrice of a sentry. Holding the necklace loosely in her hands, Amanda closed her eyes.

A silence descended over the room. Mentally Beatrice reviewed the dealers, both in the States and foreign, who she knew traded in illegal weapons. Had Joe found the connection he was looking for through one of them or was it someone new? She prayed Amanda could help her. The possibilities were too varied and she was afraid she might already be too late.

"I see a sign. It reads Tehuacán. I'm heading away from there. The terrain is mountainous and covered by dense woods. The journey is long. Ahead, on the crest of the slope, is what looks like a stone fortress. The walls, I'd guess, are close to fifteen feet high. The entrance is through a wooden gate as high as the walls. Inside are several buildings. All look well cared for. There is a catwalk around the interior of the wall and a man up there to the side of the gate. He is carrying a gun. I get the impression he is on guard. I am being taken to a passage that leads below ground. There are dungeons down here. I'm locked inside." Amanda's eyes opened. "If what I saw was real, your friend is in grave danger."

"He has a knack for that," Beatrice replied. "Only he's usually not so careless as to get caught."

"You will need help to rescue him." It was Hawk who spoke.

Beatrice heard the offer in his voice and saw the fear on Amanda's face. "No. He'll have a better chance if I do this alone. If I need help, I can get it."

Hawk nodded and Amanda looked relieved. "Now will you have some dinner with us?" she offered again. "Our housekeeper is an excellent cook."

Beatrice retrieved the necklace. "No, but thank you. I must be on my way. As you said, my friend appears to be in urgent need of help." As they walked her back to her car, she added, "It would be safest for you if you forgot I was ever here."

"You will let us know when you find him?" Amanda asked.

"Or if you need more help than others are able to provide," Hawk added.

"I will let you know if I find him," she promised Amanda, then turned to Hawk. "Thank you again for your offer. But I assure you, I know people who can give the kind of aid that will be necessary."

Driving west, she continued until she was beyond Hammond, Montana, before finding a motel room for the remaining hours of the night. From there she called Tobias.

As usual, he woke alert. She'd always marveled at his ability to come out of a deep sleep, his mind clear and ready to work. Joe had the same ability. They both also had photographic memories, a definite boon in their line of work.

"Sounds like Pedro Palma's mountain retreat in the Sierra Madre del Sur," he said, when she'd finished describing the fortress. "It's listed on the company records as a business expense. He used it to entertain some of his more nervous clients, those who preferred to remain anonymous. He'd fly them in by helicopter. They'd be masked until he got them inside the gates. The place was his version of a Spanish fortress. He had the wine cellar built to resemble a dungeon. The cell you described Joe being in could have been one of the tasting rooms.''

"So Palma has him.'' Mentally she pictured the Mexican businessman who passed himself off as a law-abiding citizen. He was plump, always dressed in the finest clothes and being chauffeured around Mexico in a Rolls-Royce. The *federales* had been after him for years. They were certain he dealt in guns and drugs, but had never gotten enough proof together to put him behind bars. He seemed to have spies everywhere. Each time a witness was willing to come forward, that witness died. Finally, there was no one brave enough to testify against the man.

"Palma is dead. Carlos Sanchez has taken over the reins.''

"Palma's right-hand man, the one we used to call The Ladies' Man because he was such a charmer?''

"That's the one.'' Tobias's voice became thoughtful. "Joe did mention him as one of the leads he was following. But as for that place in the mountains, all intelligence reports indicate that Sanchez never uses it. He prefers to do his entertaining in Acapulco where his selection of women is not so limited. According to everything in our files, that place has been deserted since Palma's death.''

"Or maybe that's just what Sanchez wants people to think.''

"It is far enough in the middle of nowhere that any activity there could go unnoticed if no one was looking in that direction,'' Tobias conceded. "It is possible that he stayed away long enough for the *federales* to lose interest in it, then began using it again on a limited basis.''

"I need directions.''

"Without contacting Harold, I can't give you specifics. And if Joe is right about the mole in The Unit, contacting him could put you at risk. But I can get you to the general vicinity."

"I'll find it from there," she replied.

He gave directions, then asked, "What makes you think Joe's there?"

"I've got to go," she said, refusing to answer.

The next morning she caught a plane for Los Angeles and made a connection to Mexico City, changing identities with each ticket. The heat was sweltering as she drove away from the terminal. Joe had taught her to be very cautious about those she was willing to trust in the field. In most cases, he'd instructed her to rely only on him or herself. But there was a man who lived in a small village northwest of Mexico City she knew Joe would trust with his life.

Manuel was a *federale*. His brother had been, as well. They'd been pursuing a band of Colombian drug dealers who were operating in both Mexico and the U.S. Their case had dovetailed into one Joe was working on and he'd joined forces with them. There had been an ambush. Manuel's brother had been killed but Joe had managed to save Manuel. After she was partnered with Joe, another case had brought them over the border and she'd met Manuel. She hoped he was home and that he remembered her.

Evening was falling and Beatrice was exhausted by the time she pulled up in front of the house she remembered as belonging to him. It looked as if no one was at home. Refusing to give up hope, she parked and started toward the house.

"No one is there," a teenage girl sitting on the stoop of the house next door called out in Spanish. She was attractively dressed, and Beatrice guessed she was waiting for her boyfriend.

"This the home of Manuel Cortez?" Beatrice asked, wanting to make certain he had not moved. Joe had worked with her until her Spanish was perfect and she spoke with an accent that placed her as a resident of the southern part of the country.

The girl's face took on a look of sympathy. "Manuel is dead, killed in the line of duty. And so young. Barely into his mid-thirties." She looked over her shoulder to the hill in the distance and made the sign of the cross. "May he rest in peace."

Beatrice recalled the dark-haired, dark-eyed man. He would have been strikingly handsome if not for the long, jagged scar across his left cheek that destroyed the symmetry of his face. The scar was a reminder of the shoot-out that had made him and Joe fast friends. After thanking the girl, Beatrice left.

She'd intended to drive directly back to Mexico City, get some sleep, then try her hand at finding the supplies and equipment she would need for her expedition. Instead, she chose to make a stop at the cemetery. It seemed only right to pay her last respects.

The grave was newly dug. Reading the tombstone, she realized Manuel had died only a few days earlier. She recalled standing beside Joe's grave. Her jaw hardened. There was a big difference. Joe hadn't been buried in front of his tombstone. He'd been in hiding somewhere, letting her think he was dead, severing all ties with her for what he thought was forever.

"Consuela said you were looking for my husband," a female voice said from behind Beatrice.

She turned to find a pretty, slender, black-haired woman, about five feet four inches in stature standing a short distance away. This was not the Elena Cortez she remembered—friendly and warm. There was nothing friendly or warm about the woman she now faced. Anger flashed in the dark eyes that raked over her. When recognition sparked, the anger increased.

"I suppose you've come seeking his help." She waved her arm toward the grave. "Well, as you can see, he can no longer help anyone."

The anger, Beatrice realized, was the only thing keeping the woman from crumbling with grief. Although aware that Elena knew some English, Beatrice continued to speak in Spanish. She wanted what was said between them to be clear. "I'm sorry."

Elena's expression became more bitter. "They are all sorry. But they have done nothing to make the man responsible pay. They say they have no evidence. But I know. In here…" She pointed to her heart. "Sanchez might not have been in the car that forced Manuel to crash into the ravine, but it was his men."

Beatrice knew that feeling. She'd been certain of the identity of the man responsible for the bombing of Joe's car, but like Elena's villain, her quarry had protected himself well. "Someday he will be punished," she said with conviction.

Elena's jaw trembled. "For days after they found Manuel's car, I prayed that somehow he had escaped death. I knew it was a futile hope. His blood was found on the front seat. Besides, no one could have survived the crash."

Beatrice's gaze leveled on the woman. "Are you saying they didn't find the body?"

"The river had been swollen for days. The car was not washed away because it embedded itself between two boulders, but Manuel's body was carried out to sea."

"Perhaps he did survive," Beatrice said encouragingly, recalling her own situation.

"He would have come home to me or, at least, gotten word to me."

Remembering how Manuel had worshiped and trusted his wife, Beatrice had to agree.

Vengeance again burned in Elena's eyes. "I wish Joe Jones was still alive. He would avenge Manuel. He would see that Carlos Sanchez pays."

Although Beatrice's instincts told her she could trust Elena, her training—Joe's training—refused to allow her to confide completely in the other woman. "I seek Carlos Sanchez. You have my word I will do what I can to see that he is brought to justice."

The woman's gaze riveted on Beatrice. "I want to help."

Beatrice had come seeking Manuel because she was uncertain where to obtain the equipment she needed. It was also important to obtain her supplies without bringing notice to herself. She made a decision. "If you could help me get the supplies I need, I would be grateful. But no one must know." She rattled off a list of food and camping equipment, then added, "I will also require an old, but reliable vehicle, something with four-wheel drive that looks much used. I don't want the kind of attention a newer vehicle would bring."

"We can use Manuel's Jeep. It is always kept packed with equipment for a night under the stars. And I have enough in my pantry to supply us with food."

Beatrice frowned. "Not *we*. Me."

Elena spread her feet, taking a firm stance. "If you want my help, you will take me with you."

"It's not safe. You want vengeance. That could make you do something rash and foolish that would only serve to get you killed." Beatrice repeated the same objection Tobias had expressed five years ago when she'd demanded the right to go after the man she was certain had killed Joe.

"I was going to go on my own, anyway. We can go together or separately. That is your choice."

That had been the substance of her response to Tobias, Beatrice recalled. He'd threatened her with a court-martial but she'd stood her ground. In the end, he'd succumbed to her wishes. But he'd assigned Eagle, a more seasoned operative, as her partner and demanded that she respect Eagle's position as senior on their team and follow his orders. Elena would have to make the same concession. "If I agree to our pursuing this together, I want your word that you will behave with caution and follow my lead."

"I will behave with caution," Elena replied.

That was as much of a promise as she'd given Tobias, Beatrice admitted. And she hadn't kept it. She'd nearly gotten herself killed. But she'd managed to capture the man in a compromising situation that even his money could not buy him out of. For a long moment she regarded Elena in silence. The woman clearly meant to pursue her quest for vengeance. Better to have her where she could keep an eye on her, Beatrice decided. "All right. We go together."

Elena smiled triumphantly. "Come. You look as if you could use some dinner and then sleep. I will call my family and tell them I have decided to visit a cousin in Honduras. They will understand. They know my grief is strong. The cousin will cover for me. That way, no one will wonder where I've gone. We'll get an early start tomorrow."

Beatrice nodded and followed the woman out of the cemetery.

Later, after she'd eaten, bathed and dressed for bed, she was too restless to sleep. She pulled on her robe and stepped out onto the back veranda.

A moment later Elena joined her. "I have made the arrangements and packed the food and water we will need."

Beatrice merely nodded. In spite of the orders she'd given herself, she was again recalling the first time Joe had kissed her. It had been on this very veranda, on a night much like this one.

"Joe's death must have been very hard on you. I prayed for you when I heard about it," Elena said with gentle sympathy.

"It is always difficult to lose a partner."

Elena gave her a "Don't try to fool me" look. "He was more than a mere partner to you."

Beatrice raised an eyebrow questioningly as if puzzled by Elena's claim. She'd been certain no one in their line of work, other than Tobias, had known about her and Joe's romantic involvement and their marriage.

"I know you were only pretending to be man and wife as part of your cover when you were last here, but I saw him kiss you. It was so quick, and you both seemed so surprised," Elena elaborated. "I, however, was not surprised. It was the way the two of you fought so hard to keep a distance between you that had me convinced you were struggling not to give in to deeper feelings. I suppose in your line of work, to care too deeply can be a disadvantage. But sometimes, the heart cannot be ruled by logic." She breathed a tired sigh. "I never wanted to fall in love with a *federale*."

"The heart does, sometimes, seem to have a mind of its own," Beatrice replied.

Elena smiled in sad agreement. "You should get some rest."

"I'll be in in a moment," Beatrice promised.

Alone again on the veranda, she looked skyward. Even now, if she closed her eyes and allowed her senses to take control, she could feel the heat of Joe's lips on hers.

They had been working together for a little over a year. When she'd first joined The Unit and Tobias had partnered them, Joe had accepted her with stoic resignation. But during their first mission, she'd realized they had a serious problem. He was treating her with deference, trying to keep her out of the line of fire. She had very forcefully pointed out to him that he could not take on the bad guys alone. She'd even gone so far as to threaten to ask Tobias to assign her a new partner.

"You'd walk over any of the others like a trooper in hobnailed boots," he'd grumbled. He hadn't looked happy but he'd added, "All right. You win. From now on you're one of the guys."

And that was how he'd treated her after that—as a comrade in arms. As senior member of their team, when she did a good job, he told her so. When she slipped, he reamed her out. But always there was a coolness between them, a barrier he never allowed her to cross and become his friend.

She'd been forced to admit to herself that she found him physically attractive. However, his lack of interest in her as a person had caused her pride to refuse to admit to anything deeper. But that night at Manuel's house, watching Joe relaxed and laughing with an old friend, she'd envied Manuel. She'd even envied Elena. Joe had treated Manuel's wife with the polite deference of a man in the presence of a beautiful woman. He'd smiled at her with masculine appreciation and complimented her on her house and her cooking. While she and Elena had been doing the dishes, she'd even heard him tell Manuel what a lucky man Manuel was.

As soon as it was politely possible, Beatrice had escaped to the veranda. There she'd been reminding herself that she was the one who had insisted Joe forget she was a woman.

But the fact that he'd been able to do that so easily was causing a strong sting of insult.

"Are you feeling all right? I know Mexican cooking is a little strong for some stomachs," a familiar male voice had interrupted her silent fuming.

She'd turned to find Joe standing a short distance away. He looked concerned but she was certain his worry was because of the mission. They were supposed to leave the next morning. "I'm fine. As you pointed out several times, Elena is a wonderful cook."

Joe raised an eyebrow and his concern turned cool.

Mentally she kicked herself. She'd sounded jealous. She turned her attention back to the star-studded sky. "Look, I came out here to be alone for a while. I'm not in the best mood for company tonight."

"I just thought I'd let you know that Manuel and Elena are retiring for the night. We should be getting some rest, too. I want to get an early start tomorrow."

"I'll be in soon." Her voice carried dismissal.

"Whatever is bothering you, I want to know about it now."

She turned to see him standing, his feet apart and his arms folded across his chest. It was his "I'm not taking no for an answer" stance. Well, this time he would just have to settle for no! "Nothing is bothering me. I simply want to be alone for a while."

The scowl on his face deepened. "We've got a tough job ahead of us. It could take days, and I'm not spending them enduring a stony silence that suggests I've done something wrong that I don't even know I've done."

"We travel in silence most of the time anyway," she retorted. "I've always been under the impression you prefer it that way."

"Silence, yes. Brooding, no. Until now we've gotten along just fine because you haven't pulled any of those 'pouty woman' moods on me."

"Well, I am a woman," she reminded him curtly.

"At the moment, I'm very aware of that," he growled back.

She'd expected icy cynicism; instead she detected an unexpected gruffness in his voice. When she met his gaze she saw heat in his eyes. "I thought you'd forgotten." Her own voice was shaky as she felt herself drawn into those dark depths.

"It's a little hard when you're dressed like that." His gaze raked over her and the heat in his eyes intensified.

She admitted to herself that she had chosen the lightweight summer dress, with a low-cut scoop neck and made of a cotton that flowed with her movements, to see if she could attract his attention. That it hadn't had only increased her irritation toward him. Now that irritation was gone. In its place excitement bubbled to life. She turned fully toward him and the breeze gently molded the fabric to the curves of her body.

His jaw twitched the way it did when he was angry or frustrated. Then, in one long stride, he breached the distance between them. His hands closed around her upper arms and he lifted her onto her toes as his mouth sought hers.

It was a hungry, demanding kiss. For a mere instant she was stunned, then her senses took over. Every fiber of her being reveled with triumph. It was as if they had been waiting for this moment all their lives.

Suddenly, as abruptly as it had begun, it ended. He released her and stepped away. "I'm sorry. That should never have happened," he said gruffly.

"I didn't think it was all that bad," she'd managed to reply, surprised that she could put a sentence together. She'd been standing near one of the round posts holding up the roof that partially shaded the veranda. She leaned back against it to steady her shaky legs.

His face had become shuttered and the cool, distant look she was so used to seeing in his eyes had returned. "It's not safe for me to be thinking about you as a woman. It diverts my concentration from more important things like keeping us both alive. I'm going to forget that kiss ever happened. I'll expect you to do the same." It was an order. He waited for no response. Clearly he expected it to be obeyed without question.

"Consider it forgotten," she muttered to his departing back as he entered the house. She was still leaning against the pillar and realized her legs continued to feel wobbly. Angrily she scowled at herself. That he could so easily put the kiss out of his mind was evidence that he'd merely given in to a moment of lust. She could have been any woman. And most likely, if she had been someone other than his partner, he would even have taken her to bed. But it would have meant nothing more to him than an enjoyable night. "Do as your commanding officer ordered," she growled at herself under her breath. "Forget it." And promising herself that she would, she went inside and to bed.

She and Joe had been tracking a cache of military weapons heisted from a base in Alabama. Their guess was that Pedro Palma was the middleman acting on behalf of the buyer, and the exchange would be taking place in the mountainous region of Mexico near the Guatemalan border.

In spite of several stern self-reprimands, the memory of the kiss continued to taunt her as they'd made their way south. She found herself covertly studying Joe for any sign he might be hiding deeper feelings for her. She saw none. He was once again the commander of their mission and she was merely his subordinate. Angry with the twinge of regret this knowledge brought, she turned her full attention to their mission.

They were to destroy the munitions and, if possible, capture Palma. But the munitions were their primary goal. There would always be other Palmas. She and Joe were on their own. He'd promised Manuel they would call in the *federales* when they located the exchange site but she knew he wouldn't do that until the charges were set to ensure that the weapons would be destroyed.

Using photos from surveillance satellites, Tobias had supplied them with a possible location. Not wanting to give up the element of surprise, when Joe thought they were still several miles from their destination, they'd hidden their vehicle and made their way through the dense forest on foot.

The going had been slow and night had fallen when they heard the sounds of voices beyond. Proceeding cautiously, they determined they'd found what they were seeking. From conversations they could hear, it was clear the men did not expect their buyers for another full day, maybe more. Most were not happy about the wait.

She and Joe were. It gave them time to work out a more effective plan of action instead of having to act immediately. It also gave them an opportunity to rest.

Both were exhausted. Even if they did find the stash and blow it up that night, they were too tired to ensure their escape. Joe led her back into the security of the forest to wait out the night. They'd traveled light on survival equipment, heavy on explosives. Between them there was only one tent. Joe found a protected spot in which to pitch it. Then he set up his own early warning system, should human or forest predator come too close. On their first assignment, she'd been amazed to learn that he'd conditioned himself to wake at the mere snapping of a twig.

"It's a trait I inherited from my Indian ancestors," he'd told her.

Experience had taught her they could rely on this ability.

After a cold meal, they climbed inside the tent, away from the multitude of insects and snakes that prowled the forest floor.

"I should have insisted Tobias send a man with me on this mission," Joe fumed as they stretched out on their sleeping bags. Because they'd stashed their explosives inside with them, there was very little room left. Their shoulders brushed and he turned away from her onto his side to place more distance between them.

She scowled at his back. Clearly he hadn't quite forgotten she was a woman. But it was equally clear he wasn't happy about this lack of discipline on his part. Well, if he thought she was lying there thinking about that kiss... She wanted to tell herself that wasn't so and toss a mental barb his way. But the truth was she had been thinking about it. However, she wasn't going to let him know that! "I thought we'd agreed that you were going to consider me one of the guys," she said frostily, her tone implying she had no interest in him other than as a fellow operative.

He shifted onto his back, being careful to avoid any contact. "That," he growled, "is getting harder and harder to do."

A curl of womanly excitement wove through her. It was quickly replaced by self-directed anger. Lust was all he was feeling. Just like the night on the veranda... he was in the mood for a woman's body and she was what was available. She attempted to build a shield of indignation. It didn't work. He wasn't trying to take advantage of her.

It was her own body that was causing the problem. She was acutely aware of him and that awareness was stirring the fires of passion to life within her. *You're going to get burned,* she warned herself. Still, she couldn't stop herself from easing onto her side for a more complete view of him. "Maybe you shouldn't fight so hard."

He frowned darkly at the nylon roof above. "I haven't got any plans for settling down or even having a long-term arrangement. In this business it's better not to look beyond the immediate present."

He was warning her that they had no future. Her conservative nature told her to lie back and go to sleep, but the feelings stirring within her were too strong to be ignored. Grudgingly, she admitted they were not new. From the first, she'd been attracted to the stoic man beside her. She'd told herself she was taking the job with The Unit because she was bored with her current assignment and found Joe an interesting study. Now, she confessed she'd become his partner because being with him felt right. It was as if she'd been looking for him all her life. "Following that line of logic, a person should live for the present and forget about tomorrow's consequences. Considering our line of work, that sounds like a reasonable attitude to take."

"Go to sleep, Tess," he ordered.

She heard the huskiness in his voice and the desire within her grew stronger. When her conservative side again tried to reason with her, tried to get her to obey his command, she argued that she could be dead this time tomorrow. "I don't feel like sleeping."

He shifted onto his side, to face her. "I don't want anything to happen between us that you'll regret."

"My grandmother used to say that life is a process of collecting memories to look back on, to learn from or to savor or both. Lately, I've been feeling a little short-changed in the ones I can look back on and savor.''

"Tomorrow could get rough." Hesitantly, he traced the line of her jaw with his fingertip. "We should get some sleep."

"To sleep, a person has to be able to relax and I'm going to need a little help for that," she replied, moving closer to him.

"Are you certain?" he demanded gruffly.

"Very." She'd never been this forward in her life. As their legs brushed and her hand came to rest on his chest, a surge of panic swept through her. Maybe this wasn't so smart, her inner voice warned. Then his lips found hers and all doubt vanished.

This time the kiss was not hungry. That element was there. She sensed it. But it was controlled. He tasted her with coaxing little nibbles, trailing them over her lips, down her neck to her shoulder, then back to her lips.

With only this mild beginning, her breathing was already ragged and her senses completely awakened. She began to ease the T-shirt he was wearing upward, nearly desperate for the full feel of him. He paused and, sitting up, discarded the shirt. When he lay back down, he lifted her toward him until her upper torso was over his. The feel of his hard firm chest beneath hers ignited a fire so intense she could barely get her breath.

"You do feel good," he said gruffly. His hands had traveled beneath her T-shirt and were working it upward. The temptation to sit up as he had and strip it off was strong but she was enjoying his touch too much. Lifting her arms, she allowed him to finish removing the garment. The effect was electric. She had removed her bra before trying to go to sleep. As the shirt came off, her soft curves molded to his hard ones.

"You feel good, too," she said, her voice a husky whisper.

She had been slowly trailing her mouth upward from his chest to his face. As she met his lips she could feel a light curl upward in one corner and knew he was pleased. She smiled, too, and deepened the kiss.

"Time to get rid of a few more barriers," he murmured.

Her breath sucked in with a tremor of delight as his hands caressed her abdomen in his search for the button on her camouflage pants. Straightening away from him, she knelt and unzipped the zipper. His gaze sultry with desire, he sat up and slid the pants down, his hands trailing along her hips. Lying back, she allowed him to complete the job. He worked slowly, kissing her newly exposed skin. When he nipped the inside of her thigh, she gasped with ecstasy and the fire within her grew so intense she was afraid of being consumed. *Not yet*, she ordered her body, but it seemed to have a mind of its own. As if he sensed he might be moving too fast, he nibbled on her knee and brought a giggle.

Her fire cooled just enough to allow her to remain in a state of heated anticipation.

"My turn," she said as he reached her toes.

"I relinquish command to you," he replied, lying back.

She had expected to feel mildly embarrassed. After all, she'd never undressed a man before. Instead, she found herself fascinated by the strength of his body and completely enjoying her work.

"I can't hold off much longer," he warned, as she discarded his pants.

She grinned at him. "I guessed that."

He laughed lightly, then, turning her onto her back, he slowly mounted her.

She braced herself as he claimed her. She'd expected some pain. It came in one sharp jab.

He cursed under his breath. "You were a virgin," he growled.

"And I would have hated to have died that way tomorrow and missed all this fun," she replied. Her body, already forgetting the pain and allowing its primitive instincts to take control, had begun to move in a massaging rhythm against his.

A guttural groan of enjoyment issued from deep within him. "I suppose what is done is done," he muttered. His hands fastened on her buttocks, adjusting the rhythm, then increasing it until she wanted to scream from pure pleasure.

"I never believed it could feel this way," she admitted. Then her breath was taken away as an explosion of ecstasy shook her to the core.

With a growl of satisfaction, he joined her. Their bodies pulsed together as one, and she hoped this would never end. Even when he did leave her to lie beside her, she held on to the lingering sensations until finally, completely exhausted, her body insisted on relaxing.

Realizing he hadn't spoken, she recalled his shock at discovering her virginity. He was probably trying to think of the words to apologize, and she didn't want that. She kissed him lightly on the shoulder. "Thanks for a learning experience I will genuinely savor for a long time. Now I can get some sleep." Shifting onto her stomach, she added a final, "Good night and thanks again." Then she closed her eyes, signaling an end to any conversation.

For a long moment, she could feel him studying her. Then he issued a gruff, "Good night," and too lay back and closed his eyes.

Beatrice jerked her mind back to the present. What had happened between her and Joe that night in the forest was ancient history. If he was alive, she would find him, tell him what a heel she thought he was for not facing her with the truth, and be on her way back to a life that did not include him.

Joe sat on the side of his cot, staring at the blank wall barely four feet in front of him. His expression was grim, his jaw set in a hard line.

For the past couple of days he'd been fed well and, although shackled hand and foot, had been allowed to go above for a couple of hours each morning and afternoon. He'd used these excursions to learn all he could about the fortress in which he was being held. He'd also learned that there was another captive in the dungeon. The guards never took both of their prisoners above at the same time, nor did they allow them to talk. But Joe had recognized his fellow inmate and knew he was a man he could depend on when the chance came for an escape. And there would be a chance, he assured himself for the umpteenth time. He never believed in giving up hope. That was what had kept him alive many times before.

But this time he had more than hope; he had anger born from a sense of betrayal that went to his very core. Since his treatment had improved, his guards had been more animated. They'd whispered among themselves and cast knowing looks his way. Last night he'd caught a name. Today, he'd heard it spoken again, along with other fragments of conversation that opened his eyes to a reality he didn't want to face.

"I forgot my own rule," he growled at himself. "Never trust anyone." The words caused a bitter taste in his mouth.

Tess's image filled his mind and his anger grew more intense. He had trusted her not only with his life but with his heart. No other woman had ever had such a hold on him. Giving her up had been like ripping a part of himself out. But when the opportunity had arisen to return her to a life where she was not risking death on a daily basis, for her sake and for his, he'd taken it. He'd felt guilt for having brought her into The Unit and even more guilty for having given in to his feelings for her. In hindsight, he'd admitted that even as they'd exchanged their vows, he'd known he was doing the wrong thing.

If she hadn't left The Unit following his faked death, he would have resurfaced to protect her. But she had and he'd told himself he'd done the right thing.

Afterward there had been so many nights when he'd lain alone in his bed, remembering the feel of her, the scent of her perfume, her soft giggle with its curious quality of seductiveness. So many times, he'd wanted to hold her once more. Cynically he recalled that it was her image that had kept him sane during those first days of his captivity and torture.

Ironic, he thought, then tried not to think of her for a while.

Chapter Five

"I still remember in detail the day Manuel proposed to me," Elena said, breaking the silence that had been between the two women during the first couple of hours of their drive.

From the hard set of her companion's jaw, Beatrice had been pretty sure Elena was thinking of her husband, and she'd been willing to leave the woman to her memories. As for herself, she'd been concentrating only on the present. "Was he as romantic as Spanish men are rumored to be?" she asked, sensing the other woman's need to talk.

"Very." Elena's chin trembled. "He knew I didn't want to marry a *federale*. Still, he came courting. He brought flowers and candy. He even hired a band to serenade me. Once, to everyone's amusement except mine, he literally carried me out of my house and took me on a picnic. But he had such a wonderful smile and there was a boyish mischievousness about him, I couldn't stay mad at him."

Elena sighed. "When I realized how deeply I was beginning to care for him, I told him not to come around anymore. For two weeks he stayed away. This convinced me his feelings were not as strong as he'd claimed. If they had been, he would have ignored my demand. I told myself I was glad to be free of him. Then I learned that he had not come because he'd gone into the mountains after a murderer."

Beatrice frowned at the road ahead. "And you were as scared for him as if it was your own life that was in danger. More scared. You would rather have risked your life than see his on the line."

Elena nodded. "Clearly, you know that feeling."

The image of Joe, laden with explosives, crawling toward Palma's encampment, came sharply into Beatrice's mind. With it came the memory of the terror she'd always experienced when he'd placed himself in danger. "Yes, I know the feeling." Realizing her palms were sweating from the intensity of her remembered fear, she silently cursed herself for allowing him to continue to affect her so strongly. "You were telling me about Manuel," she said.

"I prayed every morning and night for his safe return. At the same time, I vowed that I would avoid him at all costs. I did not want to face the prospect of a life filled with that kind of worry. When I heard he was back, I rejoiced silently, then went to visit an aunt who lived in the country. There, I learned through friends that he said he would respect my wishes not to see him. I returned home. That very day, I was walking down the street when I saw him on the other side. Our eyes met and the next thing I knew, I was running to him."

"You'd decided that you'd rather live with the worry than face life without him," Beatrice said, recalling making that same decision.

Elena nodded. "I loved him with all my heart. And now I will avenge him. Sanchez will learn what true wrath is."

The hard set had returned to her jaw and silence again fell between them.

Her gaze on the road ahead, Beatrice recalled Joe's courtship of her.

They'd completed the mission without mentioning or repeating their tryst. The munitions were blown. Palma had escaped, but Manuel and his men had managed to capture the buyer and several of Palma's men. Their mission accomplished, Joe and Beatrice had flown home.

It was during the second leg of their flight that Joe's silence had finally become too much for her to bear. He had never been a talkative man, but the stillness between them was different than in the past. It held a tension that caused her nerves to grow more and more on edge. If they were to continue to work together, she knew she had to defuse the situation.

"I don't regret what happened," she said.

He looked at her then. There was purpose on his face. "I've been thinking that we should get married."

She'd expected him to attempt to apologize and was prepared to be indignant just enough to let him know she really meant it when she said she didn't regret their tryst. Admittedly, deep down she did feel a twinge of remorse, but only because of the tension it had created. And, she confessed, because it had whetted her appetite for more; and that, she'd convinced herself, was not going to happen. She stared at him in disbelief. Then pride caused true indignation to rise to the surface. "That's a pretty drastic way to apologize, especially when you have nothing to apologize for."

He continued to regard her grimly. "I'm not apologizing. I'm asking you to marry me."

How much she wanted to marry him, shocked her. "If I thought you really wanted that, I'd consider it."

He cupped her face in his hands. "I do want to marry you." His mouth sought hers with a persuasive passion that convinced her he was being truthful.

As their lips parted, she grinned crookedly. "In that case, the answer is yes."

Tobias hadn't been pleased. "If the people I send you after found out you two were romantically involved, they would know they could use each against the other as a weapon," he grumbled. But in the end, because Joe was determined, Tobias had relented.

As a compromise, they'd been married in private, with Tobias, the minister and his wife the only ones present at the ceremony. Beatrice had written her family about the marriage and promised to bring Joe home for them to meet. But that meeting had never taken place. Almost as soon as their vows had been exchanged, Tobias had assigned them to track down a ring of drug dealers who had managed to develop a shipment-and-distribution system within several naval bases extending across the country. Although Joe had insisted she take a few days off during Christmas, he'd remained on the scent, fearful of losing their quarry or missing an important connection.

She'd told herself he was merely very adamant about his job. But she'd already begun to wonder if he'd been truthful about wanting to marry her. When that assignment ended, he'd taken her to meet his grandfather. But he'd found excuses for not visiting with her family.

In bed, in his arms, she could convince herself they were truly lovers. No man could have been more passionate. But during the day he was distant toward her, much the way he'd been when they'd first begun to work together. Even at his grandfather's, he'd never entirely relaxed, and when they returned home he was more tense than when they'd left. In the field, he became much too overly protective, as if the full responsibility for her welfare rested on his shoulders.

"I've chosen my own path," she'd told him once, when he'd tried to insist on handling a highly dangerous meeting on his own. "As far as I'm concerned, we're partners in every respect. We have a fifty-fifty arrangement. We help each other equally."

"Out in the field, I'm the one in command. It's up to me to make certain you don't get hurt," he'd replied.

She tried to convince him that he was wrong, but the strain between them continued to grow stronger. More and more of the time he made her feel like a nuisance he was forced to put up with. Just days before the bombing in which she'd thought he'd died, she'd again accused him of not truly wanting to be married to her, and he'd admitted that perhaps their marriage was a mistake. To her ire, the pain that admission had caused still stung.

"We turn here." Elena's voice cut into Beatrice's thoughts.

Again ordering herself to forget the past and concentrate on the present, Beatrice slowed and made the turn.

It was past noon when they arrived in a small village west of Tehuacán. Elena guided Beatrice to a house on the outskirts. It belonged to a *federale* by the name of Rafael Ortagea. Rafael had been Manuel's superior when Manuel first joined the force. A bullet lodged in his spine, causing partial paralysis of his left leg, had forced him into retirement.

He greeted Elena warmly, like a father seeing a long-lost daughter. Tears wet his eyes when he told of his grief at the news of Manuel's death.

"He will always live in my heart," Elena vowed.

Hearing those words, Beatrice grudgingly admitted that Joe had always remained in hers. However, once this mission was over, she planned to exorcise him completely!

Rafael turned to her. When she and Joe had been in Mexico the first time, she'd met the *federale* briefly. A flash of recognition showed on his face. "So you are the friend with whom Elena is taking this sight-seeing tour." His voice remained friendly, but she noted that his smile no longer reached his eyes and she knew he'd guessed the women were not on a vacation. "Welcome. My niece has prepared lunch for us and will serve us. Come in."

They had made this stop because Elena knew Rafael could give them specific directions to the place they sought. Also, they hoped he could provide information about how the interior was laid out. Ellen had explained that when the *federales* had finally built a case that would hold against Palma, Rafael had been one of the men sent to the mountain retreat to arrest him. However, Beatrice had not wanted Elena to mention their real purpose to the man over the phone. So now they had to play the part of two women on vacation until the niece left.

While they ate, Rafael reminisced about the times he and Manuel had worked together. His voice was gentle and his manner warm. But when the meal was over and he'd sent his niece home, his expression abruptly hardened as his gaze turned to Beatrice. "I never forget a face. This is not a sight-seeing trip, is it?"

Elena looked solemnly at Rafael. "I need your word that what is said from this moment on will be kept a secret."

For a moment he frowned reprovingly as if to say he knew he would not like what he was going to hear, then grudgingly nodded. "You have my word."

"She has come seeking Sanchez," Elena said, keeping her voice low as if in fear of being overheard.

The man turned to Beatrice, anger written on his face. "You should not have involved Elena in this. She is not trained. She will get killed."

"I needed supplies from someone I could trust," Beatrice explained, her voice carrying apology. "I have been in retirement. I didn't know of Manuel's death. I didn't want to bring her along but she gave me no choice."

"Do not talk about me as if I am a child who needs to be watched over!" Elena snapped. "I was planning to come look for Sanchez on my own as soon as I found out what rock that snake had crawled under." She smiled dryly at Beatrice. "Why do you think Manuel's Jeep was so fully stocked?"

Rafael's expression became fatherly. "Vengeance is dangerous. I would not want to lose you as well as Manuel."

Elena's jaw firmed. "I will not change my mind."

Shaking his head, Rafael turned to Beatrice. "I have been in touch with my friends on the force. They have no evidence they can use to arrest Sanchez. Do your people know something we do not?"

"I am working on my own," Beatrice replied.

"For vengeance, as well?"

She merely shrugged.

"You will help us, won't you?" Elena said, insistently. "For Manuel's memory."

"Finding Sanchez will not be difficult. He does not fear being found. He is at his home in Acapulco and better guarded than any dignitary. You will never reach him there. For any hope of success you will need help."

Beatrice shook her head. "We will be operating outside the law, breaking and entering a private home. I will not ask a *federale* to do such a thing. Besides, who would suspect two lone women? We are safer on our own."

"I have friends who would gladly help. There are many who would like to see Sanchez behind bars. I would go myself—" He scowled down at his bad leg "—if I did not think I would be more of a hindrance than a help."

"We must do this alone," Beatrice repeated more firmly. "The fewer people who know what we are planning, the safer we will be."

Rafael turned to Elena. "You must see that this is suicide."

Elena's gaze locked on his. "I agree with Tess. If others discover what we plan, like you, they might try to dissuade us and we will lose precious time." Her voice lowered conspiratorially. "Also, although I do not like saying this, I am fearful that Manuel was betrayed by one of his own. He was too good, too careful, to walk into an ambush."

Mentally Beatrice congratulated the other woman for not being naive. Apparently a few lessons of the trade had rubbed off on Elena.

For a long moment Rafael was silent, then he nodded. "You could be right. Perhaps the fewer who know of your mission, whatever it is, the better." Authority returned to his voice. "However, there are those I know I can trust. It could not hurt to have them at the ready in case you need rescuing."

"Part of my reason for stopping here was to arrange backup," Beatrice admitted. "But it must be on my terms."

"And what are those terms?" Rafael asked.

"If I find what I am seeking, I will radio a location to you where your people can meet us and provide safe passage back to Mexico City. Or, in the event my plan does not go well, they will meet with Elena and get her safely home."

"Done," he replied.

Elena frowned at Beatrice. "We will be coming back together or not at all."

Beatrice ignored the other woman's vow. She would deal with Elena when the time came. Right now, she had more important business. "I need information about the mountain retreat Palma built in the Sierra Madre del Sur."

Rafael frowned in confusion. "That place has been deserted for years."

"It is still listed as part of the assets of the company Sanchez now runs."

"Yes. But he never uses it. He has a helicopter pad at his home in Acapulco and high walls around the estate. He's convinced those he deals with that they are safe to do their dealing there."

"Still, I am convinced that what I seek is at the mountain retreat."

"I think you are on a wild-goose chase, but I would rather you found wild geese than Sanchez," Rafael said.

"Then you will give us directions?"

"Of course."

"And we will need to know what you know of the interior of the estate." Elena spoke up. She glanced sympathetically toward his leg. "You were inside, were you not?"

He, too, glanced at his leg. "Yes. I was inside." Finding a map and some paper, he began giving directions while Beatrice jotted them down. When he finished, he frowned at them. "Those mountains are no place for two women alone."

Continuing to worry about leading the other woman into danger, Beatrice turned to her. "It is very possible that Sanchez is not at the mountain retreat."

"I had a report just yesterday that he was in Acapulco," Rafael interjected, corroborating Beatrice's assumption.

"So it would serve no purpose for you to accompany me," Beatrice continued in a reasoning tone.

"I am coming with you." A comradeship showed on Elena's face. "Even if it is only evidence against the man which we find, that will be enough for me. I want to be a part of his downfall."

Seeing the determination in the woman's eyes, Beatrice knew arguing would be futile.

Elena turned to Rafael. "Will you contact your friends and have them at the ready, should we need assistance?"

His smile returned. "You sound like Manuel. Yes, I will see that you have your assistance."

Elena's eyes glittered with triumph.

"It is well into the afternoon. Why don't you stay the night here and get an early start tomorrow?" he coaxed. "The roads you will be traveling are treacherous after dark to those who are not familiar with them. They are even dangerous for those who travel them regularly. Also you can easily get lost."

"Your invitation is most kind, but we are impatient to be on our way," Elena said, rising from the table.

Grateful that her companion was as restless as she was to continue their journey, Beatrice rose also. "Thank you for your help. We are in your debt."

Rafael placed a restraining hand on her arm. "You are both behaving foolishly," he warned sternly.

"Perhaps," she conceded. Her jaw firmed. "I will leave a radio here with you and call if we have a confirmation."

His gaze traveled between the two women. "I will pray for your safe return."

While Elena gave Rafael a final hug, Beatrice climbed in behind the wheel of the Jeep and turned the key. Nothing happened. She tried again. Cursing silently, she popped the hood and got out.

"What is wrong?" Elena demanded, joining her to peer at the engine.

"I haven't a clue," Beatrice replied.

"My brother-in-law is a mechanic. I'll call him," Rafael volunteered, already on his way back inside.

"We have to find another vehicle," Beatrice said, fighting the urge to kick the Jeep. So far, she'd been able to keep her anxiousness under control and operate coolly and efficiently. But her hold was tenuous. Samantha's description of Joe was never far from the forefront of her mind. If she was correct, he needed help and he needed it quickly.

Elena frowned down the dirt road that was the main thoroughfare of the small village. "This is not Mexico city." She looked to the house they had just left. "Perhaps Rafael will have one he can loan us."

"I have nothing that I would trust to get you where you want to go," he said, stepping out onto the porch at that moment. "But my brother-in-law has promised to come within the hour." His gaze turned to the horizon. "It appears you will have to accept my offer of lodgings for the night."

"So it appears," Beatrice conceded, her growing fear that she would arrive too late to save Joe made her want to scream in frustration. But screaming, she knew, wouldn't help. The thought of setting out on foot even occurred to her. But that, she knew, would be even more foolish. Curtly, she reminded herself that her only chance to help Joe was to behave rationally. Turning to Rafael, she said, "You are most kind."

"I will have my niece prepare something special for dinner." He tucked a finger under Elena's chin and lifted her face upward. "Do not look so unhappy. Alonso is an excellent mechanic. He will have you on your way by sunrise."

"I hope so," she replied. "I must do this for Manuel."

He smiled. "Manuel is a lucky man." Releasing her, he motioned for them to follow. "Come inside out of the heat."

Beatrice gave the engine a final grudging glance, then slammed the hood shut and obeyed.

Although Alonso was not as punctual as Rafael had promised, he was as good of a mechanic as Rafael had bragged. He did not show up until the sun was on its way down, but he did find the problem. A couple of wires had jarred loose.

He'd refastened them and vowed they would not loosen again. Just to be on the safe side, Beatrice made him show her the repair, in case it had to be done again.

"Manuel did take this Jeep places where even mountain goats feared to tread," Elena said, watching also. "But he usually checked it out thoroughly afterward." Tears suddenly welled in her eyes. "I guess he didn't have a chance after his last trip." She glanced over her shoulder at Rafael who was standing behind her. "He died just days after he was here to see you."

Rafael nodded solemnly. "We went driving in the mountains. A hunting trip."

Storing that information, Beatrice waited until she could confront Rafael alone, then asked him bluntly if that hunting trip had taken them to the fortress.

"No. We were out merely for pleasure and relaxation." For a moment, he looked hesitant, then added, "He wanted to talk to me about his suspicions. Elena has guessed correctly. Manuel was certain there was an informant on the inside."

Beatrice thanked him for being candid.

"And now we will have a wonderful dinner and a quiet evening," he said boisterously, clearly happy to have the continued company of the two women.

At the crack of dawn the next day, Beatrice and Elena were on their way. The roads they followed were unpaved and Rafael had been right about them being treacherous. They were narrow, in some places more ruts than road, with sharp hairpin curves and drops of a hundred feet or more off the side, causing the going to be slow.

But they drove hard, and just as night was falling they reached the turnoff Rafael had described as being the entrance to the estate. It was a single lane wide with a tall iron gate barring access. A sign attached to the gate stated that this was private property and trespassers would be prosecuted. According to Rafael, the fortress lay a full four miles or more beyond. Beatrice was certain the barred road showed some signs of recent use, giving her hope that she was right in the assumption Joe was there.

"Looks like we found the place," she said, continuing down the public road, looking for a break in the forest that would allow them drivable access onto the land.

They found it in the form of a shallow stream. Turning into the water, she drove upstream as far as she dared, then turned onto the bank and into a small clearing. Even if she had wanted to, the trees were too thick to drive through. Besides, the motor of the vehicle could be heard for quite a distance. The only safe way to proceed from here was to hide the Jeep and continue on foot. But it was dark now. Grudgingly, both agreed the only reasonable action was to camp by the Jeep for the night.

The next morning, they found the private road leading to the fortress and followed it, keeping several feet to one side so as not to alert anyone of their presence.

Beatrice was worried about Elena keeping up the pace, but the other woman was clearly being driven by an inner force. When Beatrice would pause for a rest, Elena was anxious to go on.

Choosing to travel light for better mobility, they'd left the backpacks in the Jeep. Still, the going was slow. They didn't want to leave a trail that would be easily followed back to the Jeep by anyone other than themselves. It was noon before they saw the fortress in the distance. Changing direction, Beatrice found a sheltered position opposite the large stone structure. They were not high enough for a view of the interior but they could see the length of the front wall and a large portion of the west side. Kneeling behind a boulder, Beatrice scanned the area.

"It looks deserted," Elena whispered, disappointment evident in her voice.

Beatrice had been slowly surveying the top of the stone bulwarks. They had been solidly built. According to Rafael there was no back exit of which he was aware. That left the tall wooden gates to which the road led, as the only visible entrance. Beatrice, however, was certain there was a hidden passage. Neither Palma nor Sanchez would back themselves into a hole from which there was no escape. But it could take her days to find that entrance and she did not have days.

"Perhaps they are away on a buying or selling trip," Elena suggested, hopefully. Disappointment returned as she added, "Or perhaps your informant was wrong."

"Perhaps," Beatrice conceded, a sinking feeling in the pit of her stomach. Then, above the wall, to the left of the gate, she saw part of a man's head and shoulders emerge. "The place isn't entirely deserted," she informed Elena, continuing her inspection of the man. He looked as if he was there to stay for a while. He had a gun slung on his back and was leaning in a relaxed position on the wall, smoking a cigarette. Had there been another sentry there moments earlier and she'd missed seeing him? She didn't think so. She guessed nature had called and the man she was now watching had left his post for a short while. The fact that he'd had no one to replace him encouraged the assumption that the fortress was not fully manned. "I'm going to get closer. After dark, I'll try to make my way inside."

"I'm coming with you."

Beatrice saw the firmness of the other's woman jaw but this time she was not going to give in. "I need you to stay here. I'm trained to go in. If I have to look after you, we could both end up getting caught."

"I can look after myself," Elena hissed.

Beatrice's gaze narrowed on her and her voice took on even more authority. "In any operation, each person plays an essential part. I need you here, guarding my back. If I do not return by this time tomorrow, you call Rafael and have him send help. Then follow the path I marked back to the Jeep and get out of here."

Purpose etched itself into Elena's features. "If you are not back by this time tomorrow, I will call Rafael and then come looking for you."

Beatrice could see that telling her not to come would be futile. "Just be careful," she ordered.

"Manuel saw that I know how to use a gun and a knife," Elena replied.

Beatrice handed the binoculars to the other woman. "I will see you tomorrow, if not sooner."

Elena nodded. "And if I see danger ahead of you, I will make the sound of a frightened bird. In these hills it should carry to you."

Beatrice held out her hand. "May we both find what we are looking for," she said.

Elena smiled as she accepted the handshake.

* * *

Beatrice made her way carefully to the fortress. Keeping hidden in the fringes of the forest, she began to circle it slowly, hoping to find another way in. She had brought a rope and grappling hook but the men inside were certain to hear the hook hitting the rock and scraping against it unless they held a loud party tonight, and she didn't like counting on that. To her relief she saw no sentry on the west wall, adding proof to her assumption that the place was minimally staffed.

Rounding the corner to the north side, she was making her way along that wall when she noticed a few of the stones along the top had been knocked loose. A cut-up pine tree lay nearby and she realized it must have fallen against the wall, causing the damage. A slow smile spread across her face. There was a barrel for mixing mortar and a pile of stones nearby. Obviously, someone was planning to repair the damage. And that someone had left a ladder lying by the side of the wall.

"How very convenient," she murmured. Carefully, she continued around the perimeter to satisfy herself that the sentry she saw was the only one posted, then she returned to the north wall to wait until dark.

Night brought with it a full moon, and she cursed lightly under her breath. She'd wanted more darkness. Making her way to the foot of the wall, she listened. From inside she was certain she heard the faint sound of voices, but they were nearly drowned out by the sounds of the wind in the trees and the animals and insects of the woods.

To her relief the ladder was wooden and she was able to prop it up without making any noise. Climbing until she could peep over the walls, she paused and peered around the interior. The main house was easy to spot. It was the widest and longest structure and was directly below her. Along the west and east walls were smaller dwellings—servants' quarters, offices, bunkhouses, and maybe a few guest cottages, she guessed. From her vantage point, the main house looked completely dark. Only two of the dwellings, both to her left, had lights. It was from one of them that the voices were coming.

Looking to the wooden gates, she saw her sentry still in place, his back toward her. Quickly slipping over the wall onto the catwalk that circled the interior perimeter, she crouched low and began to make her way toward a ladder leading down. A man came out of the doorway of one of two lighted buildings below.

"Quiet night." He addressed the sentry.

"Very," the other man replied.

Their Spanish was a strong southern dialect, but Beatrice had no trouble making out the words. Their manner was comfortable, as if they were not the least bit worried or concerned. She drew a relieved breath. Surprise was on her side.

"Why don't you come in and play a hand or two?" the man who had just come out encouraged. "Pablo has been winning all evening. Poker is no good with only five. We need a sixth person to change the odds. Besides, it is a waste of time to post a guard here. These walls and that gate will protect us from any predators, and no one is going to come looking here. The *federales* only concern themselves with where Señor Sanchez is."

The sentry glanced back over the wall, swatted at an insect that had chosen to bite him on the neck, then gave a snort of disgust. "You're right. If I remain here much longer, I will probably fall asleep from boredom and fall and break my neck."

Climbing down from his perch, he accompanied the other man inside. Beatrice heard yells of welcome.

Their lack of concern caused her to fear that, even if Joe had been there when she'd begun her search, he'd been moved to a new location. Or, he was dead. Her jaw tensed. She refused to give up hope. "As long as I'm here, I might as well have a look around," she murmured under her breath.

Making her way down, she continued her search. As she had suspected, the main house was unoccupied. Weeds had taken over the flower gardens, giving the impression that, as Rafael had said, this place was no longer used by Sanchez on a regular basis—or at least, not to entertain customers. After a cursory inspection of the other dwellings to assure herself that either they were unoccupied or the residents had retired for the night, she turned her attention to finding the wine cellar. Rafael had said it was reached by a stone stairway along the west wall. She found the staircase answering his description easily. From below she heard nothing and saw only darkness. Again hope waned.

Flicking on her flashlight, she descended the stone steps. At the bottom was a small room from which two corridors led in opposite directions. Down one, she thought she detected a flickering of light.

Cautiously she made her way in that direction. Rows of empty wine racks lined the right side of the passage. Solid wooden doors with small barred windows fronted rooms to her left. Peering inside the first room she saw it was small, rectangular in shape, with a table in the center and wineglasses on a rack on the wall. Clearly, it was a tasting room. But if the furnishings had been different, it would have matched Samantha's description of Joe's prison perfectly.

The flickering light was coming from beyond the third door. Practically holding her breath she made her way to it. Keeping her flashlight aimed at the ground, she peered inside. A kerosene lamp, its wick set low to conserve energy, was the source of the light she had been following. Her gaze shifted from it to the man on the cot.

She thought she had prepared herself for seeing Joe again. She hadn't. Her breath locked in her lungs and tears welled in her eyes at the sight of his long frame stretched out on the cot, his feet hanging off the end. "Joe." She said his name in a voice barely above a whisper.

He did not move.

Fear raced through her. Was she too late? Anger replaced the fear. She wasn't going to go through that feeling of loss a second time. "Damn you, Joe, you'd better be alive!"

"A threat like that would scare the soul back into any man," came a low growl of an answer.

Chapter Six

A tear escaped and ran down Beatrice's cheek. She brushed it away. She'd promised herself Joe Whitedeer would never cause her to cry again.

He was now up, facing her from the other side of the bars. "I thought you had retired, Thistle."

The cynical edge in his voice hurt. She hadn't expected him to be overjoyed at seeing her again, but he was in need of help and she'd thought he would be at least a little pleased by her arrival. Clearly he would have preferred to be rescued by anyone else but her. Her anger returned. "And I thought you were dead."

"It seems we were both mistaken."

"No time for touching reunions," she said dryly. "We have to get out of here before one of the guards decides to come check on you." The locks were of the heavy bolt variety. She began to take out a small explosive pack. "Stand back and get ready to travel fast in case they hear this above."

He frowned, then his expression became shuttered. "You won't need that. The keys are on pegs in the anteroom. Get the one for the next cell, as well."

Her back muscles tightened with indignation. There had been an underlying impatience in his voice as if he'd expected her to have noticed the keys and picked them up on her way in. Well, nobody was that perfect, she thought acidly, hurriedly retracing her steps. Grabbing the keys on the pegs labeled for cells three and four, she rushed back and quickly released Joe, then moved to the next cell.

As the prisoner housed there stepped out, she flashed her light on his face. A gasp escaped. "Everyone thinks you're dead."

"That cell did feel like a coffin," Manuel said. Unlike Joe's cool reception, his voice held a warm greeting. "It's good to see you again, Mrs. Jones . . . Tess."

"It's good to see you, as well," she replied. His face was bruised, indicating that he, like Joe, had been beaten or had put up one heck of a struggle before being taken. The sleeve of his shirt had been ripped off and she saw a thick bandage around his upper arm.

"A bullet wound from when they captured me. They brought in a physician to administer to it," he said, noting the direction of her gaze. "I guess they wanted to make certain they kept me alive until they could break me down and make me tell them the names of our informants. Or maybe they had a prisoner exchange in mind."

"We'd better get going." Joe's voice indicated that he considered himself in command. "How many are above, Tess?"

"I only saw six. They're playing poker in a building across the courtyard. One is the guard who is supposed to be watching the front gate." She allowed her voice to take on a cynical edge that matched his. "I guess they didn't feel they needed to take any special precautions to ensure you didn't escape."

Manuel looked surprised by the obvious tension between his two comrades. "They may be few, but they have more weapons than we do. I suggest we leave before they decide to check on us."

"What's the best way to make good our escape, Tess?" It was Joe who spoke.

"The same way I came in," she replied. "Over the wall."

Stepping to one side, he made a sweeping flourish with his arm. "Lead the way."

An uneasiness rippled through her. Joe's behavior was almost flippant. That wasn't like him. Maybe one too many brushes with death had left him indifferent to his survival, she reasoned. Well, even if he didn't really care if they got out of this alive, she did. She had a few things she wanted to say to him and she was determined not to get robbed of the opportunity.

Abruptly, as if a thought had just occurred to him, he put his arm out, barring her way. "How about if I carry the gun?"

Well, at least he wasn't entirely unconcerned, she thought. He'd remembered that she didn't like using a gun and that he was a much better shot. Quickly, she slipped off the shoulder holster and handed it to him.

Then, moving stealthily, she led them out and to the ladder she'd used to get down from the catwalk. To her relief, the guard who had been on the gate had not returned to his post. Once on the catwalk, the three made their way to the ladder against the outer wall and down.

Following the same route that had led her to the fortress, Beatrice guided the men back to where Elena waited. When they drew near the other woman's hiding place, she chirped lightly and waited for a response. An answering chirp let her know everything was well.

"Wait here," Beatrice instructed the men.

Joe caught her arm before she could proceed farther. "Who's out there?" he demanded.

The depth of suspicion in his voice startled her. Then she remembered his rule about never trusting anyone. Still, she felt a jab of pain that he was no longer willing to rely on her judgment. Furious with herself for feeling anything, she ignored him and turned to Manuel. "It's Elena. She insisted on coming along. I don't want her shrieking when she sees you and, perhaps, making the guards aware that something is wrong."

"Elena is here?" Fear for his wife was evident in Manuel's voice.

Joe's hand tightened around her arm. "You brought Elena!" he growled angrily.

His unmasked concern for the other woman caused a flash of jealousy. "She gave me no choice," she snapped back, more angry with herself than with him.

"My wife has a mind of her own," Manuel said in Beatrice's defense. He made a shooing gesture toward her. "Warn her quickly. We must be on our way."

"I'll just stick close to watch your back," Joe said, releasing her.

The impression that he'd issued a warning rather than an offer of help, mystified her. She was overreacting to his displeasure at her reappearance in his life, she chided herself. Well, she didn't plan to stay long. Silently, she made her way forward.

"Well?" Elena demanded impatiently when Beatrice showed herself.

"I found what I came looking for. It was a man, someone I suspected Sanchez was holding hostage."

"A hostage? Who?"

"Joe."

Elena's eyes rounded in disbelief. "Joe is dead. He's been dead for years."

"That's what he wanted us all to think."

The fire returned to Elena's eyes. "He will help me avenge Manuel."

Beatrice smiled softly. "That's another thing. I found someone else there, as well."

Elena's breath sucked in. Fear to believe what she wanted to believe showed on her face. "Who?" The word came out barely above a whisper.

"Manuel. He's been wounded, but he's fine."

Tears rolled down Elena's cheeks. "Where is he?"

"Follow Tess." It was Joe who spoke. He'd crept out from his hiding position to join them. His gaze was on the equipment beside Elena. "I'll bring the radio and binoculars."

Elena nodded, already on her feet and waiting.

Moments later, tears of happiness welled in Tess's eyes as she watched the husband and wife rush into each other's arms—tears that were accompanied by a sharp jab of envy.

Unable to control her joy, Elena buried her face in her husband's shoulder to smother her sobs while he kissed her hair and crushed her to him with his good arm.

"Your car was found at the bottom of the ravine near the elbow in the river. We all assumed you had been killed in the crash and your body was washed out to sea," Elena choked out. "How did you survive?"

"After I was wounded, I ran into a ditch and blacked out. When I came to, I was bound and gagged and on my way here. They must have pushed my car over the ravine afterward to make it look as if I'd been killed.''

''At least it wasn't his choice to play dead,'' Beatrice muttered under her breath, just loud enough for Joe to hear.

He responded with a shrug of indifference.

''Who knows you are here?'' Manuel abruptly demanded, lightening his hold on his wife enough to look into her face.

''Rafael Ortagea,'' Elena replied, then glanced to Tess for any further names.

''Only my immediate superior,'' she added.

''Good.'' Manuel sounded relieved. ''I have reason to believe my partner is one of Sanchez's men. We will see how he reacts when I return.''

''Juan betrayed you?'' The promise of vengeance was strong in Elena's voice.

''That will be our secret until I can entrap him,'' Manuel ordered her.

''*We* will entrap him,'' she corrected.

''I—''

''You two can work that out later,'' Joe interrupted. ''We need to get going.''

''Tess marked a path back to the Jeep,'' Elena said.

''Then she can lead the way. I'll guard our rear.'' Joe motioned for them to get moving.

The hairs on the back of Beatrice's neck bristled. His tone suggested he thought she'd left a trail anyone could follow and was fearful the guards might be right behind them once they learned of the men's escape. She tossed him a haughty glance and looked for the first marking. The method she'd used had been one Joe had taught her. Her chosen guideposts were never the same. And no one would have noticed them unless they knew exactly what to look for.

She was tired but proud of her trailblazing when they finally reached the Jeep.

Before she could climb inside, Joe caught her arm. "Manuel, you and Elena take the Jeep and head home. When they find out we've escaped, they'll have people looking for two men."

Elena looked to Beatrice with concern. "But what will you do?"

"Tess and I will make our way out on foot." He tossed the radio into the back of the Jeep. Seeing the black leather satchel, he pulled it out, sorted through the contents, took out what he thought would be useful, then tossed it back. Next he turned his attention to the camping equipment the women had brought along in case they'd had to spend several nights in the wild. "Are these backpacks fully loaded?" he asked Elena.

"Fully," she replied.

"Grab one," Joe ordered Beatrice.

Next to getting caught by Sanchez's men, the very last thing Beatrice wanted was to spend time alone with Joe in a tent in the woods. "We could hide in the back of the Jeep."

His expression hardened. "Our work here isn't done."

"Surely you need nothing more to bring Sanchez to justice. He held you and Manuel captive. You have merely to testify to that in court," Elena said.

"I never saw Sanchez." Joe looked to Manuel.

The *federale* shook his head. "Nor I."

"And although I am certain these men work for him, he can claim they were merely bandits who used his property without his knowledge or consent," Joe finished. "I want to go back to see if I can find any evidence that he cannot slither away from."

"I'll help," Manuel volunteered. "Tess can make sure Elena gets home safely."

"I am not a child who needs to be baby-sat," Elena interjected.

Joe looked to Manuel. "Take care of your wife. Your arm isn't healed enough to be fully reliable. Besides, Tess and I are used to working together."

Beatrice could barely believe what she was hearing. She knew Joe liked working alone. And considering his hostile greeting, she'd expected him to try to get rid of her as quickly as possible. But he wasn't doing that. He was insisting that she stay with him. Had the past few years caused him to have some regrets about walking away from her? Maybe what she'd thought was hostility was merely frustration and embarrassment on his part. Maybe he wanted to apologize, start over, and didn't know how to say it.

Or maybe he realizes that what has to be done can't be done alone, and while he'd rather have anyone else help him, I'm the only healthy specimen that's available, she added cynically, refusing to allow the feelings she'd buried deep inside to bubble to the surface. Either way, she knew she had no choice but to remain. "A hike in the mountains is always fun," she said, forcing a cheerful face as she picked up the nearest backpack and slipped it on.

Manuel's stance stiffened. "I still think I should stay."

"You have business to take care of back home," Joe reminded him.

For a moment longer he hesitated, then nodded. "Yes, you are right."

Relief showed on Elena's face, then concern as she turned to Beatrice. "You will stop by and say hello when your work is finished, won't you? Or at least, get a message to us to let us know you are all right?" Abruptly she smiled. "You left most of your luggage behind. You will have to come pick it up."

"Yes, of course," Beatrice promised.

Joe looked toward the east. "Come on, we need to get going. It will be daybreak in a couple of hours."

"You'll need your radio." Manuel picked up the piece of equipment and extended it toward Joe. "I've got one in the Jeep. If you run into trouble, call me."

Joe shook his head. "That radio could be more of a danger than a help. They could be monitoring all the bands."

Manuel did not look convinced and Beatrice had to admit she was a little surprised by Joe's argument. Even if Sanchez's men were monitoring the bands, a prearranged message that would be nothing but gibberish to them could have been agreed upon.

But Joe gave neither of them time to argue. "I'll be in touch in a few days," he said over his shoulder, already heading back into the forest.

Chapter Seven

At midmorning, Beatrice found herself again on the slope across from the fortress. Exhausted from her treks through the woods, she sat leaning against a tree eating stale bread and chewing on a leathery strip of beef jerky while Joe knelt a short distance away, peering through the binoculars.

"Doesn't look like they're very concerned about Manuel's and my escape." He'd been silently studying the stone bulwarks and surrounding landscape for the past half-hour. Now he turned to Beatrice as if he expected her to come up with an explanation.

"Maybe they sent a search party out before we got back. Or maybe they called Sanchez and he ordered them to remain on guard at the fortress while he sent some of his other men here to conduct the hunt."

"Or maybe you were *supposed* to rescue us," Joe added another possibility. "A few days ago, I was certain they were going to let me die. Then suddenly, they were giving me food and water, and allowing me a lamp and daily excursions to the courtyard. Also, until the day before yesterday there were at least thirty of Sanchez's soldiers here. They had an arsenal of stolen weapons stashed, in preparation for a sale. And I'm certain that sale wasn't to take place for a few more days. Then, late afternoon three days ago, they began to evacuate men and equipment. By yesterday morning, the place was nearly deserted. And don't you think finding that ladder on the outside perimeter was an amazing stroke of luck? That tree had fallen before I was even brought here. I saw the top of it resting on the wall. No one paid any attention to it. I got the distinct feeling they liked it there. It added to the look of the place being unused and uncared for. Then, yesterday morning they suddenly began to show signs of preparing to repair the wall.''

She had to admit he had a point. She'd been too preoccupied with seeing him again to spend any time sorting out the events of the rescue. All the while he'd been watching the fortress, she'd been unable to keep herself from watching him. He looked much older and grimmer than the last time she'd seen him but that was, no doubt, due to his imprisonment. And he could muddle her emotions. As angry as she was at his deception, there was an equally strong joy that he was alive. "Sometimes a person gets lucky," she replied, but without conviction. Glancing around, she wondered if she'd walked into the spider's web, been snagged and didn't even know it.

"How did you find out I was still alive?" He was sitting back now, leaning against a tree, studying her, his expression unreadable.

"I didn't know for sure until I spoke to Tobias a few days ago," she hedged.

"And what prompted that? We all thought you'd retired."

Her shoulders stiffened. He was questioning her as if she were suspect. "I had retired and I'd accepted the fact that you were dead." The anger that had been near the surface burst forth. "How could you do that to me? Even if you didn't care for me, I cared for you. I wouldn't have held you to a marriage you didn't want. I would have set you free. You didn't need to fake your death to be rid of me."

"It seemed like a reasonable solution at the time," he replied coolly.

"I must have been nuts to have fallen in love with you."

"You seemed to have gotten over it."

She was about to ask him how he would know what she was feeling, but bit back the words. That could make him think she still cared, and she refused to give that impression. "We all mature. It just takes some of us longer than others."

He grinned wryly. "So it would seem." The grin vanished and his expression once again became shuttered. "You never told me what made you, after all this time, begin to suspect I might still be alive."

She knew he would detect a lie. He'd always been able to read her. "Do I have your word this will go no further?"

He shrugged. "Sure."

"A psychic acquaintance of mine told me."

He smiled cynically. "You have learned to lie expertly. Your gaze never wavered and you showed no signs of discomfort."

"I'm not lying."

His smile disappeared and his eyes seemed to bore into her. "And how did this acquaintance know about me in the first place?"

"I've never talked about you, if that's what you're implying," she snapped back. "And she didn't know about you, not in the way you mean. She had no idea who you were. The only reason she made the connection between us was because she saw me in her crystal ball as well."

"So you came looking for me because a psychic saw me in that fortress in a crystal ball." Skepticism dripped from his voice.

"Actually, she didn't see the fortress. All she knew was that you looked as if you'd been beaten and were being held in some sort of underground cell."

"And from that you deduced that I was here." His voice mocked her.

She continued to meet his gaze with proud defiance. "No. To locate your whereabouts, I contacted someone else whose psychic powers lean toward finding things. She described the mountain fortress. Tobias recognized it from what she said."

"And you expect me to believe that?"

"The police are using psychics more and more."

"You have changed, or maybe you were never the honest, straightforward woman I thought you were."

Righteous anger flared in her eyes. "Don't talk to me about honesty. You were the one who sneaked out of my life by a back door instead of confronting me with the truth."

He stretched and rose. She figured he was going to go looking for some privacy, when suddenly he approached. Before she could react, she felt a prick on her neck.

"What? Why?" she managed to gasp just before the world went black.

She woke to find herself in the tent, stretched out on a sleeping bag. Dusk had fallen. Out of the corner of her eye, she could see that Joe was stretched out on the other sleeping bag. Groggy and confused about his actions, she tried to bring her hands up to rub her face, only to discover something pulling on her left wrist. She looked down and saw the bracelet of a handcuff. The other bracelet was attached to Joe's wrist.

"So you're awake." Sitting up, he unfastened the cuffs and set them both free.

Rubbing her wrist, she maneuvered herself into a sitting position, as well. "Why did you drug me and then handcuff me?" she demanded.

"I needed to get some sleep, and I didn't want to have to worry about what you were up to."

She glared at him. "What did you think I was going to do? I was as exhausted as you. More, even."

"You've always had a knack for finding trouble."

"Me? I'm not the one who spent the last few days in a wine cellar."

"Anytime you're ready to tell me the truth about how you knew to look for me here, I'm ready to listen," he replied over his shoulder as he left the tent.

"I told you the truth," she said to his departing back. Following him outside, she noticed that night had fallen.

Remaining silent, he concentrated on the walled estate.

"According to Rafael, the *federales* believed this place was abandoned by Sanchez. I don't understand how he could be using it and no one knew," she said.

"Maybe you should ask your crystal-ball seer."

She scowled up at him. "If you know the answer, why don't you humor me and tell me?"

He gave an indifferent shrug. "If anyone decides to send a plane over to check for activity, there's a radar system that warns the men when it's near. An alarm sounds and they duck underground. Some of the buildings were gutted to provide garage room for the trucks and other vehicles. When they're not in use, they're kept inside. Any that are out when the alarm sounds, are quickly hidden. When the plane flies over, the place looks deserted. As for the locals, the population around here is sparse. Those who do live near, Sanchez has either intimidated into silence or paid to keep their mouths shut."

"So what do we do now? Do you think he'll actually come here to conduct the search for you?" she asked. "Then you'll have your evidence that he was involved in your imprisonment."

Joe frowned at her. "Sanchez never comes here. That's another reason the *federales* think he has no interest in this place. He only uses it to stash whatever illegal goods he has to barter."

"Then why are we here?" His reticence was grating on her nerves. When they'd first started working together, all the information he'd given her had been strictly on a need-to-know basis. Later, once he'd learned to trust her, he'd discussed the operations with her beforehand. Apparently they were now back to playing by the need-to-know rules again, and she didn't like it.

"I just want to take a look around. Make certain I don't leave anything that can be used against Sanchez behind. And if I'm wrong about the arsenal they had stashed here and they haven't moved all of it out, I intend to make certain they have nothing left to barter."

She nodded. "I'll help."

For a moment he hesitated, then he tossed her a tin of canned meat and took one out for himself. "We'll eat, then get started."

She had the distinct feeling he wasn't happy about having her accompany him. "If you're worried that I might be rusty and ruin the operation, put your mind at ease. I still recall a few tricks of the trade," she assured him.

"I figured you did," came his reply.

She frowned at him. If he wasn't worried about her ability in the field, then what was his problem? She recalled how ultraprotective he'd become after their marriage. But he didn't look as if he was feeling protective. "Then how about sharing whatever is gnawing at you about me?"

His gaze turned on her. It was cold. "I want to know how you found me."

"I told you the truth."

"Yeah, right," he muttered, putting aside his emptied tin of meat. "You about ready to go?"

"Anytime," she replied, washing down her final bite with a gulp of water.

After making their way down to the fortress, they began to circle the perimeter. She was surprised to find the ladder they'd used the night before still in place. "I suppose they figured we wouldn't be coming back."

"Or they didn't care if we did," he countered. Unexpectedly, he stepped aside. "You can take point. I'll protect our rear."

Finding it hard to believe he'd given her the lead, she climbed the ladder and peered cautiously over the top of the wall. She saw and heard nothing to indicate occupancy—not a single light, not a single movement. Slipping over the wall onto the catwalk, she knelt, blending in with the shadows, and scanned the interior once again. It looked completely deserted.

He joined her. "Two four-wheel-drive vehicles pulled out soon after you were asleep—"

"After you drugged me," she corrected in a curt whisper.

"That must have been the last of them," he finished, ignoring her short tirade. "But, just in case they left any booby traps, we'll do this by the book." He motioned toward the ladder leading down into the belly of the fort. "You keep the point."

Again surprise swept through her. He'd never liked giving her the point when they'd worked together before. Now he appeared to prefer her in that position. Moving swiftly but carefully, she descended and began her exploration.

An hour later, she came out of the last building. Every munitions, every piece of radar equipment, everything was gone. "Looks like they've completely abandoned this place."

"So it would seem," he replied.

A frightening thought shook her. "If Elena and I had been a day later, we'd have missed rescuing you and Manuel." When he made no response, she looked at him. His jaw set in a hard line, he looked like a man angry with the world.

Abruptly, his gaze swung to her. "Let's get out of here."

Joe did not speak again until they'd reached their campsite. He was afraid to—afraid of what he might say. He knew what he had to do, but even with all of his training, he found this particular duty impossible to accept. Heading to the tent, he said, "It'll be dawn in a couple of hours. We'll sleep until then." It was an order. Without watching to see if she was going to obey, he entered the tent and stretched out.

He'd taken no precautions this time to ensure that she would be there when he awoke. He was giving her a chance to take off on her own. It wasn't professional. But he'd done a lot for his country. Tonight, right this minute, he would do no more. This time, duty asked too much of him.

His practical side knew that even if she did take off on her own, she wouldn't stay hidden from him for long. Eventually he would have to deal with her. But maybe later it would be easier.

Beatrice frowned at the entrance of the tent. Joe's indifference stung. His distrust hurt. Her fair side forced her to admit that her story of how she'd found him did sound far-fetched. But at one time, they'd trusted each other with their lives. She'd even trusted him with her heart. A definite mistake, she reminded herself.

The desire to take some food and water and hike out on her own was strong. She'd done her part. She'd rescued him. Now she should feel free to walk away. He'd walked away from her without a backward glance. Instead, she leaned against a tree and continued to glare at the tent, her mind on its occupant. He was still a little weak from his captivity. The pace he'd set for their hike to and from the fortress had been slower than she'd expected. Inside, when he'd thought she wouldn't notice, he'd paused to lean against a wall to steady himself a couple of times during their search.

She breathed a disgruntled sigh. Her conscience wouldn't allow her to call the rescue complete until she'd gotten him back to civilization. The frown on her face darkened. However, she had no desire to join him in that tent. She would rather sleep out here with the bugs and other creepy-crawlies.

She switched her flashlight back on and aimed it at the ground, looking for a soft spot. A beetle as thick and long as her thumb scurried over the toe of her boot. For a long moment she stood indecisively, then headed to the tent.

"So you decided to stay," Joe said as she entered, ignoring the tightening in his stomach.

That he'd guessed so correctly what was on her mind, shook her. "I figured two would have a better chance of getting out of this forest in one piece than one alone."

"You always did have a practical head on your shoulders." His tone made this sound like an insult.

"I've always considered that an asset," she snapped back.

Not this time, he thought tiredly. "Go to sleep, Tess." He closed his eyes to let her know that as far as he was concerned, this conversation was over.

Lying on her back, she turned her head to glare at his harsh profile. She was the one who had the right to feel bitter and angry. He should be grateful she'd shown up.

Her intuition told her something was wrong. He'd always been a difficult man to understand. There was a lot of himself he'd kept hidden. But he'd always been fair in his dealings with her. Although his faked death hurt, she could even understand why he'd traveled that path.

She recalled another night, long ago. It was during one of their short breaks between assignments and they'd gone off to spend a quiet weekend alone. They were lying cuddled in a big double sleeping bag under a clear, starlit Colorado sky. She'd brought up the subject of them both leaving the service, settling down somewhere, leading more normal lives, maybe even having children. That was when she'd learned what was driving him.

He'd rolled away from her and lain gazing skyward. "Those are possibilities I cannot consider," he'd said.

"Cannot or don't want to?" she'd asked, admitting to herself how much she wanted the life she'd described.

"Cannot," he'd replied.

"We all have choices," she'd argued.

"I had a brother...Sam. He had a wife and a baby daughter. He was a rancher, a peaceful man who never caused anyone any harm. He and his wife and child were on vacation when a terrorist group blew the plane in which they were flying to bits. The munitions they used were armaments stolen from one of our own bases. I vowed that I would do all that was in my power to see that never happened to another family."

He'd never spoken of his brother and his brother's family before. Now she knew why. Joe was very good at hiding his feelings. But the pain this loss had caused was evident in his voice. Behind it, she'd heard the determination to live by his vow and she'd made her choice. She would stand by him. She'd been too much in love to want a life without him.

Now, she forced herself to face the full truth about their marriage. After that night, he'd apologized several times for not being able to give her the life she wanted. Her assurances that she was happy merely being with him, had obviously fallen on deaf ears. His purported death had set her free.

And set him free, she added, more certain than ever that he'd never truly loved her. He'd married her out of guilt and then felt guilty because he'd married her and robbed her of the life he thought she wanted.

A thought struck her. Could his hostility be because he was worried that she would want to take up where they'd left off? Did he think she was still pie-eyed in love with him and wanted him back? Well, if he did, he was going to find out he was wrong. She'd learned to live without him just fine!

She shifted her gaze to the ceiling, closed her eyes and went to sleep.

"It's time to get going."

Beatrice opened her eyes to see Joe frowning down at her.

Leaving the tent, she discovered he'd heated water and made coffee. He'd also already eaten. While she gulped down a quick breakfast, he returned their sleeping bags to their backpacks and repacked the tent.

She'd considered offering to help but got the impression he preferred to work alone.

After breaking camp, he took the lead, heading directly for the road. She couldn't fault his choice. The going would be much faster than trying to make their way through the forest. And, if someone should decide to return to the fortress, she and Joe could hear any traffic approaching soon enough to leave the road and hide.

His strength was clearly returning. He set a faster pace than he had the day before, causing her to nearly jog to keep up. For the first mile, she matched his gait, then the heat began to take its toll. Giving up, she set a pace she knew she could maintain. If he wanted to hike out on his own, that was fine with her.

She'd caught a glimpse of his face before she'd begun to lag behind. He had the look of a man whose mind was elsewhere and she wondered if he would even notice she was missing.

Apparently he did, she mused, rounding a bend and finding him standing in the middle of the road, his arms akimbo, his expression shuttered. Perspiration streamed down his face. He wiped at it with the sleeve of his shirt.

"I figured it would be stupid for both of us to collapse from heatstroke," she said, coming to a halt a few feet in front of him.

He raked a hand through his sweat-soaked hair, combing it away from his face. He was giving her every chance, he told himself. Without a word, he took the lead again. At first he set a reasonable pace, then began to increase it again.

Watching him, she could sense his anger as if it was a physical force driving him forward.

Reaching the gate well ahead of her, he was again forced to wait until she caught up.

The coldness in his eyes rankled her. "If I'm slowing you down too much, feel free to go ahead without me," she told him curtly. "I can make it back on my own."

"I'm sure you can." He shoved the gate open and waited for her to pass.

That was not the response she'd expected. What she had expected was for him to give her one of his dry looks as if to say she was being foolish. The realization that he wouldn't have minded in the least if she'd taken off on her own caused a jab of hurt. Again she told herself she didn't care how he felt about her. Remaining where she was, she glared at him. "I only stayed with you because I thought you might need some help getting back. You seemed a little weak yesterday. But since you appear to have regained your health, we can part company anytime. Now seems as good as any."

A silence hung between them while she waited for him to make the next move. For what seemed like an eternity, he stood studying her icily, then said in a low growl, "I should have already killed you. But, even knowing the death and destruction your actions have caused, I can't. I'd convinced myself I could let you go. But I can't do that, either. Eventually either I or someone else will have to come after you. I'm taking you back to Tobias. He can deal with you."

Shocked, she took a step back. "What are you talking about? What death and destruction? Has the sun cooked your brain?"

"Don't play dumb with me," he sneered.

"Then stop talking crazy," she countered.

"Did you really think I wouldn't figure out you're the one I've been looking for?"

Recalling her conversation with Tobias, the pieces began to fit together. Joe had insisted they travel without a radio because he hadn't wanted her to be able to contact anyone. And he'd had her take the lead position because he'd wanted to guard his back, not hers. Anger replaced her shock. "You think I'm the traitor you've been looking for? I've been out of the loop for four years!"

"Maybe not. Maybe you've been keeping in touch with contacts within The Unit or even other branches that Tobias isn't aware of. He trusted you. He wouldn't have kept an eye on you after you retired. You're a very pretty woman. You could be carrying on secret liaisons with other operatives. Raven would be happy to put his shoes under your bed anytime. And he or any of the others would have felt safe in divulging information to you. After all, you had the highest security clearance."

"I've never been good at playing the femme fatale. You know that," she retorted.

"Maybe that's what you wanted me to think."

"Whatever they did to you in that fortress has turned you into a raving lunatic." She took another step back. Joe, she knew, could be deadly and she wanted some response time in case he decided he could kill her.

"I had begun to suspect our traitor was a woman. But until you showed up, you were never on my list of possibilities."

"My being the one you're looking for doesn't make any sense. Why would I come to rescue you if I was the person you were after?"

"Five, six, maybe seven days ago—it's been a little hard for me to keep track of the time—I was certain I was a dead man. They'd pumped me full of drugs and beaten me to get information. They knew they'd gotten all they were going to get out of me and I figured they'd decided to let me die. They hadn't fed me or given me water for days. Then suddenly they brought me clean clothes, food, water and started taking me up into the daylight to get exercise."

"So maybe they decided you were more valuable alive than dead. Maybe they figured they could use you, like Manuel, for a hostage exchange."

His gaze became even darker. "You should have warned Sanchez to tell his men to be more discreet. I heard a couple of them talking, joking about how I was being spared as a favor for someone important. And that this someone had a soft spot for me...that this someone had been my partner once."

"And you thought I'd been pining over you all these years...that you still had a hold on my heart?" Her voice took on a cynical edge. "You do have a gigantic ego."

"You had me convinced you were in love with me," he returned with equal cynicism.

That he thought she'd been lying about her feelings stung deep. "I was in love with you, but that was a long time ago. Like I said before, I've matured. I have a new life I'm very content with."

"And a seer with a crystal ball told you I needed help, so you left this new life you're so content with and came to rescue me."

"We were partners once. I figured I owed you."

"I'm not buying your story." He took a step toward her. "We're going back to see Tobias and see if he buys it."

She took another step back and held up her hand like a cop stopping traffic. "You're not getting any closer to me until we've talked this out."

He continued toward her. "I'm wise to you, Tess. You're not going to fool me this time."

She continued to move backward, keeping a distance between them. "You said their behavior toward you changed six or seven days ago. That would be about the same time I contacted The Unit trying to see Tobias to find out if you were still alive."

He stopped and regarded her icily. "They called you by name. One said it must have been real interesting working with Thistle. Then they laughed about how truly dangerous your thorns are and that they'd never want to get close enough to get pricked. 'A deadly flower' was how they described you."

"They were setting me up!"

He raised a disbelieving eyebrow.

"You'd never heard them mention me until then, right?" she demanded.

He shrugged a noncommittal yes.

More pieces of the puzzle began to fit together in her mind. "Your inside person must have learned that I'd resurfaced and saw an opportunity to point you in my direction. If I hadn't shown up to rescue you, they probably would have arranged for you to escape just so you could 'expose' me and dispose of me. Then you'd think you were free of your traitor and whoever the real traitor is would be free to get on with their life, especially if they chose this time to retire."

The disbelief remained on his face. "If you aren't in league with them, how did they know exactly when to evacuate their camp? Until two days before you arrived, they showed no signs of thinking of changing locations, then suddenly they moved everything out, leaving the place nearly deserted. There were just enough men left to make it look as if Manuel and I were still being guarded. Once we were gone, even they left. Clearly, they assumed we wouldn't return."

"I must be rustier than I thought. They must have picked up my trail." An uneasy chill ran along her spine. "Or they had someone watching Elena and I missed the tail."

His gaze continued to remain cold. "There is one way you could possibly convince me of your innocence. You could tell me the truth about how you found me."

Her jaw firmed. "I've told you the truth."

"You will never know how much I'd like to believe that, but my scenario makes more sense."

"You still think that I'm the bad guy and that I rescued you because I'm still in love with you?"

"No. You've managed to convince me that isn't the case. But maybe you needed someone new on the inside. Maybe your contact retired or died and when you found out I was still alive, you decided that I could be your patsy. Even better, maybe you figured you could guide my search for the mole and lead me to some poor innocent scapegoat who could take the rap."

"You're wrong."

His expression became shuttered. "I'm taking you back to Tobias."

She knew that look; it was the one he used to hide what was really going on in his mind. She also knew Tobias expected Joe to take care of problems in the field, not bring them home to roost. "Don't come any closer," she warned.

He continued toward her. "If you're innocent, you've got nothing to worry about."

Again she backed away from him. Her fair side admitted that she could not blame him for not believing her. "All right. I'll tell you the truth. But I want your word that it will remain between us, and only us. You won't even tell Tobias. There are other lives involved."

He stopped. "You have my word." Inwardly, he hoped she did have a reasonable explanation. Outwardly, he continued to regard her skeptically.

"What I tell you will remain strictly between you and me?"

"Strictly between you and me."

The one thing she had never doubted about Joe was that his word was his bond. "There is something about myself I've never told you."

"Now why doesn't that surprise me?"

Ignoring his cynicism, she continued stiffly, "I can trace my ancestry back to the ancient Druids. And I know others who can as well."

"The Celtic priesthood that was purported to have magical powers?" He regarded her dryly. "I was under the impression that even those 'powers' could not save them from extinction. It's always been my guess that they were merely extraordinarily charismatic people or so naturally cruel, they were able to intimidate the masses into believing whatever they wanted them to believe."

She scowled at him. "You're wrong on all counts. They were not exterminated, they merely scattered and blended into other cultures. And the 'powers' were real. In ancient times they were seen as magical. Today, society refers to them as a sixth sense or ESP."

The cynicism on his face deepened. "Can I assume we are heading back to the crystal-ball gazer once again?"

"In a way." She could see he was going to need some convincing.

Impatience mingled with his cynicism. "I hope you're not going to try to convince me that you're the seer."

"No. As I've already told you, that 'talent' belongs to an acquaintance." For a moment she hesitated. But she had no choice. Even if she got away from Joe this time, he would hunt her down. "My talent lies in another area." She looked toward a rock about the size of a coconut lying at the side of the road. Slowly the rock began to lift from the ground. She maneuvered it until it floated between them, then let it drop.

Joe stood in silence, staring at her.

"Do you remember the grenade that somehow flew out my hospital-room window?" she asked him. "Or the time the gunman had a bead on us, then mysteriously fell backward and ended up firing into the air?"

For the first time in all the time she'd known him, Joe looked shaken. Abruptly his expression became shuttered. "You've always had this ability?"

"Since I was around fourteen."

"And you never mentioned it when we were together." There was accusation in his voice.

"People have a tendency to fear what they don't understand. I was afraid you wouldn't be able to accept me, that you would be uncomfortable around me."

He continued to study her as if seeing her for the first time. "Does the rest of your family have this ability?"

"No, not all of them. Most don't. And until recently, none of them knew I had it. I had a brother, Hallam, who was born without it. He wanted it badly and became envious of those who had it. The envy led to trouble, a great deal of pain and anguish for others, and eventually his death. I felt it was best if I kept my own counsel. But before I left on this trek, I did tell my grandfather—to ease his mind." Her gaze leveled on him. "You gave me your word you would tell no one."

"I'll keep your secret." He turned back toward the gate. "We need to get going." Without looking to see if she was following, he took the lead once again. From the moment he'd walked into her hospital room all those years ago, he'd known that Beatrice Gerard was special. But he'd never expected anything like the power she'd just demonstrated. Still, even it couldn't always protect her, or she wouldn't have wound up in that hospital bed. His jaw firmed with resolve. He would get her out of this safely and then they would go their own separate ways once again.

Chapter Eight

Beatrice didn't think water had ever felt so good. About midafternoon, Joe had left the road to follow a shallow stream that wove its way down the mountain. "We need fresh water," he'd told her. "And I could use a bath."

An hour's hike had brought them to a waterfall with a small but deep pool at its base. The water was icy cold and Joe had stripped and dived in. Beatrice had hesitated for a moment, then, reminding herself that he'd seen her in the nude before, had followed his example. She did, however, choose a position as far away from him as possible. But not far enough, she admitted.

Even with her back toward him, she found herself watching him out of the corner of her eye. The sun glistened on his raven hair and she recalled how much she'd enjoyed running her fingers through it. The remembered feel of his lips returned to taunt her.

She'd expected him to relax in the water, let the swirling current wash away the weariness of their trek. Instead, his behavior was businesslike and brisk. After diving beneath the surface a couple of times, he reached for his clothes, dragged them in with him and began rinsing them out. When he'd finished, he tossed them back onto the rock, climbed out and hung them over a bush to dry. And never once did he look her way.

Ordering her mind elsewhere, she pulled her own clothes into the water and rinsed them. Behind her she heard him returning to the pool. While she climbed out and spread her things to dry, she could hear him diving under the water several more times. The urge to look over her shoulder was strong. She fought it, but lost the battle. Catching a glimpse of firm buttocks, she felt the embers of a long-ago fire threaten to spark to life.

Slipping back into the water, again she ordered herself to ignore him. Instead, she remained acutely aware of his movements. When he climbed out and stood on the rock, allowing the sun to dry him, covertly her gaze traveled upward along the sturdy columns of his legs. In spite of the frigid water, her temperature rose. He looked as good as ever, she thought, forcing her attention beyond his manhood to his flat abdomen and muscular chest.

As if sensing her attention, he turned until his back was toward her.

She'd never known him to be shy. *I suppose he's worried I'll start lusting after him and try to take advantage of him,* she mused sarcastically. Uninvited, the memory of being in his arms overpowered the anger she was attempting to direct toward him. Smoldering embers burst into flame. *Traitor,* she silently grumbled at her body. Glancing back, she discovered he'd taken his still-damp clothing off the bush and was putting it on.

She waited until he'd dressed and had begun setting up the tent before she climbed out and pulled on her clothes. As added insult, he behaved with indifference to her presence.

Clearly he wanted to be certain she understood that he had no intention of ever returning to the intimacy they'd once shared. And that was fine with her, she asserted. "I'll hunt some wood," she said, heading into the forest.

He made no response other than a quick cool glance and a nod.

When she returned he had cleared a circle for a fire. Lying on the ground nearby was a large black snake, its head smashed.

"He came calling while you were away. I invited him to stay for dinner," Joe said with a wry smile.

This display of dry humor was the first glimpse she'd had of the Joe she'd fallen in love with. But when she grinned back and looked from the snake to him, his expression abruptly became cold and shuttered. The message couldn't have been clearer if he'd had a No Trespassing sign stapled to the front of his shirt.

Building the fire while he cleaned the snake, she couldn't help wondering if her "talent" was another reason he was acting so coolly. The stunned expression on his face came back to haunt her and she recalled that when Ryder had begun to show signs of telekinesis, their mother had become uneasy. Although Edie Gerard had loved her son, she'd been intimidated and frightened by his ability. It had caused a distance between mother and son that had never been fully breached. And that distance was another reason Beatrice had kept her own counsel.

She frowned at Joe's back. So what if her "gift" bothered him! Curtly she admonished herself for the curl of disappointment that wove through her. She hadn't come here seeking to start a new life with him.

While the snake roasted, she turned her mind to their current situation. Piecing together puzzles had always been an effective diversion, especially when their lives were on the line. And she had no doubt that they were.

"You said the men holding you prisoner suddenly began to desert the fort two days before Elena and I arrived?" she asked, breaking the silence between them.

He nodded. "One moment they were lazily going about their usual business, the next they were packing up trucks as quickly as possible and pulling out."

"As if they knew we were on our way and didn't want to present any obstacles to your escape." She paused and corrected herself. "Yours and Manuel's escape."

He met her gaze. "I suppose so. If they'd wanted to keep Manuel they could have taken him with them or, if they considered him of no further use, they would have killed him. They had to know that if they left him behind, I'd take him with me."

"They set you up to believe I was the traitor. I wonder how Manuel discovered Juan was his traitor."

Realizing where her train of thought was leading, interest sparked in his eyes. "You think Manuel might have been set up the same way I was?"

"That seems reasonable."

"Assuming they were setting us up to go back, expose those we thought were traitors, thus taking the heat off the real traitors, would explain why they began to treat us better, feeding us, letting us come outside so that we could get an idea of the layout of the place, seeing that Manuel's wounds were taken care of."

"Their unexpected exit has to have been because they learned Elena and I were on our way and they wanted to clear the path for the rescue. But how did they know we were coming? I could have sworn, we weren't followed." Her frown deepened. "I suppose her house could have been bugged. We did discuss our destination there."

Something nagged at her. She toyed with the fire, going over her actions for the past days in careful detail. Abruptly, a thought struck her. "I reached Elena's house three days before she and I arrived at the estate. Why did they wait until the day before we got there so that they had to rush to evacuate? And was it luck they left in a different direction so that they didn't pass us, or did they know which roads we would be taking?"

Joe regarded her thoughtfully. "I get the feeling you think you know the answer to those questions."

"We stopped at Rafael Ortagea's home on our way here. Elena said Manuel trusted him implicitly and that he knew the exact location of the place plus the layout. He was one of the *federales* sent there in search of Palma. We'd only meant to stop for lunch but ended up spending the night. Some wiring on the Jeep suddenly came loose." A speculative glimmer caused the blue of her eyes to deepen. "While Rafael kept us occupied at the table, his niece could have seen that we were delayed. Rafael recognized me immediately. He could have given the woman some sort of signal that he wanted our departure to be postponed."

Joe regarded her skeptically. "You think Rafael is in with Sanchez?"

"The timing is right. And he was the one who mapped out the roads—if you could call them that—we should take. It was a roundabout route and took hours longer than a more direct route would have taken. He was very insistent we follow it. He said it would be the safest. It would allow us to arrive unnoticed. And we did want to arrive unnoticed. Now I'm wondering if he wasn't thinking more about Sanchez's men getting out unnoticed and giving them a few extra hours for their evacuation so they could set up the rescue."

"Or maybe the timing was just a coincidence," Joe suggested.

A bitter taste filled her mouth. "I find it very insulting that you're willing to give Rafael more benefit of the doubt than you were willing to give me."

His gaze darkened. "You're right. I did judge you more harshly. In your case, I was worried I would let our past relationship cause me to ignore the truth. However, I did give you a chance to prove yourself."

As she again recalled how deadly Joe could be when it was necessary, a chill ran along her spine. At any time, he could have killed her before she'd realized what was happening and had a chance to react.

He handed her one of the sticks with a piece of roasted snake skewered on it. "You could be right about Rafael. Manuel trusted him and confided in him. I suspect there are others who did the same. Rafael was well liked and a father figure to many of the younger men. I know he continues to keep in close contact with all the people he worked with, and I wouldn't be surprised if they were taking his word that the mountain retreat was not being used. If not that, most would have stopped by to see him, as you did, on their way here. That would have given him the opportunity to warn Sanchez's men of anyone checking out the place."

"Of course there is the bullet he took," she said, not wanting to jump to any wrong conclusions without thinking them out thoroughly.

Joe's expression became grimmer. "The bullet came from his partner's gun."

Beatrice stared at him in surprise. "It did?"

"After Palma was captured, it was Rafael and his partner who were designated to escort him to jail. The rest of the squad had stayed behind to clean up after the shoot-out with Palma's men. According to Rafael, Palma insisted he had to stop to urinate. They were on a side road, so they pulled off. One minute Palma was behaving docilely, even jovially, then suddenly he became violent. He got hold of Rafael's partner's gun and shot both Rafael and the partner. Rafael managed to shoot and kill Palma as the man was running away.''

"But it could have happened differently?"

"There were no witnesses. Rafael was the only survivor."

Beatrice could almost see Joe's mind working as his expression grew darker.

"Rafael claimed they were on the side road because his partner felt it would be safer to stay off the main roads. It's possible the route was Rafael's choice. He could have tried to help Palma escape and his partner tried to stop him. When the partner turned on Rafael, Palma could have used that opportunity to attack the partner, get his gun and kill him."

Beatrice shook her head. "But if Rafael was working for Palma, why kill him?"

"Maybe he wasn't working for Palma any longer. Maybe he'd made a more profitable alliance with Sanchez. And if Sanchez wanted to take over the business, he'd have wanted Palma dead. Alive, even in prison, Palma would still have been in control. Maybe the stop was a setup by Rafael to let Palma attempt an escape so he could kill him. The partner caught on and shot Rafael or Palma caught on and shot Rafael and his partner before Rafael could do away with him."

"I think we should warn Manuel." Recalling they had no immediate way of doing that, she frowned. "I suppose the reason you refused to keep the radio was because you didn't want me to have a way to contact my evil cohorts."

He shrugged and took a bite of the snake.

Tossing him a haughty glance, she turned her attention to her dinner. Around her the sounds and smells of the forest again brought forth memories of other nights spent in this wilderness with him. Angrily she shoved them out of her mind. All she'd ever been to him was a warm body in bed and a nuisance out of it. He'd even thought she might be a traitor. That stung the worst.

"You can't leave this forest alive." Joe's voice broke into her thoughts.

Startled, she looked up to meet his gaze over the camp-fire. Had he changed his mind about her innocence? Her muscles tensed in preparation for defense.

He read her body language and frowned impatiently. "I didn't mean that literally. If whoever set this up learns you're alive, they'll know I didn't buy the setup. They'll be on their guard again and you'll be in danger. I had them convinced that I'd gone out into the cold on my own, pursuing a personal vendetta. When you showed up, our mole probably assumed that you've been working with me, or, at least, knew something of my activities, especially when you contacted Tobias, then headed this way. He or she grabbed the opportunity to try to turn me against you. I want him or her to think they succeeded. Even Manuel must believe you are the traitor and that I killed you."

Beatrice turned her gaze to the fire. "I can't go back home. If you're right about there being a traitor in The Unit, by resurfacing, I might have put my identity at risk."

"Tobias was too careful for that. When he left, he made sure all of his retired operatives were protected."

She knew he was right. But she also knew that whoever he was after was dangerous and she could not make herself walk away, leaving him again with no one to guard his back. Using her family as an excuse, she said, "You're probably right, but I won't take a chance of putting my family at risk.

Looks like we're partners again until your traitor is unmasked." She was prepared to hate this turn of events. Instead, excitement brewed within her. How much she'd missed having adventure in her life surprised her.

He stared at her in a stony silence, then said, "You can stay with my grandfather. The two of you are even more of a matched pair than I originally thought."

"I refuse to climb into a rabbit hole and wait this out. This experience should have made it obvious that you need someone to guard your back."

"I thought I'd made it clear we can't leave this forest together."

"We'll leave separately and meet at your grandfather's place. If you don't show up within a day after I arrive there, I'll come looking for you."

For a long moment he regarded her grimly. Then, with a resigned air, he said, "You'd be in more danger running around on your own than by my side. I may be more than a day behind you, but I will come. Before I do, I need to contact Tobias and check into a couple of things. I was convinced the person I was seeking was a woman. Now I'm not so sure. That could have been another diversionary tactic to throw suspicion away from the real culprit. Tobias isn't going to like it, but maybe my first suspicion was correct. Whoever I am after has organized a nationwide network. They know where all our munitions are stored. They pick and choose as the market demands. They choreograph the robberies using fake personnel with legitimate-looking IDs and distribute the goods through high-ranking criminal elements in other countries."

"Like Sanchez?"

"Like Sanchez. Even more, this person has enough sway to ask for favors. My capture was because I got too close to Sanchez and his operation, but my escape had to be orchestrated by our traitor. I'm certain of that. Sanchez would not have known about you. However, being a clever man, he saw the opportunity to guide Manuel away from his spy as well, and took it."

"Who did you first suspect as your traitor?" Beatrice asked.

"Harold."

Her eyes rounded in surprise. "Harold? He's Tobias's protégé. Tobias thinks of him as the son he never had and I could have sworn Harold is unwaveringly loyal to the Old Man."

"The person I'm looking for has to have a high level of security clearance, one that would gain him or her access to sensitive files in all branches of the service. And they have to know who our people are and where they're being sent. They also have to be familiar with the higher echelons of the criminal hierarchy around the world, and those men don't deal with just anyone."

She tried to picture Harold as the traitor. It was nearly impossible. But then . . . "I didn't know Tobias had retired. When I contacted The Unit, it was Harold who responded. So he knew I'd resurfaced. But he didn't know I was looking for you. I made it clear I believed you were dead."

"And how did he respond to that?"

She thought hard, trying to picture Harold's face in every detail. "He spoke as if he believed you to be dead, as well. But then, I've never been able to read Harold."

"Is Raven still with Tobias?"

Beatrice recalled a mission they'd gone on with Raven. He'd risked his life for theirs without hesitation. "Raven is another of your suspects?"

Joe stirred the fire, his gaze hardening as he watched the flames dancing. "The problem with this business is that eventually you find yourself unable to trust anyone."

She'd never seen him this cynical. "You trust Tobias, don't you?"

His gaze met hers. "Did he know you were coming here?"

"Yes, but several days before Sanchez evacuated the stronghold."

"Then, yes, I trust Tobias."

"And you can trust me." Her head began to swim and she realized she was holding her breath, waiting for his response. He would never love her; she'd accepted that fact. But his trust was important to her.

"Yes, I trust you."

She drew a breath and dropped her gaze to the fire, fearful he would guess how much his answer meant to her.

"We'd better finish eating and get some sleep," he said, returning his attention to his food.

Beatrice did the same. She tried hard not to think of other nights spent with Joe, but that wasn't easy—not with him sitting across the fire from her. She caught a glimpse of his hands and recalled how good they could make her feel. *Stop that!* she ordered herself. Had she no pride? He'd faked his death to be rid of her. Abruptly, she rose. "I'm going to bed."

As she walked toward the tent, she noticed that her clothes were still damp. "And I'll want some privacy for a couple of minutes while I slip out of these clothes and into my sleeping bag."

Continuing to eat, he did not even look her way as he nodded his consent.

"I could probably parade around in the nude and he'd never notice," she muttered under her breath. The image of him naked suddenly filled her mind and a heat began to build within her. Angrily she shoved it out. Quickly, discarding her clothing, she climbed inside the lightweight bedding and tried to go to sleep before Joe entered. She wasn't successful.

Keeping her back to him, she heard him shifting around and realized that he, too, was stripping out of his damp clothing. She edged farther away.

"I'm not going to take advantage of you," he assured her with a touch of impatience. "Like you, I simply didn't want to sleep in damp clothing."

He made her feel like a hag he was being forced to share quarters with. She turned to glare at him and assure him that she was merely trying to find a comfortable position, but her words stuck in her throat. He was not as immune to her as he'd made her believe.

He quickly covered himself. "I gave you some privacy. I expected the same in return."

"I was under the impression that if I was the last woman on earth, you'd choose to live out your days in celibacy."

"What I choose is not to be married, and you deserve a man who can make that commitment and keep it."

"Yes, I do," she replied. The problem was, she hadn't met anyone she wanted to marry besides Joe. Furious with herself, she searched for a way to break the bond she still felt with him. "I suppose my 'talent' makes you uneasy and doubly glad we're not together any longer."

"Your 'talent' is a little unnerving. On the other hand, I can see where it could prove useful."

She studied him. He hadn't sounded intimidated or repulsed, and there was no hint of evasiveness on his face.

"What I can't handle," he continued, "is having a wife to worry about."

She told herself she should be grateful for his honesty. But she didn't feel grateful. She felt frustrated. "Your code name should have been Lone Wolf all spelled out in capital letters," she muttered. Turning onto her back, she closed her eyes and ordered herself to sleep. Instead, her body refused to relax. She heard his breathing and recalled the soothing feel of lying with her head on his shoulder while the steady rise and fall of his chest lulled her to sleep.

He didn't love her, she reminded herself. Well, she didn't love him, either, she affirmed. However, she couldn't deny that she did lust after him. And he clearly still harbored lustful thoughts about her.

Stop thinking about him! she commanded herself and turned onto her side with her back toward him. Making love with him probably wouldn't be all that exciting, anyway, she reasoned. Her memories of the nights they'd spent together had been, no doubt, exaggerated by time.

A thought struck her. She'd never wanted to admit it before, but it was those memories of times spent with Joe that had ruined her chances to find someone else. If she proved to herself that the excitement was gone, then she could get on with her life. She turned over and lay looking at him. Night had fallen and in the dark he was no more than a shadowy form, but in her mind she could see his hard, muscular chest with the knife scar running jaggedly along the ribs of his left side.

Mentally Joe cursed his ability to know when he was being watched. At other times he'd been grateful for it. It had saved his life on numerous occasions. But tonight it served no purpose other than to torment him. And to make matters worse, it wasn't the usual simple prickling on the neck. The sensation had started there, then moved through his body like an enticing caress. "Was there something you wanted to say?" he asked in irritated tones.

Beatrice had thought he was asleep. Abruptly, she turned onto her back. "No."

"Then let's get some sleep." It was an order.

She closed her eyes but his presence was like a physical force, taunting her with an imaginary touch. Shifting onto her side once again, she frowned in his direction. "I need to put an end to us, once and for all."

"I thought we had."

"You have. But I haven't. I'm sure my memories of being with you are more fanciful than real. After all, I was inexperienced. However, they're interfering with my getting on with my life."

"And what is it you expect me to do about that?"

"It has occurred to me that one final tryst could be the cure." Silently, she congratulated herself. She'd managed to get that out in a coolly businesslike tone.

"I don't think that's such a good idea."

His rejection hurt. Apparently, any lustful thoughts he had about her weren't very strong and were easily forgotten. But that wasn't unexpected, she chided herself. After all, he'd had no trouble walking away from her before. He'd probably become bored with her in bed a long time before he left. "I'm sure you're right," she said frostily.

Silence descended over the interior of the tent. Again she closed her eyes and ordered herself to sleep. Instead, anger brewed within her. She wasn't sure who it was directed at the most—herself or him. She now had her proof that he'd never honestly cared for her; that it had been only guilt and a sense of duty that had led him to the altar. Tears burned at the back of her eyes and she was forced to admit that all these years she'd harbored the hope that he'd cared for her, maybe even loved her a little.

Joe told himself he'd handled the situation well. He'd done the right thing. But Tess was not like any other woman he'd ever known. She wasn't the kind a man could forget. Memories of her tormented him. Several times during the past years, he'd considered going to Smytheshire—secretly, without her knowledge—to see if she'd remarried and gotten on with her life. A part of him had argued that seeing her with another man would be the cure he needed. Another part hadn't wanted to see her making a life with anyone but him.

He frowned at her shadowy form. Maybe she was right. Maybe their memories were more fanciful than real. Maybe a tryst was the answer. "Damn it, Tess, you shouldn't make offers like that!" he said in a low grumble.

The husky edge in his voice told her he was reconsidering. Well, she was having second thoughts—all of them hostile. "Consider it withdrawn." She told herself to say no more, but the bitterness she was feeling was too strong. "I was never more than a warm body to you, was I?"

For a long moment there was only silence. Then, sounding like a man who'd been struggling with himself and had grown tired of the battle, he said, "No. You were a great deal more than a warm body to me. That was the problem."

Her heart skipped a beat. "I was?"

"From the first, I found myself caring about you more than I wanted to. When we went into the field, we were both risking our lives. That was part of the job. But I found it more and more difficult to place you in a position of danger. After we were married, my anxiousness for your safety became acute...so acute I was afraid I'd make a mistake and get you killed. I tried to talk you into quitting but you refused."

Her tears of anger turned to those of joy. "I thought you were trying to get rid of me because you were bored with me and I'd become a nuisance in your eyes."

"You never bored me, Tess," he assured her.

"If you'd told me the truth, we could have worked something out."

"No." His voice held no compromise. "That night in Colorado when you talked about having a family, that was when I knew for certain our marriage was a mistake. I couldn't turn away from the vow I'd made beside by brother's grave. The only way we could have led the life you described would have been for you to leave the service and spend most of your time alone. There would have been months when I couldn't even contact you and always we would've had to be careful that no one in the business ever connected you to me. You deserved a more normal life...a husband who was home more than a few days a year and who could be there to help raise your children. And one who could not bring the threat of danger to your doorstep."

Happiness flowed through her. "Don't you think you should have asked me what I wanted?"

"Even if you'd chosen the kind of life I could give you, I'd have felt as if I was cheating you. Besides, I know you. You wouldn't have quit the service. You're as stubborn as a mule. You'd have insisted on staying with me."

She couldn't deny that he was right about that. "But I could have made you understand that my choice was the best for me. Living out my life in a safe, dull environment isn't living, it's merely existing. It's like being in a void. There's no zest." As she spoke, she realized that described the past few years perfectly.

Joe felt himself weakening. He quickly recalled those times when they'd faced death—and his resolve returned. He would not ask her to risk her life for him. "I can't do my job with you by my side. You're too much of a distraction."

She heard the determination in his voice. But she wasn't willing to give up without a fight. "I'm also very useful in the field. You said so yourself several times." Pushing her covering aside, she smiled when she saw he hadn't zipped his bag closed. Easier access, she thought, playfully easing herself into his sleeping bag as she ran her palm over his chest. "And we both agreed that together we had a very good way of relieving stress."

Her touch ignited a fire. Attempting to remain in control of the situation, he caught her wrist and lifted her hand away. "I can't take you back, Tess. It was hard enough letting you go the first time. But I know it was the right choice."

He was going to be difficult, she mused. She would have been a fool to expect otherwise. However, she would prove to him that he was better off with her than without her. "All right. You win. But that doesn't mean we can't enjoy each other right now . . . seize the opportunity to relive a few old memories," she coaxed, moving closer so that the entire length of their bodies touched. She felt his maleness growing, hardening. A satisfied smile spread over her face.

"You're a strain on a man's control," he growled, his hold on her wrist tightening.

"I promise, I won't hold tonight against you," she purred. "But it has been a long time since I've been in a man's arms and I have missed it. You wouldn't want to leave me feeling so frustrated, I pick up the first gigolo I see when I get back to civilization."

He drew a harsh breath as she laid her leg over his hip, then wrapped herself more tightly to him. "As long as you understand there is no future for us, I suppose once for old times' sake couldn't do any harm," he said harshly.

"No harm at all," she agreed, kissing the hollow of his neck. She felt the tremor of surrender run through him, then her wrist was released and she knew she'd won this battle.

His hand freed, he ran it along the curves of her body. "You feel as good as ever," he murmured against her shoulder.

"So do you." She sought his mouth. He tasted as good as ever, as well. She'd been wrong, she admitted, as his hand cupped her breast and a thrill so intense it made her want to cry out, shot through her. Being with him was exciting. Even more than she remembered.

With light kisses, he bade her mouth goodbye, then gently eased her off him. "I don't have as much control as I thought," he said huskily.

She'd wanted to play with him more—touching him, kissing him and having him play with her. But she, too, was feeling much too ready. "Me, too," she confessed, wrapping her leg around him and drawing him to her.

Without hesitation, he accepted the unspoken offer. Rolling her onto her back, he mounted and entered her. For the first time in years, she felt complete.

At first he moved slowly as if getting reacquainted, then his thrusts became more forceful. The fullness of his possession invigorated her. Sensations swirled within her and she joined him, adding her own strength to the age-old rhythm of man and woman uniting.

She would have liked for this to go on forever, but her body could hold back no longer. A gasp of pure delight escaped as she reached her zenith.

Joe joined her at the climax. A low male groan of pleasure issued from deep within him. This was no cure, he admitted. No other woman would ever be as exciting to him as Tess. He held her firmly against him until both their bodies went limp, then ordered himself to release her. The problem was he didn't want to. He wanted to hold her close forever. That was not an option, he told himself. Leaning forward he kissed her stomach, then eased off her and stretched out beside her.

"You are enjoyable," he said gruffly.

"You, too," she replied.

They both fell silent, allowing their breathing to return to normal. She expected to feel relaxed and ready to sleep. Instead, she felt stimulated. Her legs tingled and the embers of desire, instead of slowly dying, began to glow once again.

She turned her head toward him. "Once was not enough."

He grinned wryly. "I always did like that wanton side of you." The desire to accept her invitation was strong, but even he had his limitations. Apology entered his voice. "However, the past couple of weeks have worn me down. I don't have the energy."

She told herself to forget it, but her body was too stimulated. "Why don't I just see if I can revitalize you?" she suggested. "I'll do all the work."

Refuse, he ordered himself. This was playing with fire. But the flame was too enticing. "That's an offer no man in his right mind could turn down," he admitted.

Grinning mischievously, she sat up and began massaging his shoulders, then worked her way lower.

"That tickles," he protested when her ministrations became more intimate.

She nipped his shoulder, then, stretching out beside him, moved against him much like a cat seeking to be petted.

"You are a temptress," he murmured, capturing her face in his hands and seeking out her mouth for a hungry, possessive kiss.

She eased herself more fully on top of him and his breathing became ragged once again. As his maleness began to respond, she accepted him, using her velvetness to massage him to the fullest of his potency.

"You do know how to get a rise out of a man," he said huskily.

"And more," she replied, beginning to move with firmer purpose.

He let her continue for a while on her own. Then, with a sigh of regret, he joined her, increasing the rhythm of their joining until she wanted to scream from sheer ecstasy.

"Now!" he growled suddenly and pulled her hard against him, holding her there.

Currents of pleasure again racked her body as it pulsed with his, and nothing but the two of them existed in her mind.

When the world again began to impinge on her senses, she dropped a light kiss on his face, then slipped off and stretched out beside him. "Now I feel sated," she admitted around a yawn.

"I'm relieved to hear that," he replied, "because we do need to get some sleep."

Smiling to herself, she closed her eyes.

Beside her, Joe frowned. This was a one-night stand and it wasn't going to happen again, he vowed. She was much too dangerous to his resolve.

Awakening alone, Beatrice ran her hand over the place where Joe had lain. She'd been in love with him when she'd married him, and she was still in love with him. That, she could no longer deny. Now all she had to do was to convince him that they belonged together.

Hearing water splashing, she left the tent and headed to the spring. He was there. Diving in, she joined him. "Morning," she said, kissing him lightly.

He frowned at her smiling face. "I meant what I said last night. We have no future together. I thought you'd agreed to that."

Mentally she frowned. He had to be the most hard-headed man on the face of the earth. Well, he was going to find out just how tenacious she could be. Outwardly, her smile softened into a flirtatious grin. "I thought we could still be friends."

"And I think it will be wise for us to keep our distance from now on," he replied, easing away from her.

She regarded him speculatively. "A person could get the impression you were afraid of me."

"And they'd be right," he admitted. Climbing out of the water, he added over his shoulder, "I'm going to start a fire and get our breakfast cooking. I want to break camp as soon as possible."

As he walked away her chin firmed with purpose. He could run, but eventually she would catch him.

Chapter Nine

Two days later she strolled into the marketplace in Puerto Escondido. Wearing the clean change of clothing she'd had in the backpack, she looked like a tourist living out of a suitcase. The backpack itself was with Joe. She'd bidden him goodbye an hour earlier. The moment they'd parted, she missed him.

But she would be seeing him soon, she promised herself and returned her mind to her current situation. In one pocket was a portion of the large sum of money she'd stashed in her backpack before leaving Elena's. The rest she'd given to Joe. Along with her money was a passport for a Clarissa Adams.

From the other pocket she extracted the beaded necklace Joe had given her all those years ago, and fastened it around her neck. She'd intended to leave it at Elena's with the rest of her luggage but at the last minute, she'd gone back, retrieved it and slipped it into her pocket. During the drive to

Rafael's, she'd chided herself for wanting this only tangible reminder of Joe with her. Finally, she'd assured herself that the only reason she'd gone back for it was to return it to him when she found him.

But she hadn't returned it to him. No longer was it a link to a painful memory but a way of keeping him with her. Admittedly, he'd maintained his distance during the remainder of their hike back to civilization, but she was not deterred. Allowing him to win a minor skirmish would put him off his guard. Her objective was to win the war.

Continuing down the dusty street, she guessed he was already several miles away. The plan was for him to make his way to a village to the north, then catch a bus or perhaps charter a plane to Mexico City. He would tell Manuel and Elena that she'd died and he'd buried her in the forest. He would also warn Manuel about Rafael.

In the meantime, she was to return to the States and wait for him at his grandfather's ranch. She purchased a handbag, a wallet, a large straw carryall, a brightly colored skirt and a white off-the-shoulder blouse. Then, making her way to the end of the street, she hailed a taxi and asked the driver to take her to the airport.

Stopping in the gift shop, she bought some makeup, tissues, a pen and pencil and a book, and stuffed them into her purse along with her passport and wallet. The skirt and blouse were already stuffed haphazardly into the straw carryall. When she passed through customs, she wanted to look the part of a harried tourist.

At the ticket counter, she told the female clerk that her luggage had been stolen, her boyfriend had deserted her, she didn't understand a word of Spanish and was feeling completely lost. Tears welled in her eyes as she added that all she wanted was to get home as quickly as possible. The woman sympathized and put her on the first plane out.

She used the same story with the customs inspector and shed a few more tears, as well. Obviously not wanting to discourage the other tourists in line from coming back, he hurried her through. Taking her seat on the plane, she breathed a sigh of relief, sat back, closed her eyes and thought of Joe.

A shadow of worry flittered across her face. She hoped he would make it safely on his own. *He's a big boy, he can take care of himself,* she assured herself. Still, she wished she could have stayed with him.

She gave herself three days to make the trip, covering her trail as she went. Uncertain about what roles she would be playing when she and Joe reunited, while in Los Angeles she bought a small but versatile variety of designer clothes and a leather satchel suitcase. At a stop in Las Vegas, she made a few more purchases, exchanging her casually elegant slack suit and Italian sandals for jeans, a button-down shirt, Western boots and a Stetson. She also added a Western drawl to her speech. From there, she flew to Sheridan, Wyoming, and boarded a bus for the final leg of her journey.

When she spotted the large, old tin mailbox that marked her destination, a sense of familiarity similar to the one she always experienced when she arrived home swept through her. *Further proof, Joe and I belong together,* she told herself.

"You sure you know where you're heading?" the bus driver asked as she prepared to disembark. "I've been driving this route for nearly ten years. That there is Frank Whitedeer's property. Ain't let but one or two people off here before. Heard the old man's a little on the loony side."

"Frank Whitedeer is a longtime friend of my grandmother. I promised her I'd stop by and see him if I ever got out this way," she replied.

"Old Frank talks to the spirits a lot." He grinned and winked. "Don't let him scare you. He's a bit unusual but harmless."

She shrugged. "Everyone has their little idiosyncrasies."

He gave a her a friendly nod, then added, "I'll be coming back through next week about this same time."

She thanked him, left the bus and started up the long, narrow dirt road. The day was hot and the walk dusty but the urge to jog was strong. She'd missed Joe and hoped that his business had been brief and he was already here. That was wishful thinking, she knew. Still, she couldn't stop herself from hoping.

"I'm like a teenager with her first crush," she muttered to herself. But instead of frowning, she smiled. It was an exciting feeling and she liked it.

As the ranch house came into sight, she didn't see him and disappointment swept through her. *With highs come lows,* she told herself philosophically.

Ahead of her, Frank Whitedeer was sitting on his porch, rocking. His steel gray hair was long and hung loose. Deeply grooved wrinkles, the result of age and the elements, gave his face character. He wore a blue cotton shirt, jeans and moccasins. Around his neck hung several strings of beads, each with different totems attached. His expression, as he recognized her, became friendly but remained guarded. He reminded her of Zebulon, and she knew it was not just because both were elderly and lived a hermitlike life.

"Joe asked me to wait for him here," she said.

The guardedness left his face and his smile broadened. "I was hoping you would discover the truth and enter our lives once again," he said, rising to greet her. "You and my grandson belong together. The bond between you is strong. The spirits have told me so."

"I wish they'd tell him," she replied, then flushed at her openness.

He shook his head. "He listens only to his own voice."

"Has he arrived?" she asked, looking around, hoping she was wrong in assuming he was not there.

"Not yet. But soon," he assured her. "In the meantime, you must consider my home as your home."

"Have you heard from him?" she asked.

"No. But he is in no danger at the moment." A faraway look came into his eyes. "He was in danger a short while ago but I asked the spirits to help him." His gaze focused on her. "And they did."

The thought that Joe's ancestors and hers must have had something in common played through her mind. Aloud, she merely said, "I'm glad."

"You will stay in Joe's room." He motioned for her to go on into the house. "Run along and rest a bit. You look tired. If you're hungry there's rabbit stew on the stove."

"Thank you," she said as he sat back down and returned to his whittling.

As she entered the bedroom she and Joe had shared on her previous visit long ago, his presence seemed to wrap around her like a warm blanket. The room was sparsely furnished and the walls were decorated with medicine shields and dream catchers. On the dresser were pictures of his family. There was one of his parents, obviously taken by a professional. And one of his grandfather when Frank had been much younger. Another was of Joe and his brother in their teens. The casual pose and grinning faces made her certain that this one had been taken by a friend or family member. Then there was the photo, this one professional, of Joe's brother with his wife and baby daughter.

His parents, she knew, had died in a car accident when he and his brother were in their teens. His maternal grandparents had never approved of their daughter marrying an Indian and refused to have anything to do with her or her children. It had been his grandfather who had taken Joe and his brother in and raised them.

A reflection in the mirror caused her to jerk around. On the bedside table was a picture of her. Her shock turned into a smile of pleasure. That he'd kept the photo, even had it enlarged and framed, was added proof that he had cared for her. Approaching it, she picked up the framed snapshot for a closer look and recalled when Joe had taken it. She'd snapped a couple of him, as well, but he'd claimed the roll of film had been destroyed. Now she realized that had been part of his plan to erase himself from her life.

Well, she wasn't going to be so easy to get rid of this time, she vowed silently.

During the rest of that day, the old man spoke little, seeming intent on his own thoughts. She didn't mind. She'd never liked making small talk. But that evening, she grew restless and her desire to learn as much about Joe as possible increased.

She found Frank Whitedeer in the rocking chair on the porch. He was carving a bird from a piece of oak.

"I don't mean to pry and I won't be insulted if you refuse to talk to me," she said, perching on the log railing that bordered the porch. "But I would like to know more about Joe. What was he like as a boy?"

The old man looked up at her. "He could be a handful, but he had a deep sense of family and an even deeper sense of responsibility. Too much, perhaps. Because of it, he has chosen a difficult and dangerous path."

"You're talking about his brother and the vow he made," she said knowingly.

The old man nodded and returned to his carving. After a moment, he spoke again, his voice soft. "Joe was the oldest by just over a year. And his and Sam's outlook on life was as different as night and day. Sam was light of spirit. Joe was serious about everything. After his parents' deaths he felt responsible for Sam. He wasn't overbearing about it, but he was always by his brother's side when Sam needed help. And Sam, in turn, always stood by Joe. Everyone who knew them, knew you couldn't take on one without having to deal with the other. At twenty, Sam married Dawn. She was appropriately named. Just looking at her soft, laughing face reminded me of the beauty of a summer sunrise and its promise of new day. The second year of their marriage she bore a child, a girl as sweet as her mother. They named her Clare, after Joe and Sam's mother. Joe doted on her. He called her Petal because he said she reminded him of a single perfect rose petal. He even talked about having a family of his own. Their deaths changed all that." Frank Whitedeer looked up at Beatrice. "I know the work he does is important but it is time he sought happiness for himself."

"I agree," she replied.

He smiled—a knowing, conspiratorial smile—and she smiled back.

Four days later, Beatrice stood on the porch, a worried frown knitting her brow. Joe still hadn't shown up. Her jaw firmed with decision. If he wasn't here by tomorrow, she was going to contact Tobias.

Abruptly, she stiffened. She was certain she heard a vehicle approaching. An old pickup came into view. It had once been red. Now the paint had worn in spots, was missing in others, and it was coated with dust all over. Relief spread through her. It was Joe's truck.

And, like so many things about his life, it wasn't what it seemed. It had a souped-up eight-cylinder motor, was carefully weighted to hold to the road at top speed, and had an extra-heavy-duty four-wheel drive that could take a person over the roughest terrain. The suspension was of the highest quality, and beneath the bed was a stash of armaments that would have made any revolutionary proud.

"Looks like Joe's here," Frank Whitedeer said, joining her on the porch.

"Looks like," she replied, fighting to keep the level of excitement in her voice to a minimum. She didn't want to appear too anxious to see him. That would only cause his guard to become stronger.

As he stepped out of the cab, her gaze raked over him, looking for any signs that he'd been injured. There were none.

Like her, he was dressed in the typical attire of a local rancher. Unlike her, his jeans, boots, Stetson and shirt were worn comfortable by use and she guessed they were ones he'd left in the truck. She forced herself to remain on the porch but the casual smile of greeting on her face began to feel plastic as he approached at an easy, relaxed gait. By the time he reached her and his grandfather, anger had replaced her relief.

"You could have gotten a message to me to let me know you were all right," she said accusingly.

He cocked an eyebrow in an "I knew I was right" fashion. "Now you understand why I said our marriage wouldn't work even if you did retire. You'd spend your days worrying. And I'd worry that one of the bad guys would discover you."

She glared at him. "You worried your grandfather and me on purpose just to make a point?"

Joe's gaze turned to Frank Whitedeer and there was apology on his face. "Did I worry you?"

Frank grinned. "The spirits told me you were all right."

Joe turned back to Beatrice, the apology gone. "My grandfather is used to not hearing from me. He does not expect it. He understands the path I've chosen and accepts it."

"It's good to have you back, boy," Frank Whitedeer interrupted abruptly, reaching out and taking Joe's hand in his for a firm, welcoming handshake. "Now, I'm going for a walk." His gaze traveled between his grandson and Beatrice. "Appears to me that you two need some privacy to work out this little problem on your own."

In silence, Joe watched his grandfather head down a well-worn path. When he turned back to Beatrice, his expression was cool and restrained. "He has always held out the hope that you and I would get back together. Today has made it clear that can never happen."

"You have got to be one of the most frustrating men in the world," she seethed.

He frowned at her accusation. "I didn't avoid communicating with you just to make a point. Until two days ago, I wasn't covering my trail as carefully as I could have. I wanted whoever is issuing the orders to know I was alive and believe you were dead. I figured my being a little careless would also confirm their belief that I'd bought their setup and believed I'd done away with the traitor I've been seeking. It also gave me a chance to try to spot whoever was tailing me."

Mentally, Beatrice berated herself. She'd overreacted. His behavior was rational and consistent with the business they were in. She took a calming breath, then asked levelly, "And did you spot anyone?"

"Yes. Someone I didn't expect."

Sensing his hesitation, she demanded sharply, "Don't you think you should share the name with me? Whether you like it or not, we are in this together."

"Unless he has a twin, the man I saw was Knight."

"Do you think he's your mole?"

"I had eliminated him from my list of suspects. He came real close to getting himself blown up in an effort to stop the theft of some rockets. But maybe that was simply because he'd sensed someone was looking for a mole and decided that thwarting one operation was worth the price to be taken off the list of possibles. Or maybe he did it as a precaution in case anyone did discover there was a mole. Our experience with Sanchez has proved that whoever we're looking for is good at tossing out red herrings."

"Or maybe my showing up puzzled Harold enough to cause him to assign Knight to tail me." Recalling the bug in her equipment, she added, "Or maybe Tobias asked Harold to assign Knight to watch over me. I know he wanted to keep you and your operation a secret but he wasn't happy about my going after you alone. Then, after I lost Knight, because I'm certain I shook any tail, he stumbled onto you, looking for me. You just said you wanted to be spotted."

The frown on his face darkened. "I contacted Tobias. Knight's supposed to be dead. He was reported killed just a day or so after I was captured."

A chill ran along Beatrice's spine. "One dead agent tailing another dead agent. Now that's irony," she said, fighting her fear with an attempt at humor.

Joe didn't return her lopsided grin. "Looks like I was too quick to eliminate him from my list of suspects. According to Tobias, he was supposed to have died at the hands of gunrunners just off the west coast. The story was, he was following them in a light aircraft. They shot it down with a missile. His body was never recovered."

"Maybe Harold arranged for him to go out into the cold the same way Tobias arranged for you to do just that."

"Tobias contacted Harold. Harold claims he didn't."

"If Knight is the one you're after, do you think he knows you're working with Tobias?"

"Tobias is the master of deception. I've never known anyone to find out something from him that he didn't want them to know."

Beatrice was about to point out that when she'd gone to Tobias to find out if Joe was alive, she'd seen it on the man's face. But before the words could be issued, she realized that it was highly likely Tobias had wanted her to know. He was never one to pass up an opportunity and, under the circumstances, who else could he have sent after Joe? "He's also an excellent manipulator," she muttered. A thought struck her. "There's one problem with Knight being your traitor. How did he know I'd resurfaced? I never saw him or spoke to him."

"You're right. The mole has to be someone who had that information. Or Knight has an accomplice in The Unit."

"Harold. Tobias. Raven." She rattled off the names of those with whom she'd had contact.

Joe drew a terse breath. "I don't relish telling Tobias that Harold and Raven are at the top of my list of suspects."

"Maybe Tobias had begun to suspect Harold and didn't want to admit it. Maybe that's why he left The Unit and why he didn't inform Harold of this investigation," Beatrice suggested. "Or maybe he chose Raven for his bodyguard because he suspected him and wanted to keep an eye on him. Or maybe he's as suspicious of both as you are."

"Maybe," Joe conceded. "I need to think this through." Sitting down in one of the rocking chairs, he propped his feet up on the railing, closed his eyes and tilted his hat over his face to signal the end of their discussion.

Beatrice resented being dismissed. But then Joe had always kept his own counsel. However, he wasn't the only one who could fit the pieces of a puzzle together. Tossing him a haughty glance, she left the porch and strode off down a path she knew led to a large rock outcropping. Reaching it, she discovered a rattlesnake coiled in the very spot she was seeking. Normally she would simply have given the snake a light mental nudge to send it on its way. Today she gave it a shove.

As if caught by a furious gust of wind, the reptile flew off the rock. Landing on the ground, it lay as if stunned for a moment, then glided off into the underbrush.

Silently she scolded herself for behaving so coldly. Then, seating herself on the rock, she turned her mind to Joe's traitor. She remembered Knight well. Soon after he'd joined The Unit, he'd accompanied her and Joe on a mission and nearly gotten all of them killed by his attempt at heroics. Blond-haired, blue-eyed and boyishly handsome, he'd been a wrestler in high school and taken up bodybuilding while in college. He could easily have passed for one of those bronze hunks on the California beaches who were more brawn than brain. But he had as much brains as brawn— more, actually. The problem was he liked being the hero too much. He'd told her that he'd chosen the code name Knight because he thought of himself as a knight in shining armor saving the world from destruction.

However, it appears that his armor has become tarnished, she mused. What had happened? Drugs? Gambling? Or just plain greed? she wondered. Or maybe a woman. He had liked the ladies. Whatever the reason, it didn't matter.

Climbing off the rock, she strode back to the house. Joe was still sitting where she'd left him. "There is only one logical course of action," she said, frowning down at the top of his hat.

Slowly, he tipped the Stetson up so that he could see her. "I have to capture Knight. He's the key. Either he's our mole or he knows who is. I've just been trying to figure out the best way to go about it."

"*We* have to capture Knight," she corrected.

"You're staying here."

She planted her feet firmly. "Knight is not a man to underestimate. You need my help."

"He can't see you. I want everyone to think you're dead. I told Manuel it was something you said before you died that made me believe Rafael was your contact rather than Juan. Even Tobias thinks you were the traitor and I killed you. But, so that he wouldn't let down his guard, I told him I was sure you had cohorts still in The Unit."

Feeling like a kid with the opportunity to attend her own funeral, she couldn't stop herself from asking, "How did Tobias take the news of my less-than-honorable demise?"

"He found it difficult to believe, but he's a pragmatist when it comes to this business. He's seen a lot of betrayal. Still, I could tell he was deeply upset. He asked me several times if I was certain you were the one."

Beatrice was flattered. Tobias generally took such news stoically or showed anger toward the betrayer. He never displayed sympathy or regret. And he'd actually questioned Joe's judgment. That had to be a first. It was nice to know he'd thought so highly of her. And she intended to prove she deserved his respect. "I know how to be invisible. You can either take me with you and coordinate your plans with me, or I'll follow behind, doing the best I can to guard your back in the dark."

"The years have made you even more stubborn and hardheaded," he grumbled.

She grinned coquettishly and added a deep Southern drawl to her voice. "Your compliments make me blush, sir."

He scowled at her humor. "You've always been impossible to reason with, once your mind was set on a course."

A seductive heat entered her eyes. Approaching him, she placed her hands on his shoulders and leaned closer. "I consider tenacity to be one of my finest traits." She kissed him lightly, then went inside to help Frank put lunch on the table.

The scraping of chair legs on the porch told her Joe had gotten up. Out of the corner of her eye, she saw him standing in the doorway watching her through the screen door. His jaw was set in a hard, firm line of resistance.

"The bigger they are, the harder they fall," she muttered to herself, determined not to give up hope.

Joe said very little to her for the rest of the day and she didn't try to force her company on him. That would only cause him to increase his guard.

Now it was late into the night. Frank Whitedeer was asleep in his room. Joe was sleeping on a pallet on the floor in front of the fireplace in the large central room that was the main living area of the house. She'd gone to bed when they had, but fearing Joe might try to sneak out on her and she would have to waste time tracking him, she'd been unable to sleep. So she'd come out onto the porch and was sitting in a rocking chair, staring up at the clear night sky.

"I'm not going to run out on you." Joe's impatient tones broke into her thoughts. "I know you'd follow and I'd have to worry about you accidentally stepping into the line of fire."

"I would follow," she assured him.

He stood leaning against one of the rough-hewn poles holding up the porch roof. "We'll start in Boston. By now, my traitor has to be putting two and two together and coming up with Tobias. Until Sanchez's men captured me, I'm certain everyone still thought I was dead. And I had them convinced I was working on my own. Then you showed up, went to see Tobias and were suddenly hot on my trail. That, in addition to my close association with Tobias in the past, has got to have started the person I'm after suspecting that Tobias and I could be working together. If so, my traitor will have his spies watching the route to Tobias's place."

She was having a hard time concentrating. Standing there, his hair rumpled, barefoot, wearing a pair of faded jeans and a shirt pulled on but left unbuttoned, he looked incredibly sexy. "When do we leave?" she asked and congratulated herself for sounding businesslike.

"Tomorrow. So get some sleep." Straightening, he strode back into the house.

She drew a shaky breath. Taking her time pursuing him wasn't going to be easy. *Keep your mind on business or you could both end up dead*, she cautioned herself. That thought brought a chill. Going inside, she glanced toward him as she crossed the room. Her jaw firmed. They were both going to survive this assignment, because she had plans for them.

Chapter Ten

Two days later, wearing a red wig, a wide-brimmed straw hat decorated with silk flowers, an overly large dress that hung baggily to her ankles, sunglasses, sandals, and toting a straw carryall that matched the hat, she stood outside one of the gift shops in the Boston airport. Feigning interest in the window displays, out of the corner of her eye she watched the passengers heading toward the luggage area.

She'd flown in a couple of hours earlier. Joe's plane had just landed. Spotting him, she experienced a rush of pleasure. Wearing a three-piece suit, loafers, carrying an umbrella and briefcase, his hair cut away from his ears, parted on the side and short enough in the back to be an inch above his collar, he looked the part of the successful businessman.

Following him to the luggage retrieval area, she positioned herself behind a tall, overweight man and peered around her human shield to inspect the others milling around the luggage carousels. The place was too crowded, she fumed silently as groups of people passed between her and Joe, blocking her view. Afraid she would lose track of him, she moved closer, this time choosing a pillar for her shield.

She scanned the faces of anyone in a direct line with Joe. No one looked familiar. He moved to the carousel and lifted his bag off. A custodian, sweeping the floor along the wall, began to edge toward him. Her gaze held on the man with the broom. His hair was brown, but then hair color was easy to change. A burn scar disfigured his neck and a portion of his face. Mentally, she shook her head. Knight was still using his old tricks. His handsomeness attracted attention so he regularly disguised himself with scars he thought would cause people to look away. And he should never dress in a jumpsuit, she added, completing her quick appraisal. His physique was the final giveaway.

As he neared Joe, she saw him taking a pack of cigarettes out of his pocket. *The dart-in-the-fake-cigarette ploy,* she mused. Moving toward the two men, she gave the pack a hard mental jerk.

A look of surprise flashed on Knight's face as his grip failed and the pack seemed to fly from his hand to the floor.

Joe had obviously spotted her earlier, because he was already turning in the direction in which she was traveling. Seeing the pack of cigarettes hit the floor, then slide his way, he grabbed it up.

Knight's gaze swung upward, following the hand that had picked up the pack. As his eyes met Joe's, he sneered with hatred, then turned to run.

His attention focused on Joe, he hadn't been aware of Beatrice's approach. "Not so fast," she said in his ear, her hands clasping his arm. Then, in a voice loud enough for those passengers nearby to hear, she added with gushing delight, "Why, if it isn't Jerry Gyles. Imagine running into you like this. Don't you know cigarettes are bad for your health? What will your mother say? She's such a health nut. Please, say you have time for a cup of coffee. It's so nice to see someone from home."

The color drained from his face. "Thistle," he gasped.

Continuing to smile, she again lowered her voice. "And just as prickly as ever," she warned, drawing his attention to her hand with a flicker of her eye. She was wearing what she jokingly called her Borgia ring. Provided she wasn't trying to knock out an elephant, the tiny needle inside held enough depressant to render her foe unconscious or, at least, drowsy enough he could be easily handled.

As he followed her eye movement, understanding flashed across his face.

"I believe you dropped these." Joining them, Joe put the pack back in Knight's pocket.

Beatrice had noticed him slide it into his pocket first and knew it was now empty. As she'd continued with her ploy of one old friend greeting another, she'd maneuvered Knight into a far corner away from the crowds.

"What's going on?" he demanded in a curt whisper. His gaze swung from Joe to Beatrice. "He killed you."

"Just wishful thinking on your boss's part or yours. We're still not sure which," she returned. "But we intend to find out."

He frowned at her as if she were talking nonsense. "I was told you found out Joe was a rogue agent and came out of the cold to track him down and he killed you. I was sent to complete your assignment."

Disbelief showed on Joe's face. "You're the rogue agent. You faked your death so you could go out on your own."

Knight's chin tightened with indignation. "I've been following orders all along. It was The Manager's idea for me to fake my death."

"Harold?" Joe growled.

Indignation flashed in Knight's eyes. "The Manager," he corrected curtly.

Beatrice had to admit he was playing the part of the well-trained agent. It was policy never to use anyone's real name in the field.

"And it was 'The Manager' who sent you out to bring me in?" Joe demanded.

Knight's gaze turned to ice. "The order was for an extermination. When I was told you'd killed Thistle, I was happy to comply." Disgust etched itself into his features. "Obviously the two of you have gone rogue together. You can kill me but others will follow."

"We haven't gone rogue," Beatrice assured him.

"Hey, what's going on, man?" a male voice demanded from behind Joe.

Beatrice looked past his shoulder to see a young man in his late teens dressed in the same-style custodial jumpsuit as Knight.

"I ain't getting paid to clean this place by myself while you goof off," he complained, continuing toward them.

Suddenly there was a gun in his hand. He got a shot off before Beatrice's mental shove reached him. She'd given a hard push that sent him sideways, causing him to lose his balance. As he hit the floor, his hold on the gun slackened and it went skidding across the room. Startled, he glanced to his side to see who had knocked into him. To Beatrice's relief, a crowd of people had just come down the nearby escalator, giving him a variety of choices.

"That man had a gun!" a woman screamed, and suddenly the place was in chaos.

The shooter scrambled to his feet and ran for the exit. Joe took off after him while Knight slowly slid down the wall, blood staining the front of his clothing. Beatrice had seen the shooter's eyes. They'd never wavered from Knight. Clearly, he'd been the primary target.

"Someone call for an ambulance! There's a man shot here!" Beatrice yelled over her shoulder. Seeing a security guard begin to speak frantically into her walkie-talkie, she turned back to Knight. "Looks to me like we're on the same side," she said, gently easing him into a lying-down position.

"I don't understand," he murmured.

His eyes closed and she realized he was going into shock. "Don't you die on me, Knight," she ordered. "We have business to conclude. You haven't saved the world from the bad guys yet."

"Have to save the world," he replied, his voice barely above a whisper.

"How's he doing?" Joe was back, kneeling on the other side.

"Not good." She looked at him. "What happened to the shooter?"

"There was a convertible waiting outside. He dived in and was gone before I could catch him. Guess my reflexes aren't what they used to be."

Knight's eyes opened. "We all slow down with age, old man."

"At least you haven't lost your sense of humor," Joe said. "Hold on. Help is on the way."

"Move out of the way!" a voice ordered.

Beatrice looked up to see uniformed paramedics coming on the run. The words *trust no one* flashed into her mind. "We can't let him go anywhere alone," she said in hushed tones.

Joe nodded. Reaching into his pocket he pulled out a Treasury Department ID and flashed it at the approaching paramedics. "This man stays in my or my partner's sight at all times. He's an important government witness."

"He's not going to be any good to you or anyone if you don't get out of the way," the older of the men said.

Joe's manner had been cold and efficient. Beatrice chose to play the "nice guy" role. "We're just concerned," she said, letting her anxiousness for Knight cause tears to well in her eyes. "He's a friend and there are some very nasty people who want to see him dead."

Immediately the faces of the paramedics softened.

She moved out of their way but stayed where she could watch them work. Joe, she noticed, was also watching closely for any signs of wrong procedure. There were none.

"We need to transport as quickly as possible," the older man said. He looked to Joe. "You can help lift."

An hour later, Joe joined Beatrice in the observation booth above the operating room in which Knight was being worked on. "Tobias called in some favors from people he knew in other areas of law enforcement. Knight will be well guarded and as soon as he can travel, he'll be taken to a safe place to recuperate."

"You honestly think he'll be all right?" she asked, unable to take her eyes off the scene below.

"I've never seen him give up."

Beatrice nodded in agreement.

"I told Tobias about you. He was relieved to learn you were both alive and not the traitor." Joe's gaze turned to the men working below. "Do you think Knight was telling the truth? That he wasn't knowingly a rogue agent? That he was set up by Harold?"

She nodded. "That seems like the only reasonable conclusion. The shooter was after Knight, not us. I'd swear to that."

"When I was captured, Harold had to have figured that there was a fifty-fifty chance I was working for Tobias and if not working for him, that I was passing information on to him." A rueful expression darkened his face. "Some of those drugs they used on me were pretty potent. I let it slip that I knew there was a mole in The Unit."

"So Harold had Knight fake his own death so he could set him up as the scapegoat. Harold would deny having anything to do with Knight's faked demise, thus labeling Knight a rogue agent and prime suspect. Then I resurfaced and provided him with an even more convenient one," Beatrice hypothesized.

"Taking the chance I was working with Tobias, Harold gave me time to pass on the information about you. Then he ordered Knight to take me out," Joe finished.

Beatrice nodded. "With you gone he wouldn't have to worry about you conducting any more private investigations either on your own or for Tobias."

"Then he'd have 'discovered' Knight was still alive, declared him a rogue agent and ordered a kill. If Tobias hadn't entirely bought the idea that you were working alone, he'd have Knight—dead, of course—to pair you up with. A neat little package."

"But sloppy. The shooter Harold had following Knight was too slow to act. Knight had time to tell us who'd set him up."

"Son of a bitch!" Joe cursed under his breath. "Knight put his life in that man's hands. A lot of good agents have."

Beatrice turned to study his stern profile. "So what do we do now?"

"We go to Tobias's place. He's sent Raven to pick up Harold."

Beatrice scowled. "He should have given us a chance to get in position to guard Raven's back."

"Raven is used to working alone."

She gave him a dry grimace. "Just like you. But if I hadn't been guarding your back, you'd be dead by now."

Joe took out the cigarette pack he'd retrieved from Knight's pocket when he'd helped lift him onto the stretcher. From his pocket he extracted the three cigarettes with their deadly doses, returned them to the pack and slipped the pack back into his pocket. "I used to think we were the luckiest agents alive. We should never have walked away from some of those scrapes we got into. Watching you today, I realized that luck had very little to do with it."

"In your case, it had a lot to do with it." She grinned lopsidedly. "You were lucky to have me by your side."

Gently he stoked her cheek. "I've never regretted the time we had together, Tess, but you deserve more from life than what I can give you."

"You're underestimating yourself," she replied.

He shoved his hand back into his pocket and his expression turned grim. "Even your talent can't always protect you. If the shooter had chosen you for his first target, you'd be on that table now."

She couldn't deny his words, so she chose to ignore them and concentrate on the men below.

It was two in the morning when Beatrice and Joe boarded the small, four-seater chartered plane that would take them to Craftsbury Common, Vermont. They hadn't been able to talk to Knight again. Because of lung damage, he was still sedated and on a respirator.

They were both exhausted. Making himself as comfortable as possible, Joe closed his eyes and went to sleep as the plane taxied into takeoff position.

But, as tired as she was, sleep eluded Beatrice. She thought of Knight lying in the hospital bed with machines keeping him alive and pictured Joe in his place. The reality was that there could be as little as a day left to her and him, or there could be a long life. Either way, she wanted to spend what time she had with him.

As she looked at him, seeing his grim expression even in sleep, the fear that she would never be able to climb the wall he was working so hard to keep between them, spread through her. Needing to touch him, she reached over and laid her hand on his. His eyes opened and he looked at her questioningly.

Saying nothing, she continued to hold his hand while she leaned back and closed her eyes. He knew how she felt. She would let him make the next move.

She felt him tense, then he placed his free hand on top of hers. Certain he was planning to remove her hand from his and return it to her lap, she fought to control a surge of frustration. But instead of the rejection she'd prepared herself to accept, after a moment he relaxed and left her hand encased in his. Opening one eye, she looked in his direction.

"I know you're pretty shaken by Knight's condition," he said, then closed his eyes, marking the end of the conversation.

Beatrice relaxed and mentally smiled. That he needed an excuse to allow any show of closeness between them didn't bother her. The fact that he'd allowed it, gave her hope.

When the plane touched down and he released her, she felt deserted. *Success is built on small triumphs,* she told herself as she followed him to the waiting car. Approaching close enough to see the driver in shadowy detail, she didn't recognize him. Immediately she stopped and her body tensed for action.

Seeing her response, Joe stopped and whispered in her ear. "He's all right. I know him. He's Tobias's grand-nephew."

She breathed a relieved sigh and continued forward, making a thorough inspection of the man sent to meet them. She placed his age in the mid-twenties. His hair was light in color. On the dimly lit runway it was difficult to discern its exact shade. The shape of the nose and eyes were the same as Tobias's. But unlike Tobias's somewhat stout figure, the man was lean and moved with agility.

"I'm Hagen. Tobias sends his greetings and welcomes you back from the grave," he said as she reached the car and he opened the back door for her.

He also had Tobias's charmingly disarming manner, she noted. Returning his smile, she slipped inside.

"Did Raven have any trouble picking up Harold?" Joe asked, as they drove away from the private airstrip.

"None."

Joe raised a skeptical eyebrow.

"Tobias decided it was unwise to send Raven alone so he called and asked for my help. I was there. We waited until Harold was at home alone, then went in. He was his usual calm self, seemed surprised to see us, but not afraid. We told him Tobias wanted to talk to him. He actually looked pleased. He placed a call to the office to tell them that he was taking a couple of days for a short vacation. Raven hit the speaker button on the phone so we could listen in. He looked a little surprised, then muttered something about Tobias's phobia with secrecy and made no more protests."

"He probably guessed Knight had named him, and knew you and Raven would have killed him before you'd let him get away," Joe said. "No doubt he's been proclaiming his innocence since his arrival, hoping to convince Tobias that Knight was lying."

"Forcefully," Hagen confirmed.

Midmorning Beatrice sat in Tobias's living room, impatiently waiting to confront the man who had tried to have her, Joe and Knight killed. Tobias had insisted she and Joe get some sleep before meeting with Harold. Now that they'd slept a few hours and eaten, the time had finally come. Silently, she watched Harold enter, flanked by Raven and Hagen.

The desire to send an ashtray or other missile in his direction was strong. She and Joe had arrived at Tobias's to be met with the news that another attempt had been made on Knight's life. It had been thwarted but, because his presence in the hospital could be a potential danger to the staff and other patients, and because guarding him was difficult in such a large facility with so many people constantly entering and leaving, it was determined that he should be transported to a private clinic. So that his pursuers would end their chase, he'd been declared officially dead once again.

The doctor had warned that moving Knight could be dangerous and it had proved to be. He'd lapsed into a coma during transport and showed no signs of coming out of it.

As Harold started across the room toward a chair Tobias motioned for him to take, she studied him. His suit coat and tie were missing. The top two buttons of his shirt were open and she could see perspiration stains spreading in a semicircular pattern from the armpits. His hair was mussed as if he'd been raking his fingers through it. Lines of stress were etched deeply into his features. She'd never seen him unkempt or rattled. On closer inspection she decided he was more indignant than frightened.

Abruptly he stopped and she realized he'd just seen Joe.

"You're alive," he said, the words coming out in something close to a gasp.

Beatrice had to admit the man looked truly surprised.

Joe said nothing and Harold's gaze shifted to her. "I suppose you found out and that's why you resurfaced."

"Something like that," she replied.

His back straightened with dignity and he turned to Tobias. "Obviously, you never truly retired."

"I did what I had to do," Tobias said.

Continuing to the chair, Harold seated himself, then leveled his gaze on Joe. "I'd say it's good to see you risen from the grave except that I have the feeling you're the reason I'm here, accused by my mentor of being a traitor. Well, I don't care what you think you know. You're wrong!"

"Knight named you just before he was shot," Joe said in an easy drawl.

"Until last night I thought Knight was dead. He's the rogue agent. He was just covering for himself."

"Then who shot him?"

Harold's jaw tensed. It was clear he had no answer.

Joe let the silence hang between them for nearly a minute, then said, "He told us that it was you who set up his fake death and you who sent him to kill me."

"That's a lie! I had nothing to do with his fake demise and until I saw you just now, I thought you'd died five years ago."

"Did you tell anyone else I'd resurfaced?" Beatrice asked, drawing his attention to her.

He scowled. "Of course not."

"Then you, Raven and Tobias were the only possible suspects and Knight named you." But as she spoke, a thought began to nag at her.

"I suppose there is nothing I can say that will change your mind." There was bitterness in Harold's voice. "Tobias has clearly discounted his own lie-detector test and sodium-Pentothal inquisition."

"We're all trained to overcome both of those contingencies," Joe reminded him. "You, yourself, would consider them unreliable when used on a trained agent."

"And so the five of you are going to form your own little court and sanction my death." Harold's chin stiffened and he held his head high. "Well, you'll be killing an innocent man."

Beatrice's stomach knotted. She didn't like the idea of playing judge and jury. The way Joe's jaw tensed, she knew he didn't, either. Raven and Hagen looked uncomfortable, as well. All turned to Tobias.

"Once our evidence is collected, you'll be turned over for court-martial," he said.

Harold continued to maintain an air of righteousness. "It's a shame you hold such low regard for old friendships."

"Did you tell anyone else on your staff—your secretary, your assistant, anyone else—that you were meeting with me?" Beatrice asked.

"No. Your message was relayed directly to me. Although both Grace and Paul have the highest security clearance and my full confidence, I adhere to Tobias's need-to-know policy and they did not need to know. In spite of what all of you think, I'm an honest man and would never do anything to compromise your anonymity."

Tobias nodded to Raven. Raven motioned for Harold to rise. Again flanked by Hagen and Raven, Harold was escorted from the room. For a full minute no one spoke. Then Tobias looked from Joe to Beatrice and said, "Well? What do you think?"

"I don't like believing he's a traitor," Joe replied, "but all the evidence points to him." His frown deepened. "How did he do on the lie-detector test and the inquisition?"

"He passed both. But then, as you pointed out, we do exercises that are meant to help us throw off the results. He could have been conditioning himself for just such an ordeal. He's clever and has a strong mind. Those were two of the reasons I chose him to be my successor."

Beatrice had been silent, considering a new path of thought. "Another possibility has occurred to me," she announced abruptly.

Both men turned to her.

"There were others who knew I'd resurfaced. Susan recognized my voice and Julia passed Tobias's message on to me."

Tobias frowned impatiently. "They're messengers, nothing more. They answer the phones and relay coded orders. They don't even know the codes."

"They know who the agents are by sight and code name," Beatrice argued. "And they know who's in the field at any given time. That's all the edge the bad guys need to spot our people and maneuver around them."

"Their equipment does allow them to trace a call to its source," Tobias said in low angry tones, as if mentally giving himself a slap. "Any agent calling in would reveal his location to them."

"And they sit at computer terminals all day. A clever hacker would have learned how to tap into munitions files," Beatrice continued. "As for making contacts with the bad guys, they could hack into other, lower-class security files for those. Interpol, the FBI and police forces all over the country exchange information via computers.''

''I assumed we were looking for someone at the top, not someone who had worked their way up from the bottom,'' Joe admitted. ''But you're right. If one of them is the mole, they could have started small, gathering tidbits of information, learning how to beat the system. Sure. Why not? Both have been with The Unit for more than ten years. If it is one of them, they could have spent those first years learning, building connections that fit naturally into their life-style so that no security check would spot them. And any clever person could hide assets well enough that they would not be found by one of our usual security checks or even the intensive one Tobias ordered after I told him about my suspicion that there was a mole in his organization.''

Tobias nodded. ''Everyone came out clean. If I hadn't had faith in Joe's nose for sniffing out trouble, I'd have discounted his theory.''

''If our traitor is one of them, that would agree with my gut instinct. For the past couple of months, I had become convinced I was after a woman.'' Joe looked to Tobias. ''To tell the truth, I was beginning to concentrate on Grace. Her security clearance gives her access to as much information as any agent. And as your secretary and now Harold's, she was, in one way or another, always in the loop on any operation.''

''I want to believe Harold is innocent, but Knight said Harold was the one who told him to play dead and go under deep cover. And, he said it was Harold who issued the order to kill Joe,'' Tobias reminded them.

''Given enough time, anyone can break a code. If Julia or Susan used Knight's code and sent a message from The Manager, he would have assumed it was Harold issuing the order," Joe reasoned. "And anyone can get a set of false documents made up."

"That would also explain why the shooter hit Knight first." Beatrice paused as the events at the airport played through her mind. "In fact, he didn't seem all that interested in either Joe or me." She concentrated harder on the images. "It happened so fast, I missed some of the details, but I'm sure our shooter was wearing headphones hooked into a radio in his pocket. But what if it wasn't a radio? What if it was an audio amplifier? What if he was listening to our conversation. Knight named Harold and suddenly the shooter was there."

"We know our mastermind is clever at pointing us in the wrong direction." Joe picked up her line of thinking. "My capture must have been a shock. When I revealed that I was after a traitor, if that traitor is Susan or Julia, she probably figured I was in deep cover working for either Tobias or Harold and that I was on her trail. She needed a scapegoat so she set up Knight to take the fall. Sanchez was to find out all he could from me and then kill me in a way that Knight could be made to take the blame. The fact that Knight had already faked his death would be the clinching evidence that would nail him as the traitor. Then Thistle entered the picture. Our traitor tucked Knight neatly in a corner for use at a future date and set Thistle up. I was to be allowed to live long enough to erase her and tell my superiors that I'd taken care of the traitor. Then Knight was pulled out to take care of me. Once that was done, he'd be killed for real. But if we took him alive, he was to point us toward Harold, then be taken out."

Tobias began to nod. "The second attempt wasn't made on Knight so that he couldn't testify against Harold, but so that he couldn't reveal the true traitor." His gaze leveled on them. "I'll admit, I prefer your scenario to Harold being the mole. But we need evidence, not speculation, and it doesn't look as if Knight is going to be of any help." He looked to Beatrice. "What about Lucinda?"

"I never spoke to her."

Picking up the walkie-talkie on the table beside him, Tobias ordered Harold brought back.

The man entered, carrying himself with stiff dignity.

"We have a new scenario," Tobias said, motioning for Harold to seat himself.

"And what am I to have done now?" Harold asked dryly, obeying the unspoken invitation.

"In this scenario you, like Knight, were set up as a scapegoat."

"By whom?" Harold demanded, an iciness in his eyes promising retribution to whoever had done this to him.

"Susan or Julia," Tobias answered. "Both knew of Thistle's return. I am excluding Lucinda. During her shift, no messages were exchanged between you and Thistle. However, if you have information that would show she had knowledge that would include her in the list of suspects, I want to know about it."

For a long moment, Harold sat mute. Then he shook his head. "As far as I know, Lucinda knows nothing regarding this matter." Harold sank back in the chair, looking toward the ceiling, his usual thinking pose. "Susan or Julia," he murmured their names. "That doesn't seem possible. They know next to nothing about our operation and they've both kept their positions within The Unit because they've never shown any curiosity. They merely relay coded messages."

"You said the messages between you and Thistle were passed directly to you, but could Grace have found out about them?" Joe asked, not wanting to overlook anyone this time.

Harold shook his head. "No. She was out sick."

As another silence fell over the room, Beatrice glanced at Raven. A smirk of self-mockery played at one corner of his mouth. "Who would suspect the receptionist? What a perfect cover. We accept their messages as if they're machines merely relaying information. We never ask for verification."

"You will, of course, have to remain my guest until this matter is cleared up." Tobias addressed Harold.

"You have my total cooperation," Harold assured him. Again his shoulders straightened with righteous pride, and he turned his attention to Beatrice and Joe. "I am counting on the two of you to clear me completely." His gaze shifted to Tobias. "In the meantime, I want to pull all of my people in. I don't want anyone out there who could be compromised."

Tobias nodded in agreement. "We will, however, bypass the usual messenger service," he stipulated. "And tell your people to continue to check in as if they were still out in the field. We don't want to tip off any of our suspects that we're on to them."

Chapter Eleven

"Do we have a plan?" Beatrice broke the silence between her and Joe. The small chartered plane had flown them directly to Washington, D.C. Now they were weaving their way through the heavy Georgetown traffic on their way to the offices that housed The Unit.

"We don't trust first impressions or even second ones," he replied.

She nodded her agreement.

Arriving at the three-story brick duplex with Versatile Pest Control painted on a small wooden sign on the small front lawn, Beatrice entered alone.

It was late afternoon, near the end of Julia's shift. The gray-haired, grandmotherly-looking receptionist smiled in recognition.

Then Joe entered. Immediately Julia's expression became coolly professional and Beatrice saw her hand move to a position under her desk.

"He is Coyote," Beatrice said. "Under Tobias's direction, he's been under deep cover."

Julia's expression remained unyielding. She motioned toward a painting on the wall. It slid away, revealing an electronic handprint-identification board.

Joe stepped up and placed his hand on the outline. After several seconds a blue light appeared.

Tears welled in Julia's eyes. "It's good to see you," she said.

"It's good to be back," Joe replied in a casual tone, as if they were merely there for a friendly visit.

Beatrice noted that the warmth in the woman's eyes seemed genuine as had her shock at seeing Joe. However, whoever they were after was a very good actress, she reminded herself as she and Joe made their way to Harold's office.

Grace looked up as they entered. She was near Julia's age but there was nothing grandmotherly about her. She dressed sharply in tailored suits, wore just the right amount of makeup and jewelry to look stylish but not gaudy, and her shoes always matched her purse. An air of efficiency exuded from her. Very little rattled her. But when she saw Joe and Beatrice, her face paled with shock. "Thistle? Coyote?"

"I was under deep cover," Joe explained, giving her a wink.

"And I've come out of retirement. I missed the excitement," Beatrice said, glancing toward Joe to let him know she meant this.

Grace's color began to return.

Ignoring Beatrice's declaration, Joe concentrated on the secretary. "We're on our way to visit an old friend. Harold's already there."

"Yes, I got his message." Grace smiled approvingly. "It's about time he took a vacation."

"He asked us to stop by and pick up a crystal paperweight. It's a gift he forgot to take with him." This was the code phrase that would gain them access to Harold's inner sanctum. As Joe spoke the words, Grace's smile became plastic.

For a moment she sat mute, then asked stiffly, "The one I bought with the rose inside?"

"No. The one with the black widow. Our friend has a longtime interest in entomology."

Grace looked toward the door marked Private. "I'm sure it's on his desk."

Beatrice read the worry on the woman's face. "Harold will be relieved to have it," she said.

Grace forced a smile as she pressed a button on the floor that released the door and allowed them to enter.

Once inside, Joe crossed the room and opened a door on the far side. Behind it was a small alcove fronting a walk-in vault like those used by banks. He punched in the code Harold had given him, turned the large wheel and pulled the door open. Inside were filing cabinets.

They pulled Susan's and Julia's records. Both had been given thorough security checks when they'd entered The Unit and their security reviews were unblemished. But that they'd expected.

Susan was a marine. She was a master sharpshooter and had rated high in her fieldwork, but an accident during a war-games exercise had injured her back, causing her to be classified as unfit for front-line combat. Rather than leave the military, she'd opted for a desk job. Her mother, father and two sisters were still living. All resided west of the Mississippi. She had a Georgetown address that allowed her to walk to work. She'd never been married or had any children.

Julia had been recruited from the navy where she'd been an ordnance officer. She was widowed with three grown children. One daughter was divorced and living in the same small town in Maryland as she did, another was in California and the third was in Kansas. At the time of the last update, she had four grandchildren.

"Julia would know how to access ordnance records," Beatrice said.

Joe nodded. "But after her accident, Susan took several courses in computing science. It's possible she could hack into any system she wanted."

"What about Knight? Why choose him?" Beatrice asked.

Joe was already on his way back to the file vault. "Let's see if there's any connection." He pulled out Knight's file. "Interesting," he murmured. "He grew up on the tough side of Philadelphia. Had a juvenile rap sheet. He's never been married. His mother died in childbirth. Seems his dad is still alive but he lists a home for wayward boys as his sole beneficiary." Joe continued to frown thoughtfully at the contents of the file. "Knight's background and lack of personal ties made him the perfect choice as a patsy. But was choosing him simply luck or by design?"

"All offices have gossip," Beatrice said with conviction. "I think we should ask Grace to join us."

Joe returned the files. When the vault was securely closed, Beatrice buzzed for Grace and asked her to join them. "I realize that talking about your fellow workers is a breach of security," she said when the secretary entered. "However, in this instance we need to know anything you know about Knight. Did he have any contacts other than business ones with any others who work here?"

Grace frowned reprovingly and her chin tightened in refusal.

"We're not asking out of idle curiosity," Joe said sternly. "We're working with both Tobias and Harold. Knight didn't die several weeks ago. He is, however, in a coma and we need to find out what happened to get him into the situation in which he found himself."

"It would seem that death is not final—at least, where our people are concerned," Grace observed.

Beatrice rephrased her question. "Do you know anything about Knight that might help us trace his actions the past few months?"

"I know he took Susan out to lunch on her birthday. They might have dated. I don't know. But if they did, I don't think it was anything serious. When we found out about his death, she looked shaken but not really distraught. She said it was a shame someone so young had to die but everyone had to go sometime."

Grace paused to think, then continued. "I once overheard him compliment Julia on her cooking. I think she might have invited him over for a meal or two." Grace frowned disapprovingly. "She's such a mother hen." A speculative gleam entered her eyes. "Or she could have been matchmaking for one of her daughters."

"Did he socialize with any of the others?" Joe asked, when Grace became silent.

She shook her head. "No, not that I know of. I think Kristine, Paul's secretary, had an eye for him. She used to always seem to show up when he was here. But he never gave her a second glance. She's the settling-down type and I got the impression that Knight wasn't looking for any ties that bind."

Beatrice smiled her agreement. From remarks the man had made, she'd also concluded that he wasn't the settling-down type. "Thanks, Grace. And, of course, you won't mention any of our conversation to anyone." This was an order, not a request.

Grace looked insulted. "Of course not. I wouldn't have been Tobias's secretary or remained as Harold's if I couldn't hold my tongue."

"You're right and I apologize," Beatrice said quickly. "I'm just very worried about Knight."

Grace's expression softened. "What is the prognosis?"

"The doctors are making no guesses."

"I'll say a prayer for him," she said, and completed her exit.

Beatrice turned to Joe. "What now?"

"We interview Julia and Susan about their association with Knight. See if either runs or makes a slip." Joe pressed the intercom button and asked Grace to request that Julia come by to see them before leaving for the day. He then instructed her to phone Susan and ask her to come in a little early.

"Susan's on vacation," Grace informed him. "She called in yesterday and said an opportunity had arisen she didn't want to pass up. She had time coming and one of our usual replacements was available so I gave her permission to go."

"Did she say where?" Joe kept his voice casual, but Beatrice saw the hunter emerging. His expression became one of single-minded purpose and his eyes darkened until they reminded her of black ice.

"No. She just thanked me profusely and hung up."

"Forget about making the appointment with Julia. We'll talk to her later. Right now, I want to know where Susan went. Check with the airlines and see if she booked a flight out. Better check Baltimore, New York and Philly as points of departure, as well. She could have driven to any of those easily. And she might not be using her real name. Fax the ticket agents and the security people at those airports her photo to see if anyone recognizes her," Joe directed. "Also, get hold of her phone records for the past couple of weeks. I want to know who she's been talking to."

After issuing orders to Grace, he used Harold's protected line to call Tobias and fill him in. Tobias agreed to arrange for a tail on Julia in case she was the traitor and Susan's departure was another false trail or merely a coincidence.

As they left Harold's inner sanctum, Grace paused in the midst of punching a number in on her phone. "How do I contact you?"

"We'll contact you," Joe said over his shoulder.

Grace nodded and went back to work.

Beatrice had seen the curiosity in her eyes but, being the professional she was, Grace asked no questions.

A quick drive brought them to the address in Susan's file. It was the end house of a row of tall, narrow, brick town houses on a quiet side street. The small sections of lawn on either side of the walk leading to the front door had been charmingly landscaped to resemble miniature English mazes, giving it an air of quiet elegance. "Nice place," Beatrice noted.

Joe got out his lock-picking kit. "Shall we take a look inside?"

"If you're looking for Susan, she's not here," a female voice with an English accent called out from behind them.

Beatrice turned, blocking Joe's actions with her body. A pleasant-faced woman in her mid-twenties, wearing a plainly cut, brown mid-calf-length dress and pushing a baby carriage was watching them from the sidewalk at the end of the short walkway leading to Susan's door. Beatrice schooled her face into an expression of distress. "But I called just three days ago to make certain she'd be in town. I didn't tell her we were planning to come because I wanted to surprise her. I guess I should have.''

The woman smiled sympathetically. ''The chance for her to go on a trip came up unexpectedly.''

Beatrice heard the click and knew Joe had managed to open the lock. Free to move, she approached the woman and held out her hand. ''I'm Tess. My husband Joe and I are old friends of Susan. We all grew up together. Joe and I've been promising her for years we'd come visit and now here we are and you say she's gone? On a trip?''

''I'm Nancy. Nancy Rupert.'' The woman accepted the handshake. ''I'm the Petersons' nanny.'' She nodded toward the house on the other side of the narrow alleyway separating Susan's place from the next row of homes. ''I take care of Susan's cats when she's gone.''

''Then you're a friend?''

Nancy gave a noncommittal shrug. ''As much as possible. We've shared a cup of tea a few times and gone to the movies a couple of times. But her working schedule and mine don't mesh too well.''

''She didn't mention where she was going, did she?'' Beatrice asked.

''I don't think she knew for certain. Someplace warm. She said something about not knowing what to take so she'd packed every lightweight piece of good clothing she had.''

''Then she plans to be away for quite a while?''

''Just a week.'' Nancy smiled conspiratorially. ''It's a man. She met him a couple of weeks ago and they really hit it off. I got the impression this trip was so that he could introduce her to his family.''

Beatrice grinned back and added excitement mingled with curiosity to her voice. ''She didn't mention a name, did she? Have you seen him? What's he like?''

Nancy grimaced with disappointment. "She refused to talk about him and he never came to her house. I used to kid her about him being her phantom lover." A hint of embarrassment tinted the nanny's cheeks. "In fact, I once kidded her about making him up. She got a little steamed with me over that."

Beatrice looked worried as if concerned about Susan's mental health. "But now you're certain he does exist?"

"The limo that picked her up was definitely real."

Beatrice noticed a gleam of female admiration enter Nancy's eyes and realized that Joe had joined them. She saw him smiling at the nanny and experienced a twinge of jealousy. Then he slipped his arm around her waist and a glow of pleasure spread through her. Right there was where she belonged. All she needed to do was to convince him of that.

"Well, what do you want do?" he asked, looking down at her, his expression that of a husband ready to bend to his wife's wishes.

Several salacious thoughts raced through her mind. They must have been reflected in her eyes because he gave her a "Stick to business" kind of frown. Breathing an exaggerated sigh, as if uncertain what action to take, she said, "Well, she did give us a key and tell us to make ourselves at home anytime we were in town. We could spend the night here and then head on up to New York tomorrow."

Joe nodded. "You can leave her a note saying we'll stop by on our way home."

In keeping with her role of longtime friend, Beatrice grinned mischievously in the nanny's direction. "That'll give me a chance to find out about this mysterious boyfriend. Maybe I'll be wearing a bridesmaid dress at her wedding, yet."

"Maybe," Nancy replied with a matching grin.

They'd learned all they could from the nanny, Beatrice decided. "It's been a real pleasure meeting you," she said. Joe smiled once again at the woman, then both headed to the front door of Susan's place. Beatrice was aware of the woman's continued watchful gaze. Joe took out his keys, rattled them a little, then opened the door.

"Is the boyfriend real or a cover?" she asked when the door was closed behind her.

"Flip a coin," Joe replied.

Meticulously, they began going through the house. Two hours later, they sat in the living room, reviewing their discoveries.

"I don't know how much of a clotheshorse Susan is, but when she told the nanny she'd taken nearly every stitch of lightweight clothing she owned, she wasn't lying. And there were very few panties and bras left, either," Beatrice said.

"So you think she's planning on staying away longer than a week—like forever?" Joe asked.

Beatrice shrugged. "Maybe she was being honest when she said she was too nervous to decide what to take or not to take so she took everything. That's not unreasonable to believe if the boyfriend is real and she was worried about making a good impression on his family."

"There were Spanish-language tapes in the recorder on her bedside table, along with a *Spanish for the Beginner* book."

Beatrice nodded toward a stack of books on the coffee table. "All of those are about Belize and Mexico—their history, traditions, modern-day politics."

Joe picked up the phone and dialed Grace's number. Hanging up a few minutes later, he was frowning. "A security guard at Dulles recognized her. He said she asked him where the ladies' room was. She left on a private jet. Its flight plan was for Mexico City."

"She left an awfully hot trail," Beatrice noted.

"Just what I was thinking." Joe's frown deepened. "Would the person we're after be so careless?"

"The question is, is she being careless or clever? By moving around so openly, she could hope to point the finger of suspicion away from herself while at the same time getting out of the country in case we have evidence against her."

"The only way we're going to know the truth is to find her." Joe's frown darkened. "There is one other possibility. This could be a trap set up to snare us, with her as innocent bait."

Beatrice knew that look. "If you're considering trying to leave me behind, forget it."

"There's no reason for you to go. I can handle this on my own."

Her voice letting him know she would not be dissuaded, she said, "I am not staying behind."

With a shake of his head as if to say she was the most stubborn woman he knew, he reached for the phone.

Five hours later, in large glasses, a curly brown wig and wearing a fake pregnancy bulge that made her look as if she was at least six months along, Beatrice boarded a flight for Mexico City. Joe was several passengers behind her, dressed in flowing robes and giving a very good impression of being an Arab diplomat.

He'd contacted Manuel and they hoped the *federale* would have a lead on Susan's whereabouts by the time they arrived. Sleep was her number-one priority at the moment. As soon as the plane was off the ground, she tilted her seat back and closed her eyes. She wished Joe could be sitting beside her but he was two aisles away, playing the part of a complete stranger. Her hand sought out the beaded necklace in the oversize pocket of her dress and closed around it.

A feeling of rightness swept through her. Joe was just going to have to get used to having her in his life. Focusing her mind on the feel of being in his arms, she slept.

At the airport she complained of pains after disembarking and was immediately guided to the infirmary. Manuel was there, waiting for her. She discarded her pregnancy bulge, wig and glasses and pulled on a long white lab coat. Looking like a nurse being led to an emergency, she accompanied him out a side exit and into his waiting car.

"It's good to see you alive and well. Both Elena and I found it difficult to believe you were a traitor and even more difficult to believe Joe disposed of you," he said as they drove away from the airport.

"It's good to be alive and well, and one of the good guys again," she replied with a grin.

"Joe gave me permission to tell Elena the truth. He said the people you seek saw you when the attempt was made on Knight."

"No sense in my playing dead after that," she confirmed.

"Elena was angry with Joe for not trusting us but I explained that the fewer people who knew the truth, the safer you were. When this is over, she wants you and Joe to come visit. You, she wants to hug. I think she's still harboring enough anger to give him a scolding."

Beatrice smiled softly. "I would like to see her again." Her voice took on a hard edge. "What about Rafael?"

Manuel looked like a man betrayed. "I've been checking more closely into his activities. He is Sanchez's man."

She could see the pain this discovery had cost him. "I'm sorry."

"I'm just glad we know the truth. Rafael and many of his family have been aligned with Sanchez all along."

"Were you able to discover anything about Susan's whereabouts?"

"A helicopter met the private jet and took off toward the south. A close business acquaintance of Sanchez by the name of Federico Fernandez has a vacation estate just outside of Belize City. We think that's where she is. We managed to get come aerial photos of the place just before dark."

They had left the city and were heading due south. After a while, Manuel turned off onto a dirt road. It led to a clearing. There a helicopter was waiting.

He glanced at his watch. "Joe should be here soon. The pilot will fly you to a place near the border. I've got equipment and supplies waiting for you."

Beatrice was only half listening. She'd known Joe would probably arrive after them. Still, she worried.

"Elena wants to have a child."

Beatrice had been looking down the road. Now she turned to Manuel. Surprise that he'd spoken of his private life to her showed on her face.

"I thought, you being a woman and someone who understands the kind of life I lead, you might be able to give me some advice," he said. "I know Joe trusts your judgment."

Beatrice had never felt comfortable advising others on how to live their lives. She preferred to force them to face their own feelings, make their own decisions. "And you don't want a child?"

Manuel leaned against the car and stared up at the sky. "It's not that I don't want a child. It's just that I can't be certain I will be around to help her raise one."

"I see." Beatrice kept her voice noncommittal.

"But she says it is that uncertainty that makes her want a family even more strongly. She tells me that when she thought I was dead, the one thing she regretted most was not having a child that was a part of me to love and care for.''

''She's a brave, intelligent woman who knows her own mind.''

Manuel nodded. ''You're right about that. Besides, I have a feeling I may have little say in this decision.''

Beatrice recalled her and Joe's brushes with death. ''I think you should enjoy your life from day to day. That's all any of us can be certain of, anyway. If you really want my advice, I'd say do what you can to ensure a future for Elena and any children the two of you may decide to have, but to constantly worry about the what-ifs will serve no purpose.''

Manuel's gaze turned to her. ''What about you and Joe? Elena is convinced the two of you have feelings for each other.''

Beatrice frowned. ''Like you, he worries too much about the what-ifs.''

Manuel suddenly grinned. ''You and my Elena are a lot alike. I can see you plan to give him little choice.''

She grinned back. ''I plan to give him *no* choice.''

The sound of a vehicle approaching caused them all to tense. Manuel and the pilot drew their weapons as the single headlight of a motorcycle came into view.

Pulling up beside the car, Joe cut the engine and dismounted. He'd discarded his Arab attire for the clothes of a Mexican peasant.

''Let's get going,'' he ordered.

As Beatrice boarded the helicopter, Joe extended his hand to Manuel. ''Thank you, my friend.''

''Have a safe journey.'' Manuel looked beyond Joe to Beatrice. ''Good luck.''

She saw the smile on his face and knew he wasn't talking only about the mission. ''Thank you,'' she called back.

"Why do I get the feeling I missed something?" Joe yelled in her ear as the pilot started up the engines.

"Manuel thinks we make a good team," she yelled back. "You seem to be the only one who needs convincing."

He frowned. "I never said we didn't make a good team."

"You don't know how happy it makes me to hear you admit that," she replied, giving him a quick kiss on the lips.

He frowned. "That doesn't mean we should stay together."

"What if Laurel had said that to Hardy? Or Roy had said that to Dale? Or Rogers had said that to Hammerstein? Or Charles had said that to Nora?"

"What if Anthony had said that to Cleopatra?" he countered.

"You are a difficult man to convince." She smiled. "However, I don't give up easily."

Groaning, he leaned back and closed his eyes.

The morning sun was high by the time the pilot landed in a clearing near a cabin not far from the border of Belize. A *federale* by the name of Carlos Mendeze met them.

Joe and Beatrice both agreed that the trail was too hot for those who had left it not to know they could be easily followed. That left them with the time of their arrival as their only element of surprise. It was for that reason they'd worn disguises during their flight. It was also the reason Manuel had not accompanied them to the border. His absence in Mexico City was certain to be noticed.

"The jeep is behind the cabin," Carlos informed them. "You will find the supplies you requested in it." He nodded toward the cabin. "Inside you'll find the aerial photos taken yesterday and a map to the estate. The photos have been blown up to give you as much detail as possible. There are also several shots taken at other times of Federico Fernandez.''

"You have the coordinates for the rendezvous points?" the pilot asked.

Joe nodded.

"Beginning in three days, I'll start making passes over them in sequence, one a day, between three and five in the afternoon," he said.

Beatrice knew they'd decided on changing the location of the pickup each day so that, should Sanchez's people spot the helicopter on one day, that would not tip them off as to where the helicopter would be the next. It might, in fact, give Joe and her an advantage. With luck, Sanchez would send his men to the region used the previous day.

Having confirmed their arrangements, the pilot climbed back into the helicopter and, taking Carlos with him, left.

Inside the cabin, they found not only the map and photos but a basket of food. While they ate, they began examining the aerial shots. The estate was a large sprawling affair on a cliff overlooking the sea. A wrought-iron gate with a manned guardhouse fronted the private drive, while a high wall formed a partial exoskeleton around the compound. On the sea side, the wall stopped at the cliff edge, allowing the sheer drop to protect the property from uninvited guests. Within the compound, a drive about a quarter of a mile long led to the main house. To the rear of the house, on the ocean side, was an extensive terraced patio with a pool on the upper level. Tennis courts were to the left of the main structure. Several smaller houses were to the right. They guessed these were the living quarters for the help.

"Dogs. I hate trying to outrun dogs," Joe grumbled, pointing to a guard patrolling the compound with two Dobermans on leashes.

"That looks like Susan." Beatrice's finger came to rest near a female stretched out in a swimming suit on a chaise longue beside the pool.

Joe nodded his agreement, then turned his attention to the map of Belize. Manuel had given him directions to a border crossing where they could enter the country undetected. In case they were stopped during their journey, their passports were stamped as if they'd entered legally two days earlier. But the hope was that they would go unnoticed by the authorities. No doubt, Sanchez had someone in their ranks on his payroll who would inform him of any travelers matching their descriptions. The longer it took for them to be detected, the better their chances of success.

Beatrice turned her attention to the photos of Federico. He was a handsome man, in his early forties, very Latin-lover looking with his dark hair and dark eyes. "It's not difficult to see how she could be attracted to him," she mused.

Joe glanced at the photo and frowned. "If you find that gigolo look attractive."

Beatrice grinned at him. "A person could get the impression you're jealous that I think he's handsome."

"I simply thought you had better taste in men," he returned dryly.

Beatrice wasn't buying that. She added another point to her tally in this battle between their wills.

Joe bit back a yawn. "I suggest we take fifteen more minutes to memorize the layout, get a couple of hours' sleep, then get going."

"I could use a couple of hours of actually lying down," she admitted.

Joe glanced around the interior of the small cabin. "You take the bed. I'll bunk down on the floor in here."

She frowned at him. "You'll rest better on the bed. It's a double and I promise I won't try to take advantage of you." Not that she didn't want to, she admitted silently. But at the moment they had business to attend to that depended on them being rested and she wanted to let him know that she could behave when it was necessary.

He frowned. "I don't think so."

"Surely a man with your control isn't afraid of a mere woman," she taunted.

A flicker of fire escaped from the shuttered depths of his eyes. "I've never considered you a *mere* woman."

A curl of pleasure worked through her. "I'm flattered." Then her expression became serious. "But we both need our rest. I insist you share the bed."

For a moment he looked as if he was going to continue the protest. Then, with a grimace of resignation, he said, "All right. But I want your word, you'll stay on your side."

"Cross my heart." She made a huge crossing gesture on the front of her chest.

Not looking totally convinced, he returned his attention to the photos.

A few minutes later as they stretched out on the bed, Beatrice ordered herself to behave. She wanted to prove to him that she was an asset, not a thorn in his side. Forcing herself to concentrate on the layout of the estate, she fell asleep.

Joe's watch alarm woke her. Even before she opened her eyes, she knew where she was. There was only one place where she felt this comfortable, this secure—it was in Joe's arms. Refusing to give it up too quickly, she issued an impatient groan and snuggled her face into his chest.

Joe ordered himself to ease away from her. Instead, he reached around her to turn off the alarm. He couldn't deny how much he liked waking with her in his arms. And he slept better when she was there. But if he allowed her to stay with him, her life would be in nearly constant danger, he reminded himself sternly.

Wanting to remain near him for as long as possible, Beatrice fought to keep her breathing regular as if she were still asleep. That he hadn't immediately risen after turning off the alarm, encouraged her to believe his resolve was weakening, and a smile threatened to give her away.

Knowing that if he lingered there for even a moment longer, he would be kissing her, Joe again ordered himself to get up. This time he obeyed.

His departure caused her smile to turn into a frustrated frown. For a moment longer she lay still. Then, schooling her face into an expression of innocence, she yawned widely and shifted into a sitting position, pretending that it was his movements rather than the alarm that had jarred her awake.

"We'll eat on the way," he said, his back toward her.

She knew he was rebuilding his wall of resistance but assured herself that a wall, once cracked, was never as sturdy as the original. This might not be really true, but it was what she wanted to believe.

Chapter Twelve

Late afternoon the next day, they sat on the deck of a small cabin cruiser, covertly studying the cliff face below the compound. Manuel had arranged for the boat and private dock and they were playing the part of honeymooners lazily cruising the Caribbean.

"It's too sheer and too high to be a feasible path of access," Beatrice said.

"I agree." Joe began to guide the boat back to its dock. "We'll wait and watch for a couple of days."

Beatrice frowned. "She was too easy to find."

"And her trail led practically directly to Sanchez."

"Maybe she's decided to retire and live off her ill-gotten gains."

"In that case, we snatch her and take her back to Tobias. We don't have any solid evidence to use against her for the munitions thefts, but he should be able to trace some of the money she's made. We'll nail her for tax evasion."

"Or maybe she's been set up the way Knight and I were," Beatrice cautioned.

"True," he agreed. "In that case, we still have to snatch her because once they're certain we've seen her here, they'll kill her."

Beatrice looked at him. "But how do we find out the truth?"

"One step at a time."

"In other words, we play it by ear."

He winked at her to let her know she'd stated the situation correctly.

"Looks like our quarry is on the move," Beatrice announced. She and Joe had been taking turns with the binoculars, watching the comings and goings of the occupants of the compound from a hidden vantage point across from the guarded gate. It was nearly eight at night.

Joe had been asleep. In an instant he was alert. "Is she alone?"

"Chauffeured in an open convertible. Federico is with her. They look like they're enjoying each other's company," Beatrice replied.

"Dinner in town?"

"That'd be my guess."

"Bodyguards?"

"There was another man in front with the chauffeur. A second car followed. It was a sedan. I couldn't tell for sure, but I think there were two inside."

Joe was already on his way to their vehicle. Beatrice hurried after him. They caught up with the two cars at the bottom of the hill. Entering town, the convertible led the way to one of the nightspots. The second man from the convertible and the two men from the sedan followed Susan and

Federico inside, flanking them in a protective manner. The chauffeur remained with the cars.

Four hours later, Beatrice was asleep when the sound of the engine starting woke her.

"Looks like they're calling it a night," Joe said, giving the convertible and sedan a chance to get a little ways ahead, then pulling out after them.

Back at their vantage point across from the compound, as she sat watching the gate once again with Joe stretched out beside her, sleeping, she smiled at herself. She was actually happy. No one in their right mind would enjoy kneeling in the midst of bushes and underbrush, with insects the size of her fingers, maybe even hands, and who knew what else crawling and flying around in the dark, their eyes glued to a pair of binoculars for hours on end. But she didn't mind because Joe was there with her. This was definitely love.

After a couple of hours, she woke him. "Looks like they're settled in for the night. How about if we go back to the boat and get some sleep?"

She saw him hesitate and knew it wasn't the risk of losing Susan that worried him. "I have promised to behave myself."

"I suppose it's safe. At least we'll have separate bunks," he said, pushing himself to his feet and offering her a hand up.

That he was so concerned about their close proximity was a sure sign she was wearing him down, she told herself. "You can't run away from your feelings forever," she warned him as they drove to the dock.

"I'm not running from them. I'm controlling them for both our sakes."

"You don't have to strain yourself on my behalf."

He said nothing but she saw his jaw harden into a resolute line. *Don't go too fast,* she cautioned herself once again. But later, as she lay alone in her bunk, she fell asleep cursing his single-minded resolve.

"She's on the move again," Joe said.

This was their third day of watching Susan's movements. Only today would be different. After an intensive investigation and the calling in of several favors, Tobias had traced an account in the Cayman Islands to her. It contained a hundred thousand dollars. This was only a small portion of what she would have acquired through the years. The rest, he was certain, was scattered around the world in other accounts. He was continuing his search. In the meantime, he'd ordered her brought home.

Beatrice had been lying back going over the various plans she and Joe had discussed to accomplish their assignment. Now she sat up, her mind alert. "How many companions?"

"Just the chauffeur and one bodyguard."

Beatrice smiled. "Shopping again?"

"Let's hope so," Joe replied.

Each of the past two days, Susan had gone into town for a couple of hours of shopping, wandering from stall to stall and store to store while the chauffeur and bodyguard watched over her.

"Third store," Beatrice said.

"Third store," Joe confirmed.

Beatrice stayed close. Joe hung back. The bodyguard and chauffeur, they'd noted, were not as alert as they could have been. They allowed Susan to go into the shops alone, preferring to wait outside on the street. Either they were bored by their job or felt confident about being in control on their home turf.

Silently, Beatrice groaned. Susan seemed more interested in window-shopping than going into stores today. Glancing over her shoulder at Joe, she gave him a single wink.

He winked back.

They would take her in the first store. Returning her attention to her quarry, she saw Susan disappearing into the entrance of a dress shop. Quickly she followed her inside.

Waiting until Susan was as far to the back of the store as possible, Beatrice approached her. For the benefit of the salesgirl standing nearby, she smiled broadly. "Susan, what a pleasant surprise to see you here."

Shock registered on the blonde's face. "Thistle?"

"Why don't we go have coffee and talk? I haven't seen you in ages." Beatrice let her gaze drop to her pocket for a second to let Susan know she had a weapon.

"Yes, of course," Susan replied, still looking and sounding confused by Beatrice's unexpected appearance.

Turning to the salesgirl, Beatrice smiled beseechingly. "I was with a gentleman but he's gotten to be a bore. I ducked in here to get rid of him. Is there a back door to this place?"

The girl smiled knowingly and pointed toward the rear exit.

"Thanks so much." Beatrice slipped her a ten-dollar bill. "And if he comes in looking for me, you'll tell I'm trying on dresses?"

The girl's smile broadened. "You saw many you loved," she said.

Beatrice was counting on the bodyguard simply asking about "the woman" who had entered the shop. It would take a while for him and the salesgirl to figure out they were talking about the wrong person. All Beatrice and Joe needed was a couple of minutes' head start. "Shall we go get that coffee?" she said, motioning for Susan to precede her to the exit.

"Would you please tell me what's going on?" Susan demanded as soon as they were outside.

"Just keep quiet and do what I say." Deciding that a threat was the best way to gain cooperation, she added, "Tobias wants to speak to you. If we can't bring you back to him, he wants you dead. At the moment, I don't think he cares much which way. It's your choice."

Susan paled. "I don't understand."

"Just come with me." Beatrice guided her to where Joe was waiting with the car.

Seeing him, Susan gasped. "Coyote? But you're dead!"

Beatrice had to admit Susan looked as if she were seeing a ghost.

"Those reports were grievously exaggerated," Joe replied as Beatrice opened the back door of the car and gave Susan a nudge.

"I don't understand," Susan muttered again, following the unspoken order and climbing into the car. As Beatrice climbed in beside her and Joe drove away, tears welled in Susan's eyes. "I haven't done anything wrong."

The blonde looked terrified and Beatrice found herself feeling sorry for the woman. "What were you doing at Federico Fernandez's estate?"

"I met him about a month ago. We fell in love. He brought me here to meet his parents. We were talking about getting married." Her eyes rounded as if the truth had just dawned on her. "He isn't just a wealthy businessman like he told me?"

"He is a wealthy businessman. His business just happens to be on the shady side," Beatrice replied.

Susan looked sick. "Oh," she said weakly. Then her shoulders straightened with defiance. "I don't run security checks on all the men I date. Surely Tobias can't sanction my death just because I made a lousy choice."

Again Beatrice found herself tempted to believe the woman. But that wasn't her decision. It was Tobias's job to find out the truth. She and Joe were simply to get Susan back. Normally she would have said nothing more, but in this instance she couldn't make herself keep quiet. She'd been set up and she wasn't going to let that happen to someone else. "Your choice of companions isn't the primary reason Tobias wants to talk to you."

"What am I supposed to have done?" Susan demanded.

"Masterminded munitions thefts." As she made this statement, Beatrice studied the woman's reaction. Again the shock looked real. It was followed by indignation.

"You two are nuts!" Susan's voice held a note of panic. "I can barely organize a shopping list."

"You can plead your case once we've gotten you back home," Joe said.

"I thought Tobias had retired. I thought Harold was calling the shots now." Susan paled. "A bad choice of words, I hope."

"As long as you cooperate, no harm will come to you from us," Beatrice assured her.

Looking unconvinced and scared, Susan sat back.

Making certain they weren't followed, Joe drove to their private dock. He and Beatrice had decided to sail north to Chetumal rather than try to make a break overland.

After securely tying Susan and leaving her lying on one of the bunks in the cabin, Beatrice joined him on deck.

"I'd feel better if this thing had a little more speed," he said, steering them out into open water.

"We wanted to look like tourists enjoying the beauty of the Caribbean," she reminded him. Picking up the binoculars, she began to scan the horizon. To her relief there was nothing but blue sky and nearly deserted shoreline.

For the next hour and a half she continued to watch for pursuers. But instead of relaxing as the time lengthened and they appeared to have made a clean escape, she remained tense.

"I hate looking a gift horse in the mouth, but this was too easy," she said, breaking the silence between her and Joe. "She goes into town shopping every day. Her bodyguards let her go into the stores alone, providing the perfect opportunity for a snatch. When she first recognized me, I'd swear she was surprised and confused, but not afraid."

The sound of a helicopter caught her attention. In the next instant a bullet hit the deck beside her. "Maybe this isn't going to be as easy as I thought," she said, diving for cover.

Joe had been keeping the coast in sight. Now he turned toward it. "Get a life jacket on," he ordered.

She'd already thought of that. Tossing one to him, she pulled hers on while making a dash for the cabin with a third. "Looks like your friends might be coming for you," she said, unfastening Susan's hands and sitting her up on the bunk to put the jacket on her.

"They aren't my friends," Susan insisted.

A barrage of shots came from above and Beatrice heard the thud of bullets hitting the deck. Letting out a shriek of fear, Susan curled up on the bunk, covering her head with her arms.

Joe was zigzagging the boat to make it difficult for whoever was in the helicopter to take aim. His actions were also making it hard for Beatrice to maintain her balance. She looked down at the woman lying on the bunk. Another spray of bullets sounded and Susan curled tighter.

"They're aiming at the fuel tank. We're going to have to abandon ship!" Joe yelled from above.

Susan sat up abruptly. Tears of fear welled in her eyes. "You're not going to leave me here, are you?"

"No." Beatrice unfastened her feet. "Stay close and stay down."

"I've been working my way toward shore," Joe yelled to them, as he steered the boat hard to the right. "After the next zag I'm guiding us up onto the beach. Be ready to jump and try to keep cover between you and the copter."

"Just think of this as an exercise in amphibious landing in hostile territory," Beatrice told Susan. "According to your records, you've some training in that."

"They didn't use live ammunition in our training maneuvers," Susan returned. "And that was a lot of years ago. I've been sitting behind a desk for a long time. I'll admit I work out at my local health spa, but jogging around the indoor track is not the same as running from someone shooting at me."

Beatrice ignored the woman's nervous chatter. She was watching the shore. "Jump," she ordered, grabbing Susan's arm and pulling the blonde with her over the side. They landed in shallow water. Both were on their feet instantly, heading for shore and the cover of the trees beyond.

Behind them, they heard the helicopter, more shots, then an explosion. Reaching the trees, they each chose one and flattened against it, keeping the trunk between themselves and the shore.

Shakily, Beatrice looked back to where the boat had beached. Pieces of it were scattered in the water and along the shore. What was still intact was burning. The shooter had finally hit his mark. The helicopter buzzed overhead for a couple of minutes, then flew off to the south.

She scanned the beach for Joe. She didn't see him. Panic swept through her.

"Where's Coyote?" Susan asked shakily.

"I don't know." Beatrice marveled that the words had come so crisply, as if she was in total control.

Susan sank to the ground. "I suppose you can be calm because you and he are used to facing death. I'm not."

Her own death, Beatrice could have faced. But the thought of losing Joe was causing bile to rise in her throat.

"Even if he's out of gas, he could have called for reinforcements," Joe growled from behind her. "We have to get moving!"

Joy filled her. Jerking around, she saw him watching her. His expression told her he'd guessed she'd momentarily forgotten the first rule of survival—don't give in to emotion. And he wasn't pleased.

Her gaze met his. "It was only a momentary lapse," she assured him.

"A momentary lapse can get you killed," he returned curtly.

"What are you talking about?" Susan was again on her feet.

"Nothing important," Beatrice replied. "Let's get going."

Joe gave her a "We'll finish this later" look, then led the way into the interior.

Motioning for Susan to follow behind him, Beatrice took the rear position. As they moved north, keeping out of sight, a thought nagged at her.

"Coyote, take a break," she said.

He turned to her, an impatient frown on his face. "We should put as much distance between ourselves and that wreck as quickly as possible."

"Something is bothering me."

"Can't you talk while we keep moving?" Susan asked, glancing anxiously over her shoulder.

The impatience had gone from Joe's face. "I think we should listen to what Thistle has to say."

"I've been wondering how they knew for certain we were the ones they were looking for? Even if they had a description of me from the salesgirl, they didn't hover above for a closer look. They started firing as soon as we were in their sights."

"Maybe we weren't as clever as we thought. Maybe we were spotted before the snatch and they knew about the private dock and the boat."

"But they came up so fast. They couldn't possibly have made a positive identification before they started shooting." She was frowning at the brooch on Susan's blouse.

"It was a gift from Federico," Susan explained, following the line of Beatrice's gaze.

"Those bodyguards of yours were pretty lax," Beatrice said.

Susan shrugged. "I didn't understand why I needed them in the first place. But Federico said it wasn't always safe for a woman to travel alone."

Joe began to see where Beatrice was going. "It was if they were nothing more than window dressing."

"I'd like to see that brooch." Beatrice held her hand out.

Nervously Susan removed it. "Take it," she said, looking at it as if it were a poisonous insect.

Extracting a small pocketknife, Beatrice carefully pried the brooch apart. "Looks like a homing device. And it was well sealed. It's my guess it's still working."

"He had me bugged?" Fury flared in Susan's eyes. "I thought the man was in love with me. Instead, he bugged me and then tried to kill me!"

"With all three of us gone, that would have tied up the loose ends," Joe said, thoughtfully. "It would be assumed that Susan tried to escape and we all died in her thwarted attempt."

Beatrice was continuing to frown at the transmitter. "They knew where we were all along. Why wait until now to do us in?"

"Maybe they wanted to be certain we were in the middle of nowhere in case we escaped their attack," Susan suggested, her gaze traveling around the untamed wilderness.

"Which means they'll come looking for us." Joe took the brooch, closed it, then gave it a strong toss to their rear. "Now let's get out of here."

As if to confirm his words, from above they heard the sound of a helicopter.

"They've already found us," Susan gasped.

"Stay hidden," Joe ordered, taking his gun from his shoulder holster.

"I hate crawly things," Susan grumbled under her breath as she crouched low, staring at the ground for any unwelcome companions.

"You'll hate dying more," Beatrice returned.

"Quiet!" Joe growled.

Beatrice moved closer to his position. She always felt stronger and more confident in his presence. And the nearer, the better. "You take the north and west. I'll take the south and east," she said, squatting with her back against his, the pistol she'd had holstered beneath her loose-fitting tunic top now out and at the ready. She glanced at Susan. "You just keep very low."

Forgetting her dislike of communing with the creatures on the ground, Susan flattened herself and covered her head with her arms.

The copter hovered over a spot in the direction Joe had tossed the brooch, then went higher. Abruptly it banked to the right, then began to descend.

"If we can get to that machine, I can fly it," Susan volunteered.

Beatrice looked at her. "Are you sure?"

"I dated a helicopter pilot. He taught me. And if it's the same kind of machine Federico flew me here in, I watched the pilot and recognized the controls."

Beatrice glanced over her shoulder at Joe.

"It's probably our best bet for getting out of here," he said, already moving in the direction of the copter's descent.

As the engines of the machine were cut, they could hear men shouting to one another. Drawing closer, they saw three men with Uzis. One of the three was the bodyguard who had been assigned to Susan. He was holding a portable locator. He motioned for the other two men to flank him, each about ten feet to either side, and all three headed into the jungle.

"Nice of them to leave their transportation unguarded," Susan said. "Looks like luck is with us this time."

Joe held out his hand to keep her from moving forward. "Let's make certain they leave first."

Susan paled at her impetuousness and huddled more closely into her hiding place.

Joe counted to twenty, then with a wave of his arm motioned for the others to follow as he headed to the machine. Looking inside, he scowled. "No key."

"No problem." Susan was grinning. "My pilot friend showed me how to hot-wire one of these. But don't ask why."

"Just do it," Joe ordered.

Susan's grin disappeared.

Joe climbed into the copilot's chair. Beatrice took the seat behind him. Both kept their eyes in the direction the men had gone, their guns held at the ready.

Muttering prayers under her breath, Susan worked swiftly. "Let's hope this starts on the first try," she said. It didn't.

Beatrice heard their pursuers shouting and crashing through the undergrowth toward them.

Susan tried again. This time the engine started. The blades created a whirlwind. As the gunmen ran into the clearing, they were forced to cover their faces and retreat. Before they could recover, the copter was on its way up. Joe and Beatrice fired, forcing them to retreat farther. Only one managed to get off a round before they were totally out of range. All of his shots missed.

"This has got to be a first," Susan yelled above the engines. "The snatchee saving the snatchers. Now do you believe I'm innocent?"

"Maybe Sanchez wanted you dead. He could have been afraid you'd link him to your crimes and give the Mexican government the evidence they need to arrest him," Joe returned.

"I don't know any Sanchez!" Susan insisted.

"Head west," Joe ordered.

Chapter Thirteen

Beatrice sat in Tobias's study. Joe was there and so was Tobias. She was showered, rested and fed. The clothes she'd worn since the snatch, the only ones she had with her at the moment, had been laundered while she got a full eight hours' sleep. Joe had cleaned up also, she noted.

"Well?" Tobias said pointedly.

Beatrice knew what he wanted. He wanted to know if they believed Susan had been set up. She responded with an "I don't know what to tell you" shrug.

Joe shook his head, letting Tobias know he was undecided, as well.

"We must ask ourselves," Tobias said, his tone taking on that of a lecturer addressing his students, "what is the purpose of the exercise—of all the exercises you have been through these past weeks?"

Tobias paused but received no response. They knew from experience he was not ready for them to interrupt yet.

"The purpose has been to cast guilt in every direction, hoping it would stick. But why didn't the person we're after simply take their ill-gotten gains and flee to some country without extradition laws and live out their life in luxury?"

"Because, once they discovered Coyote was still alive, they knew he'd never rest until he'd brought them to justice," Beatrice replied, rewarding Joe with a wry smile.

"Yes," Tobias agreed. "And because they wanted the freedom to move around when and where they wished." He looked toward Beatrice. "Here is how I see the situation. Our mole is not only crafty but likes playing games. She also thinks she's smarter than we are. When Coyote was first captured, I believe that was a shock to her. He was supposed to be dead. She'd thought she had all of her bases covered. Now she had to ask herself if he was working with someone in a covert operation of which she was not aware. If so, she needed a scapegoat. That was when Knight was drawn into the game. However, Coyote was able to convince her that he was working alone. At that point, I believe our mastermind was going to simply have him killed, then you showed up. You'd been Coyote's partner in the past. The mole had to wonder if he'd fooled his interrogators and was still working with you. The plan to set him against you was devised. Next we have Knight, thwarted in his attempt to kill Coyote, he directs suspicion at Harold. Now we have Susan. Another frame? Or a very clever villain?" He nodded toward Beatrice. "Ladies first."

"You discovered money in the Caymans under her name. However, that could have been planted. It's not much if you consider what our mole must have amassed during the past years. Provided the three of us had been killed in the boat explosion and the real mole went into retirement so the activity Joe was investigating came to an abrupt halt, the most likely assumption you would have drawn was that Susan was the culprit and had caused her own death in a botched attempt to escape. Thus, our real traitor would be free to live out her life in peace without the worry of being hounded.''

Tobias shifted his gaze to Joe.

''But we weren't killed in the explosion,'' he said, taking his cue. ''My maneuvering could have been the reason we were able to beach the boat and get safely ashore. Or we could simply have gotten lucky. There have been a lot of times when luck has been a determining factor in my survival. On the other hand, if Susan is the one we're after, we could have been meant to seemingly barely escape with our lives.''

''And Susan knowing how to fly a helicopter was certainly a convenient coincidence,'' Beatrice added.

''But if she is our mastermind would she have used so many coincidences? Not only did you escape the boat, but suddenly there was convenient transportation,'' Tobias pointed out.

''She left a trail that was easy to follow. And she claims she was duped by a man. When we made the snatch, she was surprised but put up no resistance. She simply continued to proclaim her innocence.'' Beatrice frowned as another thought struck her. ''Maybe we were supposed to escape the boat and steal the helicopter. But not because Susan is our traitor. Maybe Julia knew Susan could fly and thought those coincidences would cause us to feel certain we had the right person.''

''So you think Susan was set up—that she was made to look innocent at first, duped by a clever man. Then she was made to look guilty by too many coincidences piling up on top of each other?'' Tobias asked.

"Or maybe that's what we're supposed to think." Beatrice's frown deepened. "I feel like I'm being manipulated by an expert puppet master, and I don't like it."

"Have you found anything incriminating against Julia?" Joe asked.

"She travels a lot. The Caribbean seems to be a popular spot with her, but she's gone to Europe and all over the United States, as well. She talks to everyone—the cashiers and baggers at the grocery, the attendant at the gas station, the waitresses at the restaurants she frequents, strangers on the metro. Any of them could be her way of getting messages to Sanchez."

"I never thought of Julia as being so outgoing," Beatrice mused. "At work she rarely puts more than a few words together and even then they always have to do with business."

"A lot of people are different outside their office environment." Tobias studied her thoughtfully. "I'd never have pictured you being content to be a housekeeper for your grandfather in a secluded little valley where the most exciting topic of conversation is whether it will rain or not."

"I've decided that was the wrong choice. But your point is understood."

Tobias smiled. "If that was an admission of boredom with your current life-style, perhaps you'll consider returning to The Unit. I'm sure Harold will welcome you with open arms."

"No, she won't," Joe interjected curtly.

Ignoring him, Beatrice smiled at Tobias. "As a matter of fact—"

"I think we should keep our minds focused on the case at hand." Joe cut her off.

"Coyote's right," Tobias agreed. "You and I will continue this discussion later."

Ignoring the disapproving scowl on Joe's face, Beatrice nodded.

"So, children, do you have any ideas on how we can resolve our dilemma?" Tobias asked.

"I have noticed that Harold is not present," Joe said, a question in his voice.

"Until we have positive proof of the identity of our turncoat, he is still a suspect." Tobias leaned back and sighed tiredly. "He was the one who found the bank account in the Caymans."

Joe frowned. "You think he might have set it up just so he could find it?"

"That's always a possibility. If so, he's been thinking far ahead. However, I would expect him to. After all, he is my protégé. If anyone could set up the elaborate charade we've been caught in the middle of, it would be him."

"How long ago was the account begun?" Beatrice asked.

"Five years ago. One deposit was made. There's been no activity since."

A knock sounded on the study door.

"Enter," Tobias called out.

The door opened to reveal Susan, accompanied by Raven. "She says there's something she wants to tell you," he said.

"It's about the money in the Caymans," Susan blurted. "I lied. It is mine."

Tobias motioned for her and Raven to enter the room and for Raven to close the door.

Susan's gaze shifted between those present, and her nervousness visibly increased. Beatrice couldn't fault her for that. Joe and Raven were both intimidating and, although Tobias had a fatherly air, his reputation left no doubt in anyone's mind that he could be a formidable foe. The woman's shoulders straightened and she met Tobias's gaze. "The money is mine. It was given to me by a friend."

"A very good friend, I would assume. Tell me more about this friend," Tobias said with an encouraging smile.

A light tint gave color to Susan's cheeks. Then defiance sparked in her eyes. "He was an elderly gentleman. Very wealthy. Highly respected. Widowed. But that wouldn't have mattered to his children. They would never have accepted me. Besides, he wasn't interested in remarrying. I think having a younger woman on the side gave some spice to his life." Her chin tightened. "But we did care for each other." She paused as if finding this difficult to relate.

"Go on," Tobias coaxed, when the pause lengthened into a silence.

"He told me he was worried about my future but he didn't want to cause any friction within his family. A bequest in his will would have revealed our relationship and embarrassed his children. So he insisted I take the money and put it away for a rainy day. At first, I refused. But he was insistent. In the end, believing that he was doing this because he honestly cared for me, I relented. He gave me the money in cash and told me to put it in an account in the Cayman Islands. He said his son was suspicious, and he didn't want me depositing the money in a bank here in the States where his son could find out about it." The tint in her cheeks darkened. "He also said he didn't see any reason for me to pay taxes on it. He said it was more an insurance policy than a gift."

Anger replaced her embarrassment. "What it was, was a buy off. Less than a week later, he terminated our relationship. He said it was because he was afraid his family would find out. But he'd hired a new chauffeur—a woman—and I'd seen the looks passing between them. I was tempted to give the money back, throw it in his face in front of his children, actually. But that would only have embarrassed both him and me. So I decided to keep it and just let it sit there, like he'd suggested, for a rainy day." Her back stiffened even more. "I've worked hard all my life. And I figured I'd earned the money. He wasn't the easiest person to get along with. I told myself I deserved this little reward."

"I'll need a name," Tobias said.

For a moment she hesitated, then named a prominent industrialist who had died a couple of years earlier.

"It was wise of you to tell me this," Tobias said. "Are there any other secrets I should know."

She shook her head.

"Thank you." His voice held dismissal.

She looked to Beatrice, then Joe and Raven. "Nobody's perfect. Everyone cheats a little once in a while. But I'd never do anything to bring harm to another person." Her head held high, she exited with Raven accompanying her.

"What do you think? Was she telling the truth?" Beatrice asked Tobias.

"The man she named lived a very private life but there were rumors about the possibility he was a philander. The scenario she painted could very easily be true. It would be his style. He believed in paying for what he got."

"If that's the case, she should be flattered," Beatrice replied. "A hundred thousand is no pittance."

Tobias didn't smile. "It would seem we are back to square one."

"If only Knight would come out of his coma. He'd be able to point us in the right direction." Beatrice looked hopefully at Tobias. "Has there been any change in his condition?"

"None."

"I heard the doctors think he is showing signs of regaining consciousness. They believe he could wake at any moment," Joe said unexpectedly.

Beatrice grinned mischievously. "I heard that same thing."

"I think you should share a cup of tea with Susan and pass that information on to her," Joe suggested.

Beatrice's smile faded. "In case she is merely a pawn, I'll break the news about his resurrection and current injury slowly." Her gaze leveled on Joe. "If she did feel something for him, learning that he has been alive all along will be a shock. Learning how badly he was hurt will be an added jolt."

"Deception and loss are a part of this business," he returned.

Tobias frowned at them. "Obviously you two have a few differences to work out. But you can do that later. I think you're right. It's time we played a game of our own."

Beatrice jerked her gaze away from Joe and glanced at her watch. "It's nearly four." She smiled beseechingly at Tobias. "Do you think your cook could brew a pot of tea and put a few of those sinfully rich pastries she is always making to keep you happy on a tray?"

"At my age a man deserves to have one vice," Tobias defended, picking up the phone beside his chair and punching the button for the kitchen.

A few minutes later, Beatrice stood, food- and tea-laden tray in hand while Raven knocked on the door of Susan's room.

"If you've come to bribe me into making a confession," the blonde said, eyeing the pastries, "you won't succeed but I'll enjoy the attempt." The hint of tears glistened in her eyes. "I have nothing to confess."

Beatrice smiled sympathetically. "Actually, I'm here to relieve Raven for a while. And I decided to make my guard duty as enjoyable as possible. Would you like to share this in the solarium at the end of the hall?"

"Gladly." Susan grimaced at the interior of the bedroom in which she was being held. "As luxurious as this room is, it still feels like a prison."

Beatrice smiled encouragingly, and motioned for the woman to precede her down the hall.

Raven followed, waiting until Beatrice had set the tray on the table, freeing her hands in case her weapon was needed.

"And now I'll leave you ladies," he said.

"That man scares me. Does he ever smile?" Susan asked when they were alone.

"Every once in a while," Beatrice replied. "Not often, though," she admitted.

Susan stood at the windowed wall of the second-story room, gazing out over the wooded landscape beyond. "The only thing that is keeping me sane is knowing that Tobias is a fair and just man." She turned to face Beatrice. "I am innocent."

Beatrice poured the tea. "Then you have nothing to worry about."

Ignoring the offer of the teacup, Susan paced the floor. "How much longer am I to be kept a prisoner here?"

"Perhaps not much longer." Letting her words hang in the air, Beatrice took a bite of one of the pastries.

Susan came to an abrupt halt. "Honestly?"

Beatrice set aside the pastry. "How well did you know Knight?"

Susan gave a noncommittal shrug. "I knew him by sight. It's my job to know all the agents by sight."

Beatrice said nothing, choosing to wait to see if Susan admitted to a more personal interest in the man.

Returning to the window, Susan again stood with her back toward the interior of the room. "Why did you mention Knight?"

Again Beatrice said nothing.

Susan swung around to face her. "All right. So I dated the man a couple of times. That's no crime. We're all allowed our private lives. I never asked him his real name or anything like that. And I never pried into his work or tried to get him to tell me any secrets. After a couple of dates, we both agreed we had no future so we stopped going out. That's all."

Pity more than sadness showed in her features. "At the memorial service, I felt sorry for him. Harold, Tobias, Julia and I were the only ones who attended. I guess I wasn't really surprised. There was an insular quality about him, as if he was used to standing alone...and preferred it that way."

Listening and watching, Beatrice felt certain Susan harbored no lingering tender feelings for Knight. His death had been merely the sad passing of an acquaintance. Deciding that easing into Knight's deception was unnecessary, Beatrice said bluntly, "He wasn't dead at the time of the memorial service."

Susan frowned in confusion. "What do you mean, he wasn't dead?"

"He'd gone into deep cover. He thought he was under The Manager's instructions."

"But he wasn't?"

"No. He'd been set up by someone in The Unit to take the fall in case we got too close to our gunrunning traitor."

"Just like me," Susan said defiantly.

Beatrice made no response, implying by her silence she was still uncertain of Susan's innocence.

"Do you honestly think I'd arrange for men to fire live ammunition at me and nearly blow me up?" Susan demanded.

Beatrice shrugged. "That's not my decision to make." She took a sip of tea. "However, this matter is going to be cleared up soon, we hope. The day you left the country, Joe and I cornered Knight. He was shot but not fatally. When a second attempt was made on his life, we spread the word that he'd died. This wasn't true. However, he did lapse into a coma. Now the doctors think he's coming out of it. Joe and I leave in an hour to see him. He should be able to tell us who relayed the messages, claiming they were from Harold."

"He will tell you I'm not the one."

Beatrice saw the hesitation and then the flash of icy anger in the woman's eyes and knew the truth. *Give her rope,* she told herself. "I'll be glad when this business is cleared up. It isn't easy suspecting people I've known for so long." She smiled to imply that she was beginning to believe Susan's claim, then reached for a pastry, her manner relaxed as if she were comfortable in Susan's presence and did not see any threat there.

"I haven't been able to sleep. I'm feeling dizzy." Susan clutched for the back of a chair.

"I realize this had been a terrible strain," Beatrice cooed sympathetically, hurrying to catch her.

In the next instant, Susan had grabbed the gun from Beatrice's shoulder holster. "Actually, Knight won't vindicate me," she admitted coldly. "So you and I are going to walk out of here together."

"Tobias won't let you leave," Beatrice warned.

"He will unless he wants to see you die in front of his eyes." A sly smile played at one corner of Susan's mouth. "Even if Tobias is willing to sacrifice you, Coyote won't. I've seen the way he looks at you and I've noticed how he always puts himself in the line of fire to protect you." Her scowl deepened. "Any other agent would have bought my original setup. Coyote should have believed you were the traitor, killed you and put an end to his hunt. Then I could have retired in peace. Instead, he and you have been nothing but trouble."

"I'll take that as a compliment."

Susan snorted. "Let's go." She motioned toward the door.

"You're not going anywhere," Joe said, opening the door and entering.

"I'll kill her," Susan threatened, grabbing Beatrice by the arm and holding the barrel of the gun to her head.

"It's empty." Jerking free, Beatrice took a position beside Joe.

Susan stared at the weapon with disgust. "The oldest trick in the book and I fell for it." Tobias had entered, along with Raven and Harold. She glared at them. "Knight is dead, isn't he?"

"No. But thanks to you, he's in a coma and doesn't show any signs of coming out of it," Beatrice snapped.

Susan swung her gaze to Tobias. "You owe me. If it wasn't for me, Sanchez would have killed Coyote. I'm the only reason he's alive today."

Tobias scowled. "As fond as I am of Coyote, I don't consider that a debt to be repaid. You thought you were trading his life for Thistle's in order to retain your freedom. And there is Knight to answer for, as well."

"Sanchez must have been very unhappy when your first plan didn't succeed," Joe said. "I'm surprised he allowed you to use his people again."

Susan shrugged. "Men are so gullible when it comes to money and women. I promised I'd make him rich."

"He's not going to like this turn of events," Joe warned.

"You would be safer if he was behind bars, as well," Tobias cautioned.

"If I give you information you can pass along to the *federales* that would put him away, I want a deal. I want a slap on the wrists, along with early parole."

"No," Beatrice said sharply. "No deals."

The men all looked at her, clearly startled by the venom in her voice.

Fury etched itself into her features. "I've been thinking. That hundred thousand in the Caymans, it was for tipping off the people we were after five years ago . . . the ones who tried to kill Coyote with the car bomb, wasn't it?"

Susan shrugged, then glowered at Joe. "Too bad they didn't succeed. You've been nothing but a thorn in my side."

"It seems we are definitely two of a kind," Beatrice whispered to Joe.

Ignoring her, he concentrated on Susan. "You're going to need protection. Sanchez knows you can put him away for life. He'll be willing to pay well for your death."

"When no one comes knocking on his door to arrest him, he'll know I didn't talk," she replied.

"He might not be willing to take that chance," Joe cautioned. "Especially when I fly back to Mexico to meet with Manuel at the same time word of you being taken into custody leaks out."

Susan issued a string of expletives. Then, sinking into a chair, she turned to Tobias. "He's very careful about covering himself. Much more careful than Palma. He's smarter than Palma and learned from Palma's mistakes. However, I can give you a little information that might lead to something the *federales* can nail him on. But I want protection."

"You'll have what I can offer," Harold replied.

Chapter Fourteen

"Are you going to take Harold up on his offer of reinstatement?"

Beatrice turned to see Joe studying her, his expression guarded. She'd been waiting for this question ever since they'd left Tobias's place.

Because of the fear of phone taps and informants, it had been decided that the only way to ensure that the information Susan had given Harold was delivered without Sanchez's knowledge was for it to be given to Manuel personally by word of mouth. To put Sanchez off his guard and begin providing the protection promised Susan, Harold had placed a call to Manuel, telling him that they'd learned nothing. Now Beatrice and Joe were on their way back to Mexico City.

"I haven't made up my mind," she replied.

He didn't look convinced. "I figured since you insisted on accompanying me to Mexico, you had."

"I thought I had, but I haven't," she admitted, exhausted from the argument raging within her. "I came along because I wanted to see Elena again and collect the luggage I left with her on my first trip. Manuel mentioned he was holding it for me. Besides, I was available and two memories are better than one."

His frown called her a liar. "You came because you wanted to guard my back. You're worried that Sanchez still wants me dead."

"No agent should go into the field alone," she returned sternly, knowing her words were falling on deaf ears but having to say them anyway.

"Sanchez isn't worried about me. He knows I have no authority in Mexico and as far as he's concerned, I've got no information to pass along, either. He's not going to tip his hand by putting a price on my head. And once the *federales* know what we know, he'll be too busy with them to pay any attention to me."

"You're probably right." Frustration showed in her eyes. "But I simply couldn't pass up the opportunity to make a trip with such an amiable companion."

He frowned at this dry jab.

She studied the hard line of his jaw. "Harold made his offer very tempting. He promised that you and I could work together."

"No." There was no compromise in Joe's voice.

"You'd entrust my backside to someone else?" she asked.

He groaned and leaned his head back. "No."

Beatrice turned her gaze to the clouds beyond the plane window. He looked miserable, like a man caught between a rock and a hard place. Again she wondered if forcing herself back into his life was the right thing to do. The argument she'd been having with herself raged on.

* * *

Manuel met them at the airport. "Elena is expecting you for dinner and she will be furious with me if I do not bring you," he said.

"We'd love to come," Beatrice assured him.

Joe smiled, but Beatrice noticed that the smile did not reach his eyes. Immediately he turned the subject to the business at hand. "Have you chosen your people to whom we can entrust the information we have?"

"Yes." Quickly Manuel led them to his car and they drove to a restaurant outside of town. "We want to maintain our element of surprise," he said, leading them into a private room upstairs. "It is Juan's birthday next week. Those who are not on the task force think we are merely taking him to a nice lunch to celebrate. This place belongs to Elena's father, a very honorable man."

During the luncheon, Beatrice watched Joe covertly. After the information was delivered, he appeared to enter into the jovial mood of the rest of the men present but she knew him too well. To her it was obvious that his relaxed manner was merely an act.

He was the same when they arrived at Manuel's that evening.

"Joe seems tense," Elena said.

The men were on the patio and Beatrice had accompanied the woman into the kitchen to help with last-minute dinner preparations. She'd thought Joe had been putting on a good act of enjoying himself. "You're very observant."

"In many ways he and Manuel are a lot alike," Elena replied. "To read one is to read the other."

Beatrice breathed a tired sigh. "But there is one very big difference. Manuel is not opposed to sharing his life with someone he loves."

Elena smiled. "I knew there was chemistry between you and Joe."

"But there will be no wedding," Beatrice said, forcing herself to face the truth.

Disbelief showed on Elena's face. "Surely you can work out any differences."

"I thought that, too, but I realize that was only wishful thinking."

"When Manuel and I returned after the rescue, he told me he understood my hesitancy in marrying him. He said that if he could, he would turn back time and let me find a more secure marriage. I convinced him I'd made the right choice." Her face flushed with pleasure. "I have even convinced him that it is time we started a family. Surely, if I can do that, you can convince Joe that the two of you belong together. You should, at least, tell him how you feel."

"He knows. But he also knows me better than I know myself." Hot tears burned at the back of Beatrice's eyes. "Manuel is home more than he is gone. And when he is gone, he can still contact you. You know if he is all right from day to day. You have a life together. Our situation is different. If I chose to remain behind, keeping house and waiting for Joe's visits, they would be few and far between. And when he was gone there would be no contact, or very limited contact. I've tried to convince myself I could handle that, but I realize now that I couldn't. I would worry too much and the worry would tear me apart inside. Joe realized that before I did."

"Manuel said he's never seen partners so attuned. Could you not continue to work together?"

"I thought we could. But I was wrong about that, as well. It's the thought of my continuing as his partner that has him so tense tonight. He worries too much about me. My staying could cause both of us to get killed."

Elena gave her a sympathetic hug. "I understand your dilemma. What will you do?"

"Go home." Beatrice spoke the words she'd been dreading to say.

Elena shook her head sorrowfully. "You two belong together."

"Life doesn't always work out the way we want it to." Beatrice knew she'd made the right decision, but that didn't make it any easier. Feeling the need to change the subject to something happier, she said, "So Manuel has agreed to beginning a family."

The sparkle returned to Elena's eyes. "Yes. I have already begun decorating the nursery."

For the rest of the time the dinner preparations took, they discussed Elena's hopes and plans.

When the men joined them at the table, Beatrice read the concern on Manuel's face and guessed that Joe had talked to him about her insistence on returning to work as his partner. As proof she'd judged rightly, she noticed that whenever the conversation turned to the case she and Joe had just finished, the *federale* noted how well they worked together, then seemed suddenly ill at ease as if afraid he'd said the wrong thing.

"I got the distinct impression you talked to Manuel about not wanting me back as your partner," she said bluntly after she and Joe left the Cortez home and were on their way back to their hotel.

"The subject came up. He agreed you would be dangerously distracting." His tone implied he felt his opinion had been validated and she was being foolishly stubborn to ignore his wishes.

Afraid her control would slip if she looked at him, she kept her gaze on the road ahead. "As long as you believe that, it will prove to be true. So, I've decided that the only fair thing to do is for me to go home and let you live your life alone on your own terms. Tell Harold, thanks for the job offer but I'm not accepting it.''

"You've made the right decision," Joe said stiffly. "All I've ever wanted was the best for you, Tess."

Her jaw tightened. "You want what you think is the best for me. You're wrong, but I won't risk your life trying to convince you of that."

For a long moment a silence descended between then, then he said, "I want your word that should your friend with the crystal ball see me in trouble again, you will stay out of it."

"That's asking too much!"

"I want your word!"

Dropping her hand out of his sight, she crossed her fingers. "All right, you have my word."

For the rest of the drive, they said nothing. At the hotel, they went to their separate rooms in silence. The next morning, they parted at the airport with a handshake.

In keeping with her training, Beatrice took a roundabout route home. By the time she was driving down the road leading to her grandfather's house, she knew she couldn't go back to simply being Justin's housekeeper. If Thatcher couldn't hire her on as a deputy, she would seek a job with the state police.

Parking in front of the farmhouse, she felt a sense of homecoming, but it wasn't the same as when she'd come back here the first time. That time, she'd thought Joe was dead. There had been a void within her but it was one she'd accepted. Now that void was there again, but this time it was different. It was more of an ache, a regret for what could have been.

Justin came out of the house as she mounted the porch steps, a smile of relief on his face. "It's good to have you home, girl."

"It's good to be home." The words felt hollow. This was not where she belonged. She belonged with Joe, but unless he accepted that, she would only be a danger to him.

"Looks to me like you need a shoulder to cry on," Justin observed, giving her a hug.

"Crying won't do any good."

Releasing her, he looked hard into her face. "Whenever you're ready to talk about whatever is bothering you, I'm here to listen."

"Someday," she promised. "But not today."

He nodded his acceptance and, putting his arm around her shoulders, guided her inside.

The next morning she drove into town. Before going to the police station, she made a stop at the Brant home.

"Were you able to find the man we spoke about?" Samantha asked as Beatrice entered.

"Yes. Thank you for coming to me," she replied. "I have a favor to ask. If you ever again see him in need of help, will you come tell me?"

"Yes, of course," Samantha assured her. Interest showed in her eyes. "Is he likely to need help again?"

"Perhaps." Beatrice did not elaborate and was relieved when Samantha accepted her silence with a knowing smile. Thanking Samantha once again, she left and continued to the police station.

During the next week, she placed job applications with Thatcher and the state police. There was life without Joe, she assured herself. But until she convinced her heart, she needed to keep busy.

While waiting to hear about possible placement in one of the police departments, she threw herself into the physical labor of farming.

She was at Ryder's, mucking the stables, when a familiar male voice said, "Looks like you know what you're doing."

Jerking around, she saw Joe standing in the doorway. "I was under the impression you didn't want our paths to cross again," she said stiffly.

"I've been thinking that a man shouldn't press his luck. I've been tempting Fate for a lot of years."

There was a warmth in his eyes that caused hope to grow within her. Don't go assuming anything before he says it, she cautioned herself. "Sounds reasonable."

"I also figure a man would be equally foolish to give up a good thing when he has it."

"Real foolish," she agreed.

"I've decided I've done my duty to my brother and his family. I'm retiring from the service and buying the place next to my grandfather's. I grew up ranching and I've decided it's time I went back to it. I could use a wife who knows her way around a barn."

She frowned at him. "If that's a proposal, it's the least romantic one I've ever heard of."

A plea entered his voice. "I've missed you, Tess. And I'm not talking about just the past couple of weeks. I'm talking about every minute of every day of all the years we were apart. After I recovered from the wounds I'd suffered during the explosion Tobias and I used to fake my death, I dogged your trail until you left the service. When you headed home, I followed you all the way to Boston to make certain your break was clean and none of the bad guys were following."

"I sensed your presence but I thought it was your spirit hovering over me, hounding me, until I did what you'd always wanted me to do."

"I wanted you safe. I thought watching you drive away from the airport that day, years ago, and knowing I'd never see you again, was the hardest, most painful thing I'd ever do. I was wrong. Sending you away a second time was worse. I need you, Tess. Forgive me, please. I want to spend the rest of my life with you."

A smile replaced her frown. "That's much better." She ran into his arms.

"Looks like you two found each other," Ryder said, approaching from the house.

Beatrice ignored her brother as her lips found Joe's.

"Guess I'm going to need someone else to help with the stables," Ryder lamented playfully, watching the two of them. "My sister has obviously found a better way to work off her frustrations."

A much better way, Beatrice agreed silently.

Raven parked Tobias's car in front of the log cabin deep in the Massachusetts mountains. This had been an interesting day. With Tobias's, Thistle's and Coyote's sanction, he'd gotten to know Joe and Beatrice on a real name basis and attended their wedding with Tobias. But now the wedding was over and Tobias had directed him to this secluded home on the outskirts of Smytheshire.

His hand went for his gun as the old man who'd been sitting in a rocking chair on the porch, picked up the rifle he had close at hand and laid it over his lap.

"Relax," Tobias told him. "His bark's a lot worse than his bite."

The dog that had been lying by the old man's feet, had risen and taken a snarling position at the top of the porch steps. "Which one are you talking about?" Raven asked dryly.

"Both."

Raven continued to look skeptical. "If you say so." He started to get out of the car but the dog loped toward them, barking a threat. Pulling his door closed, he looked over his shoulder at Tobias and smiled wryly. "You first."

Tobias rolled down his window. "Zebulon, call off that beast of yours and invite an old friend in for a visit."

"My eyes are as sharp as they've ever been and you don't look like any friend of mine," the old man called back, rising from his chair, his rifle cradled in his arms.

"Maybe you should have phoned first, sir," Raven suggested.

Ignoring him, Tobias merely broadened his smile. "I know I've aged a bit since we last talked, but it's me, Tobias, you old coot!"

Zebulon's eyes squinted for a closer examination, then he shook his head. "Well, I'll be darned. It is you." Laying aside his gun, he yelled to his dog. Immediately the animal's angry disposition vanished. Showing no further interest in their uninvited guests, he lumbered to the shade of an old oak and lay down.

"Wait in the car," Tobias ordered Raven.

"Tobias Smythe. Well, as I live and breathe," Zebulon said as Tobias mounted the porch steps.

"It's Smith now. I had it legally changed a long time ago."

Zebulon chuckled. "Trying to distance yourself from your Uncle Angus?"

"He was always trying to manipulate people."

"Never did fully trust him myself, but he surprised me. You'd have been pleased with the restraint he showed, once he'd gotten Smytheshire populated."

"Seems his son and grandson have shown equal restraint."

Zebulon shrugged. "They believe all those stories Angus used to tell about the power of his ancestors and those of others he brought here are just fairy tales. There was a great-grandson who caused a bit of trouble, but it's over and done with. Family managed to hush up the details." Zebulon grinned, and motioned for Tobias to be seated in a nearby rocker. Easing himself into his, he said, "Been thirty years, if it's been a day since you last set foot here in Smytheshire. Didn't expect you to ever come again."

"Despite how I feel about Angus and his ploys, there's too many of my own kind here for me not to think of this place as having a feel of home." Tobias smiled. "But I didn't come here to talk about family feuds. I came to say hello to an old friend. It's good to see you looking as spry as ever."

"I'm doing well," Zebulon confirmed.

"Looks to me like that gene for longevity in your family is strong in you."

Zebulon nodded. "Looks like. 'Course, simple country living helps." His gaze traveled to the sleek black Cadillac in which Tobias had arrived, then back to Tobias and he grinned. "Appears you ain't been living the simple life. You're beginning to show your age."

"I took up a stressful occupation. But I'm retired now."

Interest sparked in Zebulon's eyes. "You thinking of moving here?"

Tobias shook his head. "No. A young couple I've known a long time got married here today. Since no one but you'd ever recognize me, I figured I'd come pay my respects."

"That'd be Beatrice Gerard and that young man of hers, Joe Whitedeer. They brought his grandfather by to meet me yesterday. An impressive man. Could be his ancestors aren't so different from ours."

"Could be," Tobias agreed.

Zebulon frowned thoughtfully. "Could be that Angus isn't the only Smythe who likes to meddle in people's lives."

Tobias looked offended. "It was fate that brought them together. However, the combination did intrigue me and I'll admit I provided the means to keep them together. But when they chose to part, I did nothing to stop them. In fact I aided the separation. It was Fate that again brought them together." He shrugged. "And who am I to argue with Fate?"

Zebulon had been studying the man beside him. "You say you've retired, but you don't look like a man intent on a life of ease."

"I've retired from my previous occupation. However, I am considering other options." Tobias grinned. "Tess and Joe are planning to try their hand at ranching, but I know them. They'll get bored." He nodded toward the car. "And Raven, he's a man of action. I would hate to see all this talent and energy go to waste."

"Once a Smythe, always a Smythe." Zebulon chuckled. "You will keep me apprised of your future activities?"

"Of course," Tobias promised. "And you should keep an eye on whoever inherited Ada Hogan's crystal ball."

"I watch over all my charges," Zebulon assured him.

Beatrice stood on the porch of the small, rustic ranch house that was now her home. The roof had been patched and firewood stacked high. The corrals had been mended and the barn rebuilt. Above her was the star studded Wyoming sky. The whinny of a horse and the long low moo of a cow broke the stillness, and she smiled.

Joe had accomplished a great deal before the first heavy snow. More than he knew. Excitement curled through her. She had some very special news for her husband.

"Come spring, we'll break ground on the new house," he said, joining her. Standing behind her, he circled his arms around her, letting his hands rest on her stomach. "Appears to me we're going to need a bigger place pretty soon."

Startled, she twisted her head to look up at him. "How did you know? I only just began to suspect a couple of days ago and I didn't know for certain until the doctor called just a few minutes ago."

He grinned down at her. "I am very attuned to your body."

She turned back and leaned against him, luxuriating in the firm, sturdy feel of him. "I don't suppose the other morning when I turned green and made a dash for the bathroom had anything to do with your suspicions?"

"It did awaken me to certain possibilities," he conceded with a light laugh. "But I wasn't certain until my grandfather came by today. Just before he left, he told me he was going to begin a dream catcher for his great-grandchild."

"I suppose the spirits told him."

"No, he said it was the special twinkle he saw in your eyes and the glow on your cheeks."

Turning in his arms until she was facing him, she looked up into his face. "I hope you're as happy about this pregnancy as I am."

"Everything about you makes me happy." He kissed her nose. Then scooping her up in his arms, he carried her inside.

* * * * *

"Just call me Dr. Mom....

I know everything there is to know about birthing *everyone else's* babies. I'd love to have one of my own, so I've taken on the job as nanny to three motherless tots and their very sexy single dad, Gib Harden. True, I'm no expert, and he's more handy at changing diapers than I—but I have a feeling that what this family really needs is the tender loving care of someone like me...."

MOM FOR HIRE
by
Victoria Pade
(SE #1057)

In October, Silhouette Special Edition brings you

THAT'S MY BABY!
Sometimes bringing up baby can bring surprises... and showers of love.

TMB1096

There's nothing quite like a family

REUNION
HANNAH • MICHAEL • KATE

The new miniseries by
Pat Warren

Three siblings are about to be reunited.
And each finds love along the way....

HANNAH
Her life is about to change now that she's met
the irresistible Joel Merrick in HOME FOR HANNAH
(Special Edition #1048, August 1996).

MICHAEL
He's been on his own all his life. Now he's
going to take a risk on love...and
take part in the reunion he's been
waiting for in MICHAEL'S HOUSE
(Intimate Moments #737, September 1996).

KATE
A job as a nanny leads her to Aaron Carver,
his adorable baby daughter and the
fulfillment of her dreams in KEEPING KATE
(Special Edition #1060, October 1996).

Meet these three siblings from

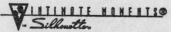

Silhouette SPECIAL EDITION®
and
VINTIMATE MOMENTS®
Silhouette

Look us up on-line at: http://www.romance.net

REUNION

This October, be the first to read these wonderful authors as they make their dazzling debuts!

Women to Watch

THE WEDDING KISS by Robin Wells
(Silhouette Romance #1185)
A reluctant bachelor rescues the woman he loves from the man she's about to marry—and turns into a willing groom himself!

THE SEX TEST by Patty Salier
(Silhouette Desire #1032)
A pretty professor learns there's more to making love than meets the eye when she takes lessons from a sexy stranger.

IN A FAMILY WAY by Julia Mozingo
(Special Edition #1062)
A woman without a past finds shelter in the arms of a handsome rancher. Can she trust him to protect her unborn child?

UNDER COVER OF THE NIGHT by Roberta Tobeck
(Intimate Moments #744)
A rugged government agent encounters the woman he has always loved. But past secrets could threaten their future.

DATELESS IN DALLAS by Samantha Carter
(Yours Truly)
A hapless reporter investigates how to find the perfect mate—and winds up falling for her handsome rival!

Don't miss the brightest stars of tomorrow!

Only from ▼ Silhouette®

WTW

The collection of the year!
NEW YORK TIMES BESTSELLING AUTHORS

Linda Lael Miller
Wild About Harry

Janet Dailey
Sweet Promise

Elizabeth Lowell
Reckless Love

Penny Jordan
Love's Choices

and featuring
Nora Roberts
The Calhoun Women

This special trade-size edition features four of the wildly
popular titles in the Calhoun miniseries together in
one volume—a true collector's item!

Pick up these great authors and a chance to win
a weekend for two in New York City at the
Marriott Marquis Hotel on Broadway! We'll pay
for your flight, your hotel—even a Broadway show!

Available in December at your favorite retail outlet.

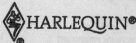 

The Calhoun Saga continues...

in November
New York Times bestselling author

NORA ROBERTS

takes us back to the Towers and introduces us to
the newest addition to the Calhoun household,
sister-in-law Megan O'Riley in

MEGAN'S MATE
(Intimate Moments #745)

And in December
look in retail stores for the special collectors'
trade-size edition of

THE
Calhoun
Women

containing all four fabulous Calhoun series books:
COURTING CATHERINE,
A MAN FOR AMANDA, FOR THE LOVE OF LILAH
and *SUZANNA'S SURRENDER.*
Available wherever books are sold.